# Mood Swings and Hockey Flings

## HOT FLASH HOOKUPS

### BOOK TWO

MARIKA RAY

SYLVIE STEWART

First Edition: April 18, 2024
Cover Designer: Sylvie Stewart
Editing: Nancy Smay at Evident Ink

Ebook ISBN: 978-1-950141-69-2
Paperback ISBN: 978-1-950141-76-0

# Nickname Key

Florida Storm Chasers:
    Banks "Benny" Bennet
    Nikolai "Druggy" Drugov
    Bobby "Roadie" Rhodes
    Pete "Forns" Fornier
    Alexi "Barzee" Barinov
    Jake "Booch" Bouchard
    Erik "Popeye" Anderson
    Danny "Dan-O" Bright
    Rich "Money" Monkowski

**In the cutthroat world of professional sports, I'm the agent who always calls the shots. Until a decade-old feud with hockey superstar Banks Bennet resurfaces, and I'm forced to play nice.**

When his agent drops him and rumors of a trade swirl through the league faster than a puck on a breakaway, I find myself in the dreaded role of Banks's new agent. There's no doubt I can save his career from crashing into the boards, but only if we don't strangle each other first.

All I need to do is whip this man-baby into shape and negotiate an epic contract that will establish me once and for all as the top hockey agent in the league. No problem, right? But between babysitting Banks, battling perimenopausal mood swings, and fighting this annoying attraction to my client, I'm facing a hat trick of challenges.

Not everything about Banks is what it seems. Under all that bravado and childish behavior lies a sensitive and considerate guy who values more than just his time on the ice—leaving me to wonder if maybe there's more to life than just wins and losses.

If I'm not careful, my emotions might have me losing control and throwing away the professional playbook for a shot at happily ever after...and that's *not* how this game is played.

# Chapter One

Kaitlyn

"I don't understand what the big deal is."

I juggle the cardboard coffee cup in my hand and the strap of my new laptop bag, getting everything settled so I can grab my suitcase and trek across the long-term parking lot to the terminal in my sky-high heels. Rolling one's eyes is not advisable when balanced on two sticks the width of a pencil, but I'm highly tempted.

"All those guys do is fight and knock out teeth. Football is a real sport." Dad never understood why I wanted to get away from football.

I nearly wipe out in a pothole, sloshing coffee through the hole in the lid of my drink, but thankfully not getting any on my suit sleeve and only a small splat lost on the concrete. Regardless of it being two in the afternoon, that caffeine is precious. "Dad, hockey is a real sport. Just because you didn't play it, doesn't mean it isn't valid. This new hockey client is a big deal for me."

Dad continues like he didn't hear me. "Besides, what's an Asian girl doing in the world of hockey?"

"Jesus, Dad." I consider telling him more Asians play professional hockey than football, but it will have no effect. He's always right.

Dad scoffs loudly in my earbuds. "Back in my day, we didn't–"

I cut him off before I can get the half an hour lecture he's famous for. "Oh, sorry, Dad. I gotta go. The tram's here. I'll text you when I get to Tampa. Love you."

The tram is not here, nor will it ever be because I parked out in long-term parking to save a few bucks, but he doesn't know that. "Fine, but don't take less than 50 percent!" he manages to bark before I stop in the middle of the lot and fish my phone out of my pocket to hit the end button.

I finally give in to the eye roll. Dad doesn't understand what I do as a sports agent or else he wouldn't suggest a 50 percent cut with a straight face. Nor would he scoff at the entire sport of hockey. He does know football; I'll give him that. He played two seasons in the NFL for Georgia back before I was born. Lord knows I've heard about those two years my whole damn life. Which is why I'm trying to branch out from football and center my career around hockey. Anything to get just a little distance from Dad and his former– and brief–career.

Shoving the phone back in my pocket, I continue to the terminal, tossing my coffee cup away after guzzling the rest and whizzing through security with very little fuss. After a stop at the bathroom, I wheel my suitcase to the bar located next to my gate. I skipped lunch in my rush between meetings and getting to the airport, but I have enough time before boarding to grab a bite to eat. I sit with a glorious sigh, my feet barking at me to at least consider a ballet flat next time. I tell my feet to shut the hell up. The stilettos are the cherry on the bottom of my professional package. I'll be dead and buried before they pry these babies off my feet.

I'm perusing the menu when I feel a presence settle in the seat next to me at the bar. A slight shift of my eyes informs me it's a man in jeans, a T-shirt, and a ballcap. I swivel slightly in the opposite direction, studying my menu with renewed focus, hoping he gets the message. It's not that I'm against meeting someone new. It's just that I recently ended a two-month-long relationship with a man who lied about being separated from his wife. At the moment, I can't emotionally handle another asshole. There must be nice guys still left on the planet, right?

My phone vibrates on the bar top and I snatch it up, scanning through the incoming email from Bella, the part-time assistant I was finally given, an extravagance only allowed because it was getting obvious my boss only gave assistants to the male agents and eyebrows were starting to rise at the unfair treatment. With any luck, I'll hit it off with my new hockey client and gain a few more while I'm in Tampa. Maybe by this time next year, I'll have my own agency and my own full-time assistant. Bella informs me that Jake, my new client, has told her that he'll be picking me up from the airport himself. My mouth quirks to the side. I wasn't expecting that. Then again, hockey is a new sport for me and maybe they do things differently.

"Tell me it's good news," comes a deep baritone next to me.

I lift my head to meet the blue-eyed gaze of a man towering over me, even though his elbows are on the bar top and he's most certainly not trying to impinge on my space. Not when he's nursing a beer that almost disappears in his large hand. His thick eyebrows quirk up and then down, a flirty twinkle in his eyes that makes me think he does this a lot. He's handsome and he knows it.

"It's always good news. I'll accept nothing less," I respond, returning my gaze to my screen to thumb out a quick response to Bella. Then I lock the phone and place it back on the bar top to finish reading the menu.

"The grilled cheese sounds like a meal for a toddler, but it's actually the best Gouda that's ever passed my lips."

The stranger next to me isn't going to shut up. That much is clear. I swivel in his direction and give him a proper once-over. The jaw belonging to the blue eyes looks like it was sculpted from granite. He looks perhaps a year or two younger than my thirty years of age. The faint scar through one eyebrow adds to the air of masculinity. He looks tall, based on the way his knees are jammed into the base of the bar top. His clothes are nothing to write home about, but the way they fit his muscular frame is. The jeans are the type that have been worn over and over again, molding to the person's body, and oh, what a body it is. He sports a ProBuild Direct hat that likely indicates he works for the local company and got his muscles the old-fashioned way. I tilt my head and decide to have some fun until I board my plane. This new contract means I've earned a little harmless flirtation in my life.

"Do you let a lot past your lips?" I lift an eyebrow suggestively and his gaze snags on mine, surprise in his eyes.

The tug on his lips is immediate. "I do enjoy the finer things in life."

"As do I. I'd say cheers, but I don't have a drink."

Just like I planned, the man lifts his hand and flags the bartender. "Dave, can we get this beautiful lady with the killer heels a drink?" He looks back at me. "What would you like?"

"Hmm." I've had at least six cups of coffee today already. Probably better to switch to alcohol before my heart flutters right out of my chest. "Wine. pinot noir, if you have it."

While the bartender gets busy finding a glass and my wine, the stranger turns to me fully, his knees barely brushing the outside of my thigh. "Should we swap names, or should I keep calling you beautiful lady with the killer heels?"

"I kind of like that nickname, but it is a mouthful." I hold out my right hand in the space between us. "I'm Kaitlyn." I purposely leave off my last name. A woman can never be too careful.

The stranger shakes my hand, his palm warm and rough against mine. "With a C or a K?"

I quirk an eyebrow. It's a pet peeve of mine when people spell my name wrong. "With a K, thanks for asking. And you are?"

He's still holding my hand, his smile open and friendly. "Ben."

"And do you come here often, Ben?" At the humor infusing his eyes, I clarify. "And that's not a pickup line. You're on a first name basis with the bartender and he sat your drink in front of you without you ordering. A girl can put two and two together." I finally pull my hand back when the bartender places my wine glass on the bar top.

As I take that first sip, I can feel Ben studying me. "I do fly through here often. My parents live in Buckhead. You?"

I smile coyly. "I don't tell strange men where I live."

Ben grabs his chest in fake agony. "I save you from ordering a subpar lunch and this is the thanks I get? I'm a strange man?"

He's actually pretty adorable and I'm feeling willing to take the risk of getting to know him. "This could be your thing. You lure women in with your talk of grilled cheese and Gouda, and then when they head to the bathroom, you strike."

His eyes widen and he puts his hand on the bar top, just an inch from mine. "I strike, huh? What am I doing in this scenario of yours? Robbing you in the bathroom? Stealing your identification and living a life as Kaitlyn with a K?"

I laugh softly, enjoying the conversation. I don't spend much time socializing outside of business dinners. It's nice to just chat with a stranger. No pretenses. No one to impress.

"I doubt that last one. You'd have to decide if your nickname would be Kait or Lyn, neither of which is a good option. So you'd live your whole life correcting people when they try to shorten your name. You'd think back on that day you robbed the real Kaitlyn and wish you'd never done it. Best to stay here at the bar and eat your grilled cheese as Ben. Impossible to shorten that one."

Ben is grinning now, his straight white teeth against tan skin reminding me of the classic American frat boy. "You're fun, Kaitlyn with a K."

I let out a snort, the loud, indelicate kind that I usually stuff down. "That's a first."

Ben tilts his head and signals for another round from our bartender. "What's a first? Being fun?"

I shrug. "Yeah, I mean, I'm mostly a workaholic. What with that and correcting people shortening my name, it doesn't leave much room for fun."

"What is it you do?" Ben tips his glass and the last of the beer slides down his throat. I watch the way his Adam's apple bobs and wonder why I find that so hot. Maybe I do need to get out and date.

I open my mouth, but Ben beats me to it, clanking his empty glass down on the bar top. "Wait. Don't tell me. You don't tell strange men what you do."

The bartender slides the beer across the bar just as a loud voice comes through the airport speakers. "Our apologies, folks, but Flight 798 to Tampa, Florida has been delayed. Right now we're looking at a two-hour delay while we wait for the plane from New York to arrive. Bad weather up there has delayed them, which delays us. Stay close to the gate and we'll give updates."

My shoulders slump. Ben bumps my leg with his knee. "That your flight?"

I nod, calculating how to adjust my dinner plans now that I'll be a few hours late. Hopefully my new client will understand.

"Mine too," Ben says, not sounding like the announcement bothers him too much. "How about we order some grilled cheese and settle in?"

I nod. It would be a shame to waste the glass of wine. "That sounds great. Excuse me while I email my assistant."

Ben waggles his eyebrows. "Wow. An assistant? You must be a workaholic." He flags the bartender yet again. "Let's see if we can fix that. At least for a few hours."

I shoot him a confident smile, liking the sound of that. If I have to be delayed here in the airport bar, at least I get to spend two hours flirting with a handsome man.

Oh, and sampling the best Gouda outside of the Netherlands.

# Chapter Two

TEN YEARS EARLIER

Banks

Damn, if this woman isn't the full package.

There's nothing unusual about meeting a woman at an airport bar–in fact, it can be the best place to strike up an acquaintanceship for the simple reason that everything in an airport is temporary. It's only a matter of time before all parties take off to their different destinations, never to meet again. Temporary has always been my MO, one I'm well-known for.

But Kaitlyn–with a K–is as intriguing as she is beautiful. Long black hair cascades over her shoulders with caramel highlights that almost perfectly match her eyes. The heels alone have me sporting wood, especially when combined with that tight designer suit that shows off her slim body while accentuating curves in all the right places.

Had I known I'd run into a beauty like Kaitlyn, I might have dressed nicer, but comfort is my only goal when traveling. And my casual attire doesn't appear to be hurting too much.

"Well, Ben, I might owe you my firstborn," Kaitlyn says as she dabs her full lips with a napkin. "That grilled cheese was life changing."

I grin, my eyes still trained on her mouth. "Saddling me with a small incontinent human doesn't sound much like gratitude. Maybe we can arrange for a different kind of IOU."

Her lips curve at my not-so-subtle come-on. "Perhaps." But the moment is broken when Dave interrupts to ask if we need another drink.

I don't know why I told her my name is Ben. While it technically *is* my name, only my parents and brother use it. I'm Banks to everyone else–or Benny when I'm on the ice. But after hearing the name all weekend with my family, I used it on reflex, and I admit I don't hate how it sounds coming from Kaitlyn's pink lips. I'd kill to hear her screaming out *any* of my names while under me.

But I doubt that's in the cards.

We both refuse the offer of another drink, and I settle up with Dave, but we've still got another hour to kill.

"Can you really walk in those things?" I ask, gesturing to her sky-high heels.

She laughs. "I could run a marathon in them if I had to."

"Then I guess walking off those sandwiches won't be a challenge." I stand and hold a hand out to help her off her stool like the gentleman my mother tried to raise–with varying levels of success.

When she places her hand in mine, I feel a tingling warmth spread up my arm. Must be an after-effect from the elbow I threw at Booch at Friday's practice. That twat might be a hell of a defender, but his mouth has a way of getting under everyone's skin, both on and off the ice.

Kaitlyn shoulders her laptop bag and I pull my carry-on behind me as we exit the bar and wade into the streaming masses in the terminal. As promised, there's not a single wobble in her step despite the two glasses of wine she drank. Gotta love a girl who can hold her liquor.

Time for a little fishing, so I tilt my head to a newsstand displaying Atlanta and Georgia memorabilia. "Need to pick up any souvenirs for anyone?"

I can't tell if she's onto me or not when she suppresses a smile and answers, "My dad *is* a big Georgia football fan."

"Sounds like your dad and I have something in common then." I'm essentially a sports addict, although hockey is obviously my favorite. I love everything about hockey–except that it sometimes gets in the way of a good nap.

"Go Tigers," she says in a voice that's way more sultry than any cheer I've ever heard.

"Are you into sports?" A hot woman who's into sports and dresses like that? Way too good to be true.

"You could say that."

I put my hand over my heart. "Will you marry me?" I'm not above begging.

Kaitlyn tilts her head back with a laugh, exposing the slim column of her throat. Fuck, my dick is going to give me away if she keeps this up. "I make it a rule to never get engaged on a first date."

"So this is a date, is it?" No arguments here. Even if we only have another hour, it's maybe the best date I've ever been on. Something about her has me hanging on her every word like I'm watching a playoff game gone into overtime.

She pretends she didn't hear me and steps up to the newsstand to pluck a pack of temporary tattoos from a display of Georgia Tigers merchandise. "I don't exactly need souvenirs from my own town, but these could come in handy next time I go to a game." Her smile tells me she knows she just gave away that she lives in Atlanta.

I swipe the tattoos from her hand and pull out my wallet.

She doesn't protest, so I pay for them but don't give up the bag.

We continue our walk, keeping conversation light until our flight is finally called to board. When they make the call for first-class passengers, I watch Kaitlyn for movement, but she stays where she is. So I do too.

"Coffee!" she suddenly and inexplicably exclaims, spinning on her heel and scanning the terminal in a panic. "I need coffee for the flight."

I smile, finding this new side of her fucking cute. "They have coffee onboard."

She whips her head toward me, lip curled like she just smelled the inside of my skates. "I'm not drinking that swill. Airplane coffee is made with *tank* water. Do you know how much bacteria is in there?"

"Well, now I do." My own lip curls.

"I'll be back." She powerwalks to a nearby coffee kiosk as the next group is called to board.

I make a quick decision and hurry to the airline counter by the gangway. A brief conversation with the attendant—and an autograph for her son—gets me exactly what I want.

Kaitlyn jogs up to the dwindling line with her cardboard cup of coffee just as they announce last call. "You're still here. I thought you would have boarded by now with that carry-on."

"I'm in no hurry." I tell her the truth and gesture for her to walk ahead of me. The attendant scans our tickets and we board the plane.

As we're about to step on, Kaitlyn turns to me. Even with her heels, I've still got a few inches on her. "Well, Ben, it was a pleasure meeting you. Thanks for the Gouda—and the conversation."

"The pleasure was all mine, Kaitlyn with a K."

Her return smile is dazzling, but I don't get to enjoy it for long, as she turns to walk down the aisle to her seat. I follow, handing my carry-on to the flight attendant, who stows it in the first-class bin above my original seat.

A glance to the seat shows a middle-aged guy with a paunch smiling like he's just won the lottery and guzzling his free glass of champagne. I hold back my laugh.

At the second row of business class, Kaitlyn stops to sit in the aisle seat to our right, coffee in one hand and laptop bag in the other. She lifts her eyes to me. "Bye."

But I don't follow the line of passengers down the aisle. Instead, I bend and point to the window seat beside her. "I think that's my seat." I don't even try suppressing my smile at her surprised expression.

She stands without a word and slides back into the aisle, her shoulder brushing my chest as she maneuvers her way out. I fold myself into the window seat, not even caring that my knees jam into the seat in front of me. I'll gladly give up legroom for another hour and sixteen minutes with her.

By the time she sits back down, she's laughing quietly. "I'm too practical to consider coincidence. You switched your seat, didn't you?"

"I have no idea what you're talking about. I always sit in..." I look up at the row number. "Seat 9A. It's my lucky number." Which is a lie. My lucky number is the same as the one on my Florida Storm Chasers uniform: 29.

"You're a terrible liar." She lowers her tray to rest her coffee on while she fastens her seatbelt. "You must lose a lot of money in poker."

"Untrue. I don't play poker." As a professional athlete, I steer clear of any kind of gambling. It's a slippery slope, and I know myself too well.

"Lucky for you." She laughs and retrieves her coffee cup. "What do you do for guys' night, then?"

I don't want to tell her we go clubbing or play video games because that will make me sound like a douchebag to someone as put-together and professional as Kaitlyn. So, instead, I tell her another version of the truth. "My friends are all my coworkers, and we work a lot of nights."

She glances at my ball cap, not for the first time, and I know what she's thinking–that I work for ProBuild Direct, the company whose logo sits on the cap. It's my dad's company, a construction supply manufacturer he built from scratch starting when he was twenty—eight years younger than I am now. It's a lot to live up to. Even as a professional athlete, I sometimes feel like I'm playing catch up with his legacy.

I could correct Kaitlyn's assumption, but to what end? She clearly wants to keep things anonymous. And, besides, she's no puck bunny who would hand me her panties when she found out what I do for a living. Hell, she'd probably look at me like she did when I suggested the petri dish airplane coffee.

"Doesn't sound like a bad gig," she responds. "Can't say that I have too many friends in my office."

"Then you obviously work with a bunch of dicks–they make awful friends. You know what they say...never trust a dick." It's sound advice from someone who has one.

"A lesson I've maybe learned a time or two." One corner of her mouth quirks. "Present company excluded, of course."

I laugh just as the captain comes over the speaker to announce we're taking off shortly. When he's done, I venture, "Still not going to tell me what you're doing in Tampa?"

I get my answer when she takes a sip of her coffee and asks, "Have you ever noticed how few airline pilots are women?"

So I give up and simply enjoy her company as we cruise thirty-thousand feet in the air to Florida. The time slips by way too fast, and before I know it, we're standing on the sidewalk outside baggage claim at Tampa International Airport.

My Porsche is parked in short-term, but I wait with

Kaitlyn for her taxi. Even I know not to offer her a ride. She's too careful for that. And it's for the best, anyway. She's the kind of woman you give all your attention to, the one you build a future with–not a casual hook-up who you forget about the minute you step on the ice or board a plane for your next away game. I'm the guy who likes to forget, and everything about her tells me she's not looking to be remembered *or* forgotten. She's got a game plan all her own.

Her taxi pulls up, and she holds her hand out to me as she grips the handle of her giant suitcase. But instead of taking her hand, I place the newsstand bag in it and lean in to place a kiss on her cheek. Half of me expects her to punch me in the face, but when she doesn't, I whisper, "Have a good life, Kaitlyn with a K."

# Chapter Three

Kaitlyn

The flight delay last night, while lovely due to my travel companion, ended up causing a kink in my plans. Jake was unable to pick me up from the airport like we'd planned. Something about a therapy appointment that he couldn't miss. Which meant I got up extra early to have breakfast with him at the restaurant downstairs in my hotel. We've had a full hour to get to know each other before he has to get to practice, but even that limited amount of time has shown me I have my work cut out for me. He's already been dropped by an agent for being a handful, and I can see why. The kid is young and mouthy. He's also sporting a bruise below one eye, and when I commented on it, the kid grinned like he was proud of it.

"I gotta head out, babe, but I'll see you at the rink?" Jake throws his napkin onto his plate and scrapes his chair back.

I stand up too, if only to not be at a height disadvantage. "Absolutely never would it be okay to call your agent 'babe.'

Remember that and we'll get along just fine. See you in two hours, Bouchard."

Jake shoots me a wink like he didn't hear me. "She's feisty. I like it." And then he walks away, his swagger thicker than the baby hair on his jaw that's just barely coming in.

I sigh and sit back in my chair, wondering what the hell I just got myself into. Jake Bouchard–known as "Booch" to his teammates–is an up-and-coming star of a player, but his maturity level is nonexistent. The payout as his agent is going to be better than anything I've seen so far in my career, but not if I can't control my client long enough to collect a check. Pretty sure strangling one's own client is frowned upon. Plus, Ed Presley, my boss, would finally have a reason for firing me like I know he wants to. He's the typical male chauvinist, threatened by a smart, competent woman.

"Just do your thing, Killer Kaitlyn," I mutter under my breath.

It's a nickname I got my first year as an agent when I "accidentally" knocked an NFLer in the balls with my umbrella after he got handsy with me. Sometimes these tough guys need more than a lecture; they need a lesson. And that's just what I'll do today when I get to the rink. I'll keep Jake in his place and show him that I can be his strongest champion if he just treats me with respect. It isn't a lot to ask in exchange for me directing his career.

I go back to my room and make sure my suit is impeccable, along with my makeup. There's a fine line between looking professionally feminine and looking like I'm going on a date. I need these hockey guys to take me seriously. Being a woman in a male-dominated arena means I have to work twice as hard to achieve the level of success I dream about. I watch some game play videos, along with Jake's highlight reels, and then grab my laptop bag and head downstairs to walk to the practice rink just two blocks north.

Ed has been to this rink a million times and gave me a curt text with directions this morning. I give my information to the security guard and get a printed name badge, and she directs me to wait outside the coach's office. The door is closed, and I hear voices inside, so naturally I try to listen in.

"You can't keep coming into practice late. You need to be an example to the younger guys," a gruff voice implores.

"Sorry, Coach. Won't happen again."

I frown. That second voice sounds familiar.

A loud sigh breaks the silence. "We both know that isn't true. Now get the hell out of here. I have an appointment."

An unseen door opens and closes and then the door nearest me whips open. Coach Kent Bowman is in a pair of khakis and a polo shirt. The guy is remarkably fit for being on the cusp of retirement. It's patently unfair that the silvery-white hair only makes him hotter when he's old enough to be my father.

"Kaitlyn Phillips?" he asks, a warm smile on his face.

I shake his hand and he steps back to let me into his office. I have a seat in one of the two cracked leather club chairs, and he sinks behind his cluttered desk. "Thanks for meeting with me. I met Jake earlier this morning and want to see how he fits with the team so I know how to best represent him."

Coach Bowman smirks and leans his elbows on the desk. "That kid is something else."

I bite back what I want to say and remember it's my job to make my client look good. Even if I might not actually agree. "Tenth pick in the 2012 draft. Nothing to sneeze at."

Coach tips his head to the side. "Hell of a player out there on that ice." He drops his hands to the desk and laces his fingers, leveling a serious gaze at me. "But he's a hothead. Gets himself in trouble on and off the ice. I won't sugarcoat it, Ms. Phillips. You have your work cut out for you."

Maybe that warning should strike terror in my heart, but

all it does is fire me up. The men in my life have always discounted me. Mostly my father and my current mentor, Ed, the biggest asshole in the hockey agent world. Not this time, fellas. I'm going to make Jake Bouchard my bitch. Okay, that's a bit extreme, but the sentiment isn't. I'll shape him up and get him the best damn contracts known to the hockey world. He's going to look like a fucking angel when I get done with him.

"Good thing I like a challenge," I say with a grin that makes the corners of Coach Bowman's eyes crinkle in amusement.

"Alrighty, then. Let's meet the team, shall we?" He stands and opens the door along the back wall, holding his arm out for me to go ahead of him. The first rush of cold air from the ice rink hits my skin and I'm so excited I can barely control my professional expression.

The sound of blades carving the ice floats up and over to the slightly raised level where we stand. Hockey players in various levels of uniforms and padding fly around the oval, moving faster than one would think possible. A puck is in motion, slicing through the air and smacking into the pads of the goalie. The player stands, wearing a shit-eating grin on his face and looking taller than any man should. Taunts and chirping fill the air before another coach in the signature gold and black colors of the Storm Chasers whistles to get every-one's attention.

"Wrap it up, boys!"

The guys all turn in our direction and skate over to their benches, pushing and shoving each other like children. I've been in a lot of football locker rooms, so I'm used to the atmosphere, but even with my background, the level of testosterone floating around this hockey team hits me like a wall when Coach Bowman and I reach the side of the rink. I prop my laptop bag against the wall, the curtain of my hair falling into my face. The bag falls over and threatens to spill its contents, which happen to include that stupid plastic bag of tattoos from the airport yesterday. I spent way too much time last night thinking about Ben instead of today's meeting. I feel my spine softening just thinking about looking into Ben's warm blue eyes. The coach's voice jolts me back to the present and I line my spine with steel, putting Ben behind me.

"Nice work out there," Coach bellows, and the guys immediately quiet down. "I expect you to be on your best behavior when you meet our guest today." Half the team lets out a groan.

My bag falls over again, and I want to drop-kick it, but instead I paste a pleasant smile on my face. Friendly, but not too friendly. Serious, but not a hardass.

And I immediately freeze. Horrified. Shocked. And feeling a little like my breakfast might come back up.

Because not only do I spot my new client shooting me another fucking wink, but next to him is the same man I had lunch with yesterday at the airport. The same man I flirted shamelessly with.

"Ms. Phillips?" Coach Bowman is looking at me, his head swiveled over his shoulder, probably wondering why I've gone whiter than the ice.

I blink and push absolutely everything aside. I have a job to do, and it does not include Ben. Fucking Ben. That's not even his name. I'd bet my life on it. There's not one player on the Storm Chasers' roster named Ben.

"Yes," I say brightly, stepping forward and standing next to Coach Bowman. "Nice to meet you all. I'm Kaitlyn Phillips."

"With a K," someone mutters under their breath, interrupting me. I have exactly one guess as to who that could have come from.

I carry on, determined to funnel all my embarrassment

and shock into doing my job. "I'm Jake Bouchard's new agent and I'd love to get to know you all."

Jake makes some noise that has another one of his teammates snickering. Ben is glaring at Jake. I can feel the respect slipping from the room and swirling around the drain at the center of my professional life. I open my mouth to try to rein in this situation, but the goalie beats me to it.

"Do you have a business card on you, Ms. Phillips?" His Russian accent is thick, but I don't detect any sarcasm or teasing in it. He's incredibly tall, his sandy brown hair a sweaty mess, which doesn't take away from his stoically handsome face. Pretty sure women have fallen to their knees over the centuries when they've gazed upon that kind of jawline.

"I do." I reach for my bag and grab one, handing it to him, grateful at least one player is a gentleman. The goalie blocks out most of the players who are back to shooting the shit and chirping at each other, each louder and more obnoxious than the rest.

"I am Niko Drugov," the goalie says, his thick finger tracing the edge of my card. "Ignore the idiots."

My smile is genuine. "I like you, Niko Drugov."

Jake shoves his way into our pleasant chat, a shit-eating grin on his face I want to wipe off. Then Ben—or whoever the fuck he is—also joins us. My gaze drops to his number, my brain flipping through the roster I memorized for this meeting. I kick myself for not recognizing him yesterday. He's Banks Bennet, first-line center for the Storm Chasers.

"Quit hogging my agent, Druggy," Jake says, shoving his elbow into Niko's side. The hulking goalie gives zero reaction.

"He's being polite, something you should try," I snap back.

Banks, not realizing that both he and Jake are being murdered in my imagination right now, continues to smile at me like we're old friends. "Where'd you end up putting the Tiger tattoo, Kaitlyn with a K?"

Our small group freezes and all eyes turn in my direction. The familiarity of that question hints at us having a history. One afternoon in the airport does not equate to a history.

The tip of my nose goes numb, but the rest of my face flushes hot. Jake is hooting and hollering now, brain immediately going in the gutter while Niko tips his head as if examining me in a new, more unpleasant light. More than one player over Ben's shoulder is staring at my body, as if they could see through my suit to the skin below, clearly having overheard our conversation. I pull myself up to my full height, tug down my suit jacket, and stand directly in front of Ben. I look him up and down, taking my time to peruse his disheveled, sweaty appearance. He looks damn good, but my face says the opposite. I sniff and look down my nose at him somehow, even though he's more than a few inches taller than me in his skates.

"If," I drawl, letting my voice carry, "I had a tattoo, you'd be the last person to find out where I placed it on my body." I lean in and give a meaningful glance at the 29 emblazoned on his practice jersey before eviscerating him with my glare. My voice is now barely a whisper. "So much for nine-a being your lucky number."

Ben swallows hard, that fucking smile finally dying on his handsome face. Jake elbows him in the gut.

"Gotta love watching Benny crash and burn." Jake doubles over laughing. If I could drag my gaze away from where it's locked with Ben's hurt one, I would glare at Jake too.

Coach Bowman clears his throat and takes back control of the group. "I'd like Ms. Phillips to observe a scrimmage if you're done acting like toddlers. Try to impress me this time."

The guys all scurry away on the ice, Ben or Banks, or

whoever the hell he is, being the last one to leave. He finally looks away from me, the tips of his ears as red hot as my temper. I have a seat next to Coach Bowman in the first row behind the big goalie.

"Sorry about that. They're not much more than little boys in grown up bodies sometimes."

I shrug. "I'm used to it."

Coach shoots me a sympathetic look. "Still doesn't make it right."

"No, it doesn't." I shake my head and watch the team play, making notes and doing my damn job–even if my heart is hammering against my ribs and my brain is scattered.

I really liked Ben last night. Today's version is on my shit list. And yet part of me hates that I put that wounded puppy dog look in his eyes.

I watch him miss a shot, and Jake gives him shit for it. The very next play, Ben slams into the back of Jake and pins him against the boards in a punishing crash. It takes three other players to break those two apart. And when Ben yanks away from his teammates to skate over to the bench while throwing me a look over his shoulder, I pretend I don't see him.

I'm here to do my fucking job.

# Chapter Four

Banks

Clearly, I'm an idiot for expecting Kaitlyn to be as happy to see me as I was to see her. I mean, what are the chances that the woman I clicked with so instantly yesterday would show up at the rink today? I thought for a second that God liked me and had finally forgiven me for that whole mess with that Nikki chick last year. How was I supposed to know she was a reporter? She looked like any other puck bunny to me. I still owe Coach for pulling me out of that clusterfuck. My agent would have dropped me if Coach hadn't stepped in.

I thought today was my lucky day. Then fucking Booch tells me he already banged Kaitlyn at her hotel last night. Half the words that come out of that asshole's mouth are bullshit, so I don't know if he's being straight or not. The guy does get a lot of tail, though.

But Kaitlyn? Everything about her yesterday said she wouldn't be the type to open her thighs for a guy like Jake Bouchard. Especially being his agent! Yeah, Booch is full of shit for sure. But I still can't believe my perfect woman is also an agent. It certainly makes things more complicated.

The second she saw me, I regretted ever telling her my name was Ben. She looked not just surprised to see me but stricken—like I'd purposefully lied to her.

It's obvious now, though, that she kept more than her last name and profession from me yesterday. The ice queen didn't show her face until just now.

Yeah, maybe I shouldn't have mentioned the tattoos, but with Booch whispering in my ear on the one side and Popeye making me laugh with a joke at Booch's expense on the other, part of me just wanted to stake my claim. Obviously, it backfired.

The ice queen dressed me down, while at the same time making it clear she wanted to erase not just the memory of our time together but my entire existence. She's obviously one of these women who only cares about proving she's better than men, and her act at the airport was just that—an act.

To think I wasted time last night reevaluating my lifestyle. Kaitlyn was on my mind the entire drive home from the airport, and when I walked into my mess of a condo, I felt like I was seeing it for the first time. Shame washed over me at living like a frat boy—dirty dishes on the counter, beer bottles on the nightstand, laundry piled up to the ceiling with nothing but jeans and workout gear in it. When I spotted the box of Lucky Charms on the counter, it was the last straw. Because I'd never get a woman as perfect as Kaitlyn if I continued to live like this.

Now I know Kaitlyn with a K was bullshit. She doesn't exist. And I'm doing just fine the way I am. Hell, I'm a professional hockey player making bank and getting as much pussy as I want. Nothing wrong with that.

This realization does not, however, keep me from smashing Booch into the boards when I get back onto the ice.

The fucker deserves it for treating his agent like shit just because she's a woman. Even if she's not the woman I thought she was.

Kaitlyn watches the rest of the practice, and while I try not to let her distract me, I know I'm not playing my best. The team counts on me as first-line center, so I need to get my shit together before Thursday night's game. I also need to get five new alarm clocks and set them up all over my condo so I stop oversleeping. If my agent hears I was late to practice this morning, his foot will be so far up my ass I'll be tasting his shoe polish.

"Yo, Banks! Come check this out." Erik Anderson–otherwise known as Popeye–shouts when I get to the locker room. His stall is right next to Booch's where Jake and his new agent have their heads together. Great.

I try waving Popeye off, but he insists, "I promise you want to see this."

With no other choice, I trudge over his way. Kaitlyn turns to send me a glare, and Booch uses the opportunity to make lewd fucking gestures behind her back.

"Fuck off," I tell him, but the shock on Kaitlyn's face tells me she thinks I'm talking to her. It's quickly covered in ice again. Probably just as well. If she's gonna dish it out like she did out on the bench, she'd better be able to take it.

"It seems I have a lot more work to do on my character judgment instincts. I don't like being wrong, and I'll see it doesn't happen again, *Ben*," she bites at me before turning back to Booch.

I've had enough of this crap, so I ignore her and focus on Popeye instead. He turns his phone screen to me and guffaws just before pressing play on a social media video of some hot girl. It looks like she's in the stands of our practice rink just down the hall from here.

"Storm Chasers just finished practice, and I'm telling you,

Banks Bennet is hands down the hottest player on the team. I'm gonna go see if he'll sign something for me." She winks and pulls the neck of her tank top down to reveal half of a full, creamy breast. "I'm comin' for you, Banks," she purrs and then kisses the screen with red-glossed lips before the video cuts off.

"Told ya you wanted to see it," Popeye crows before laughing again.

Booch pipes up, cutting Kaitlyn off in the middle of her sentence, "Lemme see. A hundred bucks says I already had her."

I stalk over to my locker stall, anxious to put distance between me and every-fucking-body at this point. Skipping both my shower and post-practice work with my physical therapist, I shrug on my street clothes and head for the door. Shouts and wolf whistles follow me.

"Try to last more than five minutes this time, Bennet!" one of the jackasses yells, followed by another shouting, "Let us know if they're real or fake!"

I ignore them all. I just want to get away from here. Away from *her*.

I have to take the back way out to avoid the puck bunny, my mood being so foul I'd undoubtedly be a rude asshole to her. But as I approach my Porsche, I slow my pace. Nothing makes me want to put distance between the ice and me. Nothing. So I'm beyond pissed I'm letting this agent woman I don't even know get into my head. This isn't me.

I resolve right now to put this shit behind me and return to business as usual. And if Kaitlyn Phillips can't do the same, I'm perfectly capable of biting right back. Game on, ice queen.

# Chapter Five

PRESENT DAY

Kaitlyn

> Ed: Your primadonna is acting up again.
> Control your clients, Phillips. It's Agenting
> 101.

I growl at the text message from Ed Presley and ignore it, cranking the incline higher on the treadmill. Sweat is already doing a number on my hair, which means I'll have to wash it before I head to the arena tonight for another Storm Chasers game. I don't go to all their games, by any means, but I do hit a lot of them since three players on the team are mine. Most of my time is spent scouting the under-eighteen hockey players, securing them with my agency before they make it big. The game has changed the last few decades, something Ed can't get through his thick skull.

Ed didn't exactly work my fingers to the bone, but I chipped quite a bit of my nail polish doing his dirty work for five years straight. Sure, he taught me how to be an agent, but he's also the reason my therapy bill is so high. The man's face is plastered next to the definition of misogynist in the dictionary. Not one day went by at his agency when I didn't endure some fucked-up comment about being a "pretty little thing" or how I should "leave this work to the boys, sweetheart." I paid my dues and left the second I felt opening my own agency specializing in hockey was feasible. It wasn't easy, but I'm finally where I want to be in my career: poised to overtake Ed Presley in the hockey agenting world.

When I hit the three-mile mark, I slow the treadmill and cool down. Lots of things have changed since I entered the hockey world. Back then, I could run a mile a couple times a week and stay in shape. These days, I require three miles five days a week, three days of lifting weights, and an obsession with lean protein and vegetables. Thankfully, I don't eat much. Don't need to when I practically have an IV of coffee in my veins.

Multiple texts come in while I get ready back in my hotel room. I ignore them all until I get to the arena and take my seat one row behind the Storm Chasers' bench before the guys are even out on the ice. My ex-boyfriend is one of the texts, asking me again to reconsider. I snort and then look around to make sure no one heard that. Thankfully, ticket holders haven't been let in yet. There's nothing to reconsider. Broderick definitely won me over and made me reconsider that romantic love actually exists, but when I broached the subject of children, he made it clear that was not in the cards for him. A lot of introspection later, I realized that it was important to me, so I made the heavy decision to break up before we entwined our lives any further.

"Looking at porn sites again, Kaitlyn?"

I glance up sharply, seeing the snarky face of Banks Bennett as his teammates file in behind him to drop off gear before the official warm-ups.

I give him a dazzling smile. "Yes, actually. Saw you banging some puck bunny. Didn't know you did sex tapes, Bennett. Is that why your agent dropped you? Again?"

His handsome face clouds over as I knew it would. He's in a pickle and there's nothing I love better than someone I dislike being at a disadvantage.

"You wish you knew, don't you? Always such a busy-body, Kaitlyn with a K." He shoots me a wink that makes me angry. For more than one reason. The man is infuriating. He's been trying to humiliate me since the day we met. Well, the day after we met. But he's also aged well and I'm not afraid to admit it. At least to myself. The man is stupid gorgeous with topaz blue eyes, black hair that has a hint of curl when he's sweaty, and a scruffy jawline that promises a good time between the sheets. Not that I'd ever give myself the chance to find out what that experience would be like. After all, I'm no puck bunny.

"Better watch out for Bobby, hot shot. Last couple games he looks like he might be taking over your job for you."

Banks's face hardens and I know I've struck a nerve. You don't get to be thirty-eight years old in the NHL and not worry about your longevity. And now that Ed dumped him as a client? Brutal timing.

"Tell Roadie and all your little hockey boys they have some big skates to fill if they want my position." Banks turns to leave and tosses over his shoulder. "And your blouse is unbuttoned."

Immediately, I look down, cheeks flaming. My blouse is not unbuttoned. Banks's laugh trails behind him as he marches back into the locker room.

"Fucker," I mutter, settling back in my seat to respond to all the texts. I'm just debating whether to answer Broderick when my friends tap me on the shoulder.

"Hey, Kaitlyn!"

I look up to see the smiling faces of Olivia Wylder and Roman LaFontaine. "Hey, guys!"

I jump up and hug them both, scooting over so they can join me. Roman retired from the Storm Chasers last year, leaving Banks as the oldest guy on the team. Olivia has quickly become my best friend this last year, which, paired with Banks and Roman being best friends, unfortunately means we end up at a lot of the same social gatherings. Thankfully I'm a mature adult and can deal with an asshole like Banks.

"You're here early," Roman says, immediately putting his arm around Olivia. These two are so adorable it makes my heart hurt. I thought I'd found that in Broderick, but our future goals weren't aligned.

"Yeah, figured I'd reply to some texts and emails while I waited for my boys to take the ice."

"Does 'my boys' include Banks?" Roman smirks.

I toss my dark hair over my shoulder. "He's not one of mine."

Olivia sighs. "You two still fighting?"

"Is the sky still blue? Did my father forget to send me a Christmas card this year? Does Ed Presley have a hair piece?"

Olivia snorts. "God, that toupee of his is awful, isn't it?"

"It really is." I giggle. "Oh! Wait. I have an invitation for you." I reach down and pull a thick, creamy envelope out of my bag and hand it to Olivia.

"What's this?" she asks, sliding her finger under the flap.

"I'm hosting my own fortieth birthday party," I announce. "Just a few friends, lots of champagne, and zero drama allowed."

"If you can promise me pedicures, I'm in." Roman looks at me with puppy dog eyes. The man isn't kidding. He can still rough up a player on the ice if he needs to, but don't come between him and his spa treatments now that he's retired.

"Pedicures can be arranged," I assure him. "Just need you

two to be there." Mostly because I don't have many friends and if they don't come it might just be me and my neighbor at my fortieth birthday party.

"Um," Roman shifts in his seat. "Speaking of being there for each other, there's something I need to talk to you about."

I frown at his nervous tone. When Olivia starts biting her thumbnail, I feel like I might need another caffeine hit before I can handle this conversation.

The noise in the arena gets louder as the ticket holders are let in and the most fanatical hockey fans stream down the stadium stairs to get to the plexiglass. Music starts pumping and the announcer's voice booms through the speakers. I have to lean over Olivia to hear Roman.

"You're scaring me," I say. When Olivia lets out a nervous giggle, I know it's serious.

Roman shifts in his seat and then swivels toward me, giving me his full attention. "We've become friends, haven't we, Kaitlyn?"

I'm about to be hustled. I can feel it in my bones. "Definitely. And now you want a favor. So spit it out already, Roman."

"I need you to pick up Banks."

I give a quick shake of my head. "I lift weights and all, but he's too heavy for me."

There's that nervous laugh from Olivia again. Roman doesn't break our stare-down. He knows that I know what he's actually talking about. But the second I acknowledge it, I'll have to deal with what he's truly asking me. And that . . . well, that's unfathomable.

Roman wants me to be Banks's agent. He wants me to take the one man who's gotten under my skin for ten straight years and babysit him full time. Because that's what being an agent is. I'm a glorified, well-paid babysitter of grown men who act like babies most of the time. Banks, especially.

"Kaitlyn," Roman sighs. "He's got no one else."

"Seems like that's his fault," I snap. "Did he put you up to this?"

Roman scrubs a hand over his face. "No. Definitely not. He'd take a stick to my balls if he knew I was talking to you about this."

I throw my hands in the air. "There you go. See? It'll never work. I can appreciate you wanting to help your best friend, but he and I just don't get along. It would be a disaster."

"It's already a disaster." Roman's eyebrows are darting all over his face, clearly agitated. "He's up for renegotiation this year and the younger guys are breathing down his neck. Everyone says Ed dumped him and it looks bad for Banks. Especially since Ed was his second agent. Banks looks like he's not a team player. A wild child who can't be tamed enough to play fair. He needs the very best agent out there to keep his dream alive for a few more years. That's you, Kaitlyn. Don't let some petty grievances crush a man's dreams."

I blow out a puff of air and sit back in the plastic seat. "Really laying it on thick, Roman." Guilt lines my veins, almost wiping out the irritation of his ridiculous request. Fuck, I hate it when people make a really good case. I project the image of a tough broad in a man's world, but lately those fucking Hallmark movies have been getting me right in the solar plexus. I have a heart, dammit. And Roman is tugging hard on the strings.

The announcers start revving up the crowd and pretty soon the Storm Chasers are taking the ice for their pregame warm-ups. The lights are flashing, and the bass of the music is thumping through the arena. Immediately, my eyes go to Banks, taking in the way he effortlessly glides across the ice, his stick handling so quick my gaze can barely keep up. I should be watching my three guys, but Banks has always drawn my gaze first.

This would be a disaster. I know it as sure as I know caffeine will one day kill me. And in both instances, I know better, but I barrel ahead anyway like a runaway train, straight for catastrophe, helpless to save myself. I look over at Roman, whose gaze hasn't left me.

"You're going to owe me so big."

Roman's infectious grin doesn't quell the anxiety eating away at my stomach.

I'm so going to regret this.

# Chapter Six

Banks

"Way to shut 'em down, Druggy." I thump our goalie on his shoulder pad as I pass by his stall in our locker room after our matchup with the Stingers. Damn, I needed that win.

"I have asked you repeatedly not to call me that, Benny," Niko Drugov, the man who delivered the shutout tonight, glares at me over his shoulder. "It is what one calls a drug addict." The guy is enormous and could reduce me to nothing but a red stain on the rubber floor beneath us if he chose to, but murdering your own teammate is a bad look.

"Right. I forgot," I lie and grin at him as I cross the floor to my stall. We've been doing this same routine for almost the entire twelve years we've both been on the Storm Chasers roster, and it never gets old—for me, at least. He needs to finally accept that a hockey player doesn't choose his own nickname.

Before I can reach my stall, however, I stop short to consider that Karma might be lurking around the arena tonight. Sitting her fine ass on my bench is none other than the devil herself, long legs crossed in a tight pencil skirt with a form-fitting silk blouse hugging her breasts. And let's not forget the stilettos. Kaitlyn always prefers to forgo the pitchfork in favor of heels that could gouge my eyes out just as efficiently.

And here I was having such a good night. I fix a saccharine smile to my lips as I walk closer. The mood in the room is high, music and chatter mixing with the usual smell of sweat, but I don't feel much like celebrating anymore.

Once upon a time, I entertained some fantasies about Kaitlyn Phillips–well, okay, I can admit she still stars in a few, and they're mostly of the hate-sex variety. But that was before. Before she threw away any potential for civility between us, much less the chance to explore our undeniable chemistry. She publicly threw down and started acting like she was chosen by the hockey gods themselves for the sole purpose of putting all of us knuckle-dragging mouth-breathers in our places. It's only gotten worse over the years. In a word, she's unbearable.

"To what do I owe the pleasure, Ms. Phillips? Or are you just taking five before luring more unsuspecting children to your house made of candy?"

Her smile is a twin of mine, except her lips are the same red as her blouse and they're shaped like a perfect heart. "Oh, hot shot, not all of us live like five-year-olds. Don't you know my house is made from the carcasses of washed-up hockey players like yourself?"

My jaw starts to tense as she pulls herself up to standing, but I force a relaxed expression. I have the height advantage in my skates, so I use it to step closer and peer down at her. Not a single strand of her glossy dark hair is out of place, and her makeup looks as if it was applied by Michelangelo himself.

Kaitlyn knows every one of my buttons, having invited herself to witness the better part of my career as she's picked up way too many of my teammates for my liking. I can admit she's a hell of an agent. Just never out loud.

I tilt my head and feign confusion. "I'm sorry, but I could have sworn that was *you* behind the bench bellowing like a rhinoceros when I scored on that breakaway."

Her laugh is caustic. "Don't flatter yourself, Bennet. A team win makes my job easier–it means I don't have to work as hard to give my clients a winning image. Something I hear you're struggling with these days," she says with another fake smile.

There she goes again, jabbing her sharp fingernail into the wound. If she only knew.

Yeah, my agent, Ed Presley, and I parted ways after nine years–so what? The guy is an asshole and everyone knows it. As is often the case with assholes, he isn't so hard to tolerate if he's working for your benefit; it's when he's opposite you that the stench gets too bad to stomach anymore. If I didn't think she'd use it against me for all eternity, I'd confess to Kaitlyn that I'm impressed as hell she lasted on his team as long as she did without taking a stiletto to his brain stem.

I don't regret splitting with Ed and his agency; it was a long time coming. I do, however, regret the precise timing, my impulsive ass having landed me without an agent right before my contract is up. I wish I could say I'm surprised with myself, but nope.

As anticipated, Ed is now out there whispering in everyone's ears–something I'd normally brush off since everyone talks shit. But this time it's keeping agents from taking my calls or signing me as a client, some with better excuses than others. Druggy's agent told me he loved me, but I was his wife's hall pass, so he couldn't afford to have me in his orbit. It's not my fault I'm handsome!

My buddy Roman's agent, Jim, is retiring and offered me a junior agent. Hard pass. Jim would have done me right for sure. Hell, Roman is retired, and Jim got him two endorsement deals–one for old-man pain cream and the other for some hotel chain. Ed was always promising endorsements, but the best I ever got was a sports drink only available in Japan. He was a hell of a negotiator when it came to my last contract, though.

Suffice it to say, I'm sweating it right about now, and Kaitlyn knows it.

"Why don't you run along and see Roadie and your other little boys?" I shoulder her aside, finally getting to my stall.

But she only crosses her arms and stands her ground. "I wish I could, *believe me*. But my competitive spirit has me backed into a bit of a corner."

"Oh, yeah?" I drop my helmet on the bench and pull my jersey over my head. "Mud wrestling match later? I'll lend you my cup."

Her nose wrinkles, and I laugh when it takes her a few seconds to shake it off.

Then she has me choking on my own saliva when she declares, "I've decided to be your temporary agent to negotiate your contract extension." When my jersey falls to the bench and I continue to cough, she rolls her eyes. "Do you need a lozenge or something?"

"More like a lobotomy," I croak, punching the pads covering my chest. "While I'm sure there's an ulterior motive here, I'll stop you right now and say thanks, but no thanks."

She'd likely negotiate a trade to a league in the Czech Republic to get rid of me. I know I'll only be getting slower and more injury-prone with age. Hell, these young pissants like Bobby Rhodes can't go ten minutes without reminding me. But I'm still a dominant player, and I intend to remain just that. I deserve a contract reflecting that fact.

"I'm not denying an ulterior motive, Banks, and it will cost you a pretty penny too. But let's cut the bullshit. We both know you're out of options, just like we know I'm fucking excellent at my job. And I'm sure it isn't hard to guess that I relish any opportunity to make Ed Presley eat dirt."

Ah. That actually makes sense. And it's something I'd enjoy as well.

But I'm not an idiot.

I pull off my pads and shirt, the surrounding air immediately hitting my sweat-covered chest and back to offer some cooling relief. Kaitlyn's eyes drop to my chest, almost like it's a reflex, but she immediately pulls her gaze back to mine, straightening her spine as she waits for my response. I don't miss the faint blush hitting her cheeks, though. Interesting.

"No." I wipe the sweat from my face and chest with a towel before tossing it with the rest of my discarded gear.

If I thought she'd push it, though, I'm wrong. Her arms drop to her sides and she simply shrugs. "Don't say I didn't offer." Then she's strutting in those mile-high heels to Roadie's stall, the young punk grinning at her like the lovesick jackass he is.

He's welcome to her. The last thing I need is Kaitlyn Phillips going to bat for me and interfering in my life. I'll figure it out on my own.

"Come on, man, you gotta have my six! I'm getting my butt handed to me!" Eli shouts.

"What do you think I'm doing? I just took one in the leg for you!"

"Right there!" he yells over me. "Two o'clock!"

I jam my thumbs into the controller, tilting my body sideways on the couch as I try hitting the sniper on the flatscreen before he hits me. My character's groan sounds from the TV just before the thud of another character's body on the dirt confirms Eli's has bitten it too.

"Dammit!" I drop the controller on the cushion next to me, Eli doing the same—but without the cursing. "I thought we had it that time."

He reaches for his Gatorade on the coffee table. "No offense, Banks, but you kind of suck at this game."

I don't take offense. He's right. I'm much better at Zombie Army. "It's because I'm hungry. You wanna order a pizza?" I ask, already knowing his answer since it's the same one any twelve-year-old boy would give.

I place the order for a meat-lover's special and relax back onto the couch, tagging the remote to switch the TV to SportsView, hoping to catch the highlights from last night's game. Eli's thumbs race over his phone screen faster than I can dangle a puck on a breakaway.

"Mom says I need to be home by seven," he tells me.

Eli is the only child of a single mom named Denise. She works two jobs, has a deadbeat ex-boyfriend, and still manages to smile and laugh all the damn time. I'm pretty sure she's either an angel or a saint. What she's not is a man, so she enrolled Eli in the Big Brothers program two years ago, and that's how he and I got hooked up. I'm supposed to be a positive male role model in his life, but I'm pretty sure our maturity levels are the same. Eli might even have the edge on me.

But I've got money and not a lot of friends, so it works out well for both of us. I take him one afternoon a week, and we either hang out like today, go hit the batting cages, or take in a game or movie.

I nod in acknowledgment, taking a sip of my own

Gatorade and muting the TV for the commercial break. "Your mouth is blue, you know."

Eli grins, his gap-toothed smile almost as blue as his lips. "So is yours."

I stick my tongue out as I roar out a battle cry and tackle Eli from the couch to the wood floor beneath. He tries working himself free, guffawing in my ear and using the defense skills I taught him to very little effect. I let him up, and we go a couple more times until I finally let him land a kick to my stomach and he declares himself champion.

The doorman calls up, and the delivery guy knocks on the door a few minutes later. Eli and I hunch over our paper plates on the couch, shoving the pie into our faces while SportsView coverage finally gets around to the hockey highlights.

"You should play football instead," Eli advises as the broadcasters cover another game.

I yank the pizza slice from his hand and toss it back into the box. "That's sacrilege. Give me back my Gatorade."

He laughs and shoves my hand out of the way to retrieve his slice. Hockey is not Eli's thing, and when I asked him why, he told me it was "a white-dude's sport." Since I couldn't exactly argue, I didn't. But I'm determined to convert him eventually.

"Storm Chasers took on the Stingers last night at Flagler Arena, pulling off a 4-0 shutout." Joe Bellvue, one of the broadcasters says, and I lean forward, watching the footage. As always, they cover each goal, but I notice they spend a lot more time talking about Roadie's and Dan-O's goals than mine. Fuck me for making it look so easy.

Joe's co-host, Andrew Heller, chimes in, "Rhodes is looking good out there this season. Storm Chasers had him as winger last year, but I like seeing him as second line center like last night."

"Agreed," Joe responds. "Banks Bennet may need to watch his back or Bobby might take his spot on the first line."

Andrew chuckles. "Well, Bennet's not getting any younger."

They start ribbing each other about their own respective ages and states of decrepitude, and I grit my teeth to keep from throwing the remote at the screen. That wouldn't exactly scream role model. Fuck! Commentators are talking shit about me now too?

I drop my pizza back onto my paper plate and jab the off button on the remote.

Eli shrugs and turns my way. "Looks like Warlords isn't the only thing you suck at." When I glare at him, he smiles. "There's always football."

<h1 style="text-align:center">Chapter Seven</h1>

Kaitlyn



"Argh!" I throw my phone on the bed and pace the window overlooking the Gulf. Not even the sight of a full moon hovering over the sparkling water can bring my mood back up. I should have left for Atlanta this afternoon, but I'm not ready to give up on the idea of taking Banks on and burying Ed. First, Banks refusing my offer of help when I didn't even want to offer it, and now Ed Presley giving me shit via text. If I didn't have to deal with him professionally from time to time, I'd block his ass and save myself the stress.

My heels snag on the carpet of the hotel room as I halt abruptly. "Someone has a big mouth!"

How else would Ed know I talked to Banks after the game? That pisses me off more than Ed's message. I swear to all the hockey gods, if it's one of my guys, I will relish tanking his career before I string up his balls as a warning to other snitches who think they can talk about me behind my back.

I sink to the bed and lean down to take my heels off. There's only one way to remedy this situation. I have to be Banks's agent and negotiate such a spectacular contract that Ed Presley is forced to eat crow and watch my career skyrocket over his. The cherry on top is that Banks will absolutely hate this arrangement. Frankly, I will too, but I can put that aside for the couple of months it will take to put Ed in his place. Nothing would make me happier than seeing the look on his face when I put him to shame.

Thanks to Bobby, Alexi, and Pete being on the same team, I know exactly when the guys are due at the practice rink tomorrow morning. That leaves me the rest of tonight to put together a plan. I'm good at what I do, and it doesn't take me long to strategize my moves over the next few months. Now I just need Banks to get on board. It won't be easy, but with my negotiating skills, I know he'll eventually succumb to Killer Kaitlyn. They all do.

One of only two doors on this level of the high rise rips open and a shirtless, half-asleep Banks Bennett appears in the crack. His dark hair is more disheveled than usual, and I don't dare look down to take in his half-naked body.

"Fuck. I'm clearly having a nightmare," he mutters before shutting the door in my face.

I knock again, louder this time. I hear a groan from the other side of the door, but he opens it, staring at me with one eye closed. He only needs one blue iris to get the point across: I'm not wanted here. Sadly for him, I don't care. I'm about to save his ass.

"I thought I paid the doorman enough to not let degenerates up here," he says, voice still rough from a nap.

"Oh, big words and everything, hot shot. I'm impressed. Now, come on. We have work to do and not enough time to get it done."

I plant my palm between his pec muscles and push. He stumbles back in surprise–I don't normally push my way unwelcome into people's homes–and I take advantage, charging into his space. I take a moment to look around. Having never been in his condo before, I'm surprised to see it doesn't resemble a teenager's bedroom as I would have assumed. There's a half-empty glass of water on the coffee table and a well-worn blanket abandoned on the back of one of the couches, along with a couple video game controllers left on the floor. The living space is vast, filled with comfortable-looking furniture and open to a luxurious kitchen. It all looks casually homey and tidy, but then again, I haven't seen his bedroom.

"What the fuck, Kaitlyn?" Banks snaps, crossing his arms over his impressive chest and looking more awake with each passing second. Good. He needs his wits about him if we're going to right the ship that is his career.

I ignore the puffed-up muscles and the gray sweatpants–even though they happen to be my Kryptonite–and throw my laptop bag onto the couch. Clasping my hands together in front of me, I get straight to the point.

"I did my homework last night. Word on the street is you're going to be traded unless you prove your continued worth to the Storm Chasers. *And* if you have a good agent to make management see that worth. I, on the other hand, have a former boss to stick it to. This is what you call a win-win situation, Banks. A marriage of convenience that will benefit us both."

Banks turns to the right and walks away, disappearing down a hallway. That isn't exactly what I was expecting. Normally Banks verbally spars with me until one of us is bleeding out on the floor or limping back to a neutral zone. I'm about to go after him when he reappears, tugging a shirt over his head and walking past me.

"I already told you, no thanks." He keeps walking and I follow this time, trailing his ass to a kitchen with all the modern appliances a gourmet chef would swoon over.

"Listen. Perhaps I didn't make myself clear the other night, which is very unlikely, but I forgot how you hockey guys need everyone to speak slowly." Banks grabs a mug out of a cabinet and shoots me a dirty look over his shoulder. "I'm motivated to negotiate the best deal possible for you to stick it to Ed Presley. You'd be a fool to turn me down."

Banks drops the lid of the coffee canister he plucked out of the cabinet and bends down to pick it up. I avert my eyes, even though most women would have gawked at his impressive backside. Instead, my gaze snags on a drawing taped to his refrigerator. It's a cyborg thing with human eyes, but a robot body. It's clearly the work of a child, but there's talent there. I tuck that away in the back of my brain, wondering why Banks has a child's drawing in his kitchen.

Banks dumps coffee grounds into the machine and clicks the on button before turning around and leaning his hips against the countertop behind him. The coffee pot gurgles to life and the aroma of roasted beans fills the kitchen. My mouth waters, but I refocus on the task at hand.

"On what planet would I ever trust you with my career?"

I tuck my hands into my pants pockets. He's got a point. I

wouldn't trust me any more than I trust him. "Look, Ed Presley is my nemesis. Even more than you, hot shot, so trust me when I say I want to bring him to his knees. The best way to do that is to pick up the client he dropped and beat him at his own game. Help me help you."

Banks studies me, his gaze taking in every detail of my appearance. My heart rate begins to hammer at his thorough inspection, but I school my entire body into an air of nonchalance. The machine behind him beeps and he ignores it.

"If we do this—"

My face breaks into a brilliant smile. I knew I'd get him to come around. Banks holds his hand up, cutting off my enthusiasm. "*If* we do this, what did you have in mind?"

This is where I shine. I hold up my hand and count off my fingers. "One, you have a terrible reputation for being late. Two, you need to step up as a leader for the younger guys on the team. Three, you've missed important meetings, which projects an image of not caring. And four, the only thing the fans know about Banks Bennet personally is that he prefers blondes."

Banks grins. "You sound like a jealous girlfriend, Ms. Phillips."

I huff. "Don't be ridiculous. I'm your agent now. That means I rule your life. No detail is too small. We have to make you out to be the man every woman wants to bring home to their mama but who also happens to have phenomenal hockey skills with several more years of playing left in him. I'm not a jealous girlfriend. I'm a fucking miracle worker."

Banks drops the grin and spins back around, pouring himself a cup of coffee. When he turns to face me, his eyes are narrowed. "I would have said no and laughed you right out of my condo."

"Except?" I move one step closer, feeling certain victory is within my grasp.

He levels a serious look at me, one I rarely see directed my way. He isn't smirking or looking like he wants to tear me limb from limb. "Roman called me last night and told me he heard the same rumor about me being traded."

I want to gloat, but for the sake of our budding professional relationship, I hold it in. I revert to the teasing we've engaged in for ten years now. Reaching out, I walk my fingers up his chest. "And now you *desperately* need me?"

Banks watches my fingers for a moment before flicking them off his chest and giving me a deadpan look. "We need each other, Kaitlyn with a K. A win-win, remember?" Then he extends the hand holding the coffee.

My eyebrows scrunch together as I look at the cup of steaming hot coffee, black as my soul. "What is this?"

"I poured you a cup of coffee," he says, tone implying I'm dumber than a doornail. "Did I say it slow enough for you?"

I give him a scathing look, but take the coffee and enjoy the first sip. "I'm going to regret this," I say to no one in particular.

Banks's infectious laugh makes my lips tug at the corner. "Oh, believe me. We're both going to regret this."

I consider it a good start when I leave ten minutes later, and we haven't strangled each other. We agreed to meet after his game tomorrow and hash out the details of my plan. In the meantime, I need to see if I can extend my stay at the hotel in Tampa and move my birthday party to Florida. Considering I only invited four people, that shouldn't be too hard. With everything we need to do to change up Banks's reputation, I won't be home for my birthday next week like I thought. All I have to do is envision Ed Presley's face when I trump his ass and the sacrifice is completely worth it. I fire off a text to my assistant and have her clear my calendar. Operation Humiliate Ed is underway.

# Chapter Eight

Banks

"They say talking to yourself is the first sign of senility," I say as I step up behind a murmuring Kaitlyn where she sits at a booth nestled in the back of Salvatore's, my favorite mom and pop Italian place in Tampa. To my utter delight, she jumps in her seat.

I pin her with a grin as I assume the seat opposite her and cross my arms on the table. It's after our game against the Snow Devils, which ended in a 2-1 loss in overtime earlier this evening. I wasn't at my best, which frustrates the hell out of me, and Roadie scored our sole goal. The only thing that can put a dent in my mood is Sal's linguini and a good sparring match with the woman seated across from me.

Clearly not here to enjoy the homemade pasta, Kaitlyn ignores my dig and gets right down to business. "Have you read over the terms I sent?"

I don't answer, instead preferring to be the one to lead this little sit-down. Sal's wife Lucia appears beside us, smile wider than Druggy's arm span. "Banks, *caro*. Sal didn't tell me you were coming tonight. And who is this beautiful lady?"

There's no denying Kaitlyn is beautiful, so I don't even try. "My wife," I say instead.

Kaitlyn only narrows her eyes at me, lips pursed in disapproval.

Lucia doesn't miss a beat. "And what would your wife like to drink this evening?" She refuses to take the bait, and I frown at her while Kaitlyn places her order for a glass of pinot noir. Lucia doesn't bother asking me what I want before she disappears to get our drinks.

Instead of reverting to her previous topic, Kaitlyn shakes her head at me, eyes narrowing again and drawing my attention to her dark eyebrows as they scold me. "Did you seriously invite me to your hook-up trap to talk business?"

Genuine confusion clouds my brain. "My hook-up trap?"

"Don't play stupid—if that's at all possible, that is." When my expression doesn't change, she scoffs and throws a hand out to indicate the dining room. "The cute little old Italian couple that knows you by name and doesn't need to ask your order because you're 'family' to them? The burgundy leatherette booths and cozy decor landing somewhere between quaint and kitschy that tells your date you're not only a harmless, trustworthy guy, but you're so gosh darn down to earth that the rumors about you and all those women can't possibly be true?" Her voice drips with sarcasm—not unlike the overflowing candle fixed into an empty wine bottle on our table that is, indeed, both quaint and kitschy, just as she accused.

I feel my lips quirk. "Are you suggesting I use Sal and Lucia to seduce women?" When she opens her mouth to respond, I quickly continue, "And by extension, are you suggesting I brought you here to seduce you?"

Her mouth slams shut.

"I didn't think so." I slide her menu in front of her.

"Everything here is fantastic, and they have the best clam sauce I've ever tasted." The truth is, in the twelve years I've been coming here, I've never brought a date with me—unless Eli can be considered a date, but I'm pretty sure he'd nut-punch me if I suggested it.

Lucia returns with Kaitlyn's wine and my beer, and we both order the linguini with clam sauce and a house salad–me, because it's my favorite, and Kaitlyn, because she obviously just wants to get on with our meeting. Lucia compliments Kaitlyn on her choice and retreats to the kitchen, leaving us alone again.

I realize only then that this scene almost exactly mirrors the day we met and is the first time we've dined alone since. Even our drinks are the same, although I cap it at one these days. If she shares my realization, she doesn't show it, taking us back to business instead. Probably just as well.

"Well? Did you review it or not?"

I'm tempted to lie so we can avoid the inevitable—me legally tying myself to this woman, even for a short while. But it's time to get on with it. "Yeah. My lawyer's got it now."

She nods, ignoring her wine and drawing a leather folio from the bag at her side to open it on the table. "I thought we were just talking. I didn't know there'd be a PowerPoint presentation and a quiz." I scowl at the thick stack of pages inside her folio.

Her eyes flick from the pages to me, and she pauses a few unamused beats before dropping them back again. "We're not even halfway through the season, and you've been late to eight practices and almost every one of your PT sessions. You no-showed a press conference, ditched a podcast halfway through with no explanation, skipped a mandatory team meeting, and were late to two others.

I start to object, but she's not done. She doesn't even look up from her naughty list as she turns to the third page. "You've regularly and publicly antagonized Bobby, Alexi, and Pete, all of whom have less than two years on the team and are next-generation players taking cues from the likes of Drugov, Bright, and you. Not only weren't you anywhere close to being considered, but you expressed zero interest in being team captain after Roman's retirement last season. You're the oldest player on the team, and you've never even been an alternate captain, for god's sake. Your only media appearances this season include a few measly press conferences and numerous photos with puck bunnies. You've been linked to three different women in the last three months, one of whom is a college student at FSU."

Her eyes finally lift to mine again, and it takes serious effort not to growl at her as she pointedly scans me from my finger-combed hair to my artfully scruffy chin and on down to my ZZ Top T-shirt. "You dress like every day is laundry day at the frat house. Your stick work is sloppy, and —you're coughing up pucks like an old man with bronchitis."

I gasp, hand hitting my chest. "You lie." How dare she insult my play?

"Just because you don't like being scrutinized doesn't mean everything I said isn't one-hundred-percent true. I deal in facts, not fiction, and if you think Kent Bowman and Sam Macalby are any different, you're fooling yourself. Where do you think I got most of these records?"

Shit. That's not good. Coach's opinion means a lot to all of us, and Sam is the GM who holds my contract extension hostage.

Still... "My stick work is sharp as your stiletto heel. And I had something in my eye tonight when Michaelson stole the puck." The rest? Yeah, I can't really explain a lot of that, so I take a healthy sip of my beer.

And it's nobody's business how I spend my time off the ice. Yeah, I know I've got a bit of a reputation when it comes to women, but so much of that is bullshit people make up—not that I've dissuaded anyone from assuming it's all true. That sounds like a lot of wasted energy I could be spending napping.

Kaitlyn's not willing to give up her soapbox yet. "Hockey is serious business for serious people, Banks. Maybe some of this was allowed to fly when you were younger and fresher, but that time is gone. And if you're hanging out behind the bleachers with the head cheerleader while the rest of the team is sweating out drills on the field, you're going to find yourself with a lot more free Friday nights than you'd prefer."

I slam my glass down on the wood tabletop. "Why are you making football analogies? Is this the senility thing again?"

She waves me off, unoffended for once. "*Friday Night Lights* reruns were on in the hotel gym. I got a little carried away."

Lucia comes back with our salads, and Kaitlyn closes her folio and slides it aside to make room. I eat in silence as I consider everything she's said. Players get traded. It happens. But being traded now can't be disguised as anything other than being demoted. And I'm not even close to being ready to throw in the towel. The game is everything.

After a few minutes, I set my fork down and shove my salad bowl forward so I can lean into the table. "I am deadly serious when it comes to my game, and anybody who says different is full of shit. Just because I'm not the first guy on the ice doesn't mean I'm not the last guy off it. I'm at every optional practice, I work more drills than any other two players combined, I've got the game film memorized before the team review even starts. I hit the weight room at every available opportunity." I stab a finger at my leg. "These thighs can crack a watermelon! So don't you ever tell me I'm not serious about hockey."

Kaitlyn takes a sip of her wine and considers me before

swallowing. I watch the motion of her slim throat and feel it in my dick. If she's going to accuse somebody of not being serious, it's gotta be him. "Nobody ever said you aren't a great hockey player, hot shot. I wouldn't be here if you weren't. But tell me this: if what you say is true, why isn't anyone talking about *that* instead of all of this?" Her red-tipped index finger digs into the folio.

Fuck. I hate it when she's smarter than me.

I sigh and drop back, letting my head rest on the high pad of the booth behind me. "So, what's your big plan?" I don't like the defeat in my tone.

Her lips widen in a sly smile. I wonder if she knows it looks evil. "You just bought yourself a full-time governess. I'm going to whip you into shape, Benjamin Banks Bennet, and when I'm done with you, you'll be the league's golden boy, buffed to a shine so high, Mario Lemieux himself will be able to spot you from Pittsburgh.

"Sounds terrifying."

She laughs, and it's evil as well. "I'm going to make you look so good, you'll be a shoe-in for the All-Star game in March." I shoot her a skeptical look. I've made the All-Star game twice in my career, neither of those occasions being recent. She reads my expression and continues, "The fans are voting for a third of the players, dummy. You think I can't get the world behind you?"

Her explanation does nothing to relieve my skepticism. Winning the fans' affection is for guys like Roman. He can charm the pants off anyone, given the chance. Me? I'm not so good at playing that game since I tend not to care much about what people think of me.

"Give me your phone." Kaitlyn reaches an impatient hand across the table and I unlock my phone before forfeiting it to my new babysitter. She snatches it from my fingers like it's *The Precious* and we're dining in Mordor. Her thumbs fly over the screen. "This is our calendar. I've already filled it out with your usual commitments in addition to some new ones I've added. On that note, you're doing an interview on Harry Rosen's podcast next Tuesday."

Harry Rosen? That guy is a kiss-ass. "I don't pander."

"You do now." Her thumbs are back at work. "I'll need you to add any personal items to the calendar and we'll discuss to see if we'll keep or cancel those."

"Not happening." I reach for the phone, but Kaitlyn holds it to her chest, and while I consider going after it, I'm not looking to get her shoe in my groin.

"Yes, it most certainly is." God, she's bossy. "Macalby is not going to trade a member of the All-Star team—or let him loose as a free agent—so that's our golden goose."

"You're not interfering in my personal life," I demand, my index finger aiming for her right pupil. "My career is fair game, but my personal life is off limits."

The look she gives me is half exasperation and half concern. "Haven't you been listening to anything I've been saying? They're one and the same."

I mumble some expletives. "Are you going to dictate when I can take a shit too? Jack off? Call my mom?"

Her thumbs pause on their latest task and her eyes find mine. "I'm more than a little disturbed at how seamlessly you shifted from masturbation to talking to your mother."

"Now who's not being serious?" I give up and crane my neck, looking for Lucia and my linguini. It's my only possible comfort now. With no sign of her, I drain the rest of my beer. "And how are you going to do all this micromanaging from Atlanta? You'd have to move into my condo to keep me on that short of a leash. And I gotta warn you, I sleepwalk. And I don't own any pajamas."

Kaitlyn slides my phone back across the table and palms her wine glass again. "Hard pass. I'd murder you before morning, and that wouldn't help either of us. Besides, appearing to be living with your agent is a worse impropriety than your college girlfriend."

"Mandy is in grad school. And we weren't dating. It's not my fault if fans snap pics of me with people and plaster them on social media." I try not to pay attention, but I know pictures get posted by people who don't know what the fuck they're talking about. Just last month, I was pictured opening the door for some girl and the media started speculating about wedding dates.

Kaitlyn gestures with her glass, wine sloshing dangerously close to the rim. "Dating, sleeping with, same thing. Although I'm relieved to hear she isn't pledging a sorority and bar hopping with a fake ID."

She's determined to think the worst of me and it's annoying as hell. Yes, I'm aware I'm a hypocrite. "I'm not sleeping with her!" Why I find it so important for Kaitlyn to know this, I have no idea.

"Good. I'm glad you put an end to it. By the way, you're now celibate until your contract extension gets signed." She rocks her index finger back and forth in a scolding gesture. "No chance for bad press. I'll also be accompanying you to physical therapy, and my team is taking over your social media."

"No!" Fuck, am I pouting?

Yes!" she counters, mocking my petulant tone.

"No, I mean I wasn't *ever* sleeping with Mandy. She was my hypnotist, if you must know."

"What?"

"Pain relief. It was worth a try." I shrug on a deep sigh, suddenly exhausted.

Kaitlyn reaches over to pat my hand like the governess she's claiming to be. Is it normal to have sex fantasies about your governess? Yes. I'm sure it is. "You'll be thanking me in two months, I promise."

"Linguini for Mr. and Mrs. Bennet," Lucia announces with a wink as she lowers two enormous plates to the table. My mood lightens a bit, and I grab my fork after thanking Lucia.

The first bite is heaven on earth. I sneak a glance at Kaitlyn as she absently forks her first bite into her mouth, chews once, and then moans. My lips tip up, and she sends me a closed-mouth smile from across the table. She's won and she knows it. But I've still got one card I haven't played, as small as it is.

"Fine. I submit, Killer Kaitlyn."

She chokes on her linguini at my words. But that's what she gets for talking to herself in public.

# Chapter Nine

Kaitlyn



Olivia's text comes in at the worst possible time. I'm lugging my suitcase off the elevator on Banks's floor when I read it. I fire off a quick text saying I couldn't possibly let her do all the work, but she texts back that's what friends do for each other. Right there in the hallway with my suitcase halfway out of the elevator, my eyes burn. Badly. I look up to the overhead lights quickly and try to sniffle the tears away, but it doesn't work. One stupid tear escapes my eye and I dash it away before it can mess up my makeup. What the hell is wrong with me? Crying over a text message? Crying because I have a genuine friend for once? Un-fucking believable.

"Did you break a heel or something?"

Banks is leaning against his door frame, that same pair of sweatpants hanging low on his hips, chest bare. He looks like he just woke up and that pisses me off. All those warm and fuzzy tears turn to rage. I've been up since before sunrise, getting in my own workout an hour earlier than usual just so I could spend a few hours continuing to work on a game plan. The least the jackass could do is put in the same amount of effort. Well, that shit ends today.

"What the fuck, Bennett? It's nine in the morning. Are you just getting up?"

He scrubs a hand over his face and then crosses his arms over his chest. "Yeah. But only because someone held up the elevator and the dinging woke me up. Besides, our flight home didn't land until midnight."

I yank my suitcase into the hallway and the dinging stops. The doors slide shut and the elevator swooshes to another floor. Banks frowns, like he just woke up enough to see that I have a suitcase in my hand.

"Hold up. You're not actually moving in with me, are you?"

I scoff and swish past him on heels that eat up the cushy carpet. "You wish. I just rented the condo next door to you for the next three months." When I get to the door just down the hallway, I turn back around with an evil grin on my face. "Good to see you, neighbor."

Punching in the code the owner gave me, I push the door open and look around my new temporary home. The place is much smaller than Banks's condo, and everything is a shade of sterile gray. I feel Banks behind me before I hear him.

"But Pierre lives here." My door shuts behind him.

I spin, leaving my suitcase up against the wall. I'll unpack later. Right now, I have a client to whip into shape. "Oh look! You're my first visitor."

"Kaitlyn," Banks snaps.

I refrain from rolling my eyes. Barely. "Yes, Pierre owns this place. Lovely fellow. He was all too happy to rent it to me once I made my offer."

Banks groans, and while I know he's pissed at my proximity and this entire situation, the sound does something to my insides. I tell my insides to shut the fuck up. I'm probably just hungry. I went extra hard at the gym this morning, a fact my aching shoulder is reminding me with every move.

"No time for you to sit here and groan like a little baby. Did you check your calendar? We have exactly twenty minutes to buy some flowers and head over to Sunset Shores Retirement Home."

His handsome face twists into revulsion. "A staged photo op? No. Absolutely not."

I suck in a deep breath, hoping to magically inhale some patience. "It's not up for debate. Your social media is sucking wind, and we need to bulk that bitch up. I only have one photographer coming to snap some pics, so put on some respectable clothes and let's go."

I move to walk around him and open the door, but he puts his big hands on my shoulders, and I freeze. With all the sparring we do, you'd think him touching me wouldn't be a big deal, but I hate to admit that it is. Every time he's ever touched me is etched into my memory.

"I'm not doing it. If you must know, I have a standing visitation at Bay Villages already and it's not the right day of the week for that."

Nope. Didn't suck up any patience whatsoever. "What? Why didn't you tell me? Why wasn't that in your file?"

Banks lets me go, but with the door behind him, there's not a lot of room between us. Even with my sky-high heels, I'm eye level with his naked collarbone and I've suddenly developed a fetish for collarbones. The back of my neck breaks out into a sheen of sweat. Maybe I should have had some electrolytes after my workout. First tears and now obsessing over fucking collarbones? I'm clearly off today.

"Because it's something I do on my own time. No one needs to know."

I tilt my head back to glare at the ceiling and wonder if thirty-nine is too young to worry about stress-related medical events. When my head rights itself, I put my hands on Banks's shoulders, giving him a shake. The solid wall of muscle barely moves.

"You don't have any of your own time. You are a public figure, Banks. Everyone needs to know when you do something good. Don't you get it? You're in the time out corner because you haven't shown people all the good things you do. I assume you do other good things?" I wave away my question. "It doesn't matter. You do one good thing. Let's focus on that. Get dressed."

"But–?"

I shake him again. "You either get dressed and get your ass to Bay Villages or you can call Ed and beg him to come back as your agent. Your choice."

His face clouds over, and I know I've won. Banks flings my hands off him. "I'm really starting to regret this."

"That makes two of us, hot shot." I follow him back to his place, even when he lifts an eyebrow at my hovering. I wait in the living room while he changes, shooting an email to my paparazzi contact to let him know about the location change. He's not sure if he can make it, so I tell him I'll snap a few pictures for him to use.

"Does Mommy approve of my outfit?" Banks asks, stepping back into the living room. He has on a pair of jeans, a plain white T-shirt, and a ProBuild Direct ball cap. That hat threw me off ten years ago. Now I know it's his father's company and Banks is not an employee there.

"Ew. Not your mommy, I'm your governess," I clarify.

"And the outfit's fine, but lose the ball cap when we get to the retirement home. The whole point is for people to recognize you."

We argue over who drives, but Banks wins, mostly because he's got a good seventy-five pounds of muscle on me and I can't physically push him into my rental car. I have to move a kid's comic book from the passenger seat of his truck, which makes me lift my eyebrows at his maturity level, but we make it to the retirement home without killing each other.

The second we step through the sliding glass doors, the woman at the front desk hops up, all sunshine and smiles for the grumbling athlete next to me. Her name badge says Judy.

"Hey, Banks. You're early! We weren't expecting you until Saturday."

The two hug like old friends and I tilt my head, surprised Banks hadn't lied about his visits. Why the hell didn't Ed know about Banks visiting the old folks' home on a regular basis? This is perfect gossip to leak to the press to help his image. I shrug, happy I'll be the one to let this secret out. I can just picture Ed's face seeing the news story.

"Beatrice isn't expecting me either, but I hope it's okay I dropped by? If not, I can wait and come back Saturday."

"Oh gosh, no! She'd love to see you. Though she might cry if you don't show up for your regular Mahjong tournament on Saturday."

My jaw drops and Banks's ears turn red. "Oh, I'll be back for that, don't worry. She beat me last week and I can't have her thinking she's better than me."

I step forward, wanting to pump this woman for more nuggets like Banks being a regular Mahjong player. This is PR gold. Banks puts his hand on my back and the gesture feels... almost...intimate? I fling off that thought and shake the woman's hand as Banks introduces us. She gets us settled at a round table in one of their activity rooms before walking off to find Beatrice.

I gape at Banks. "How did you come to be a regular Mahjong player with the over sixty set, hot shot?"

Banks is studying his hands like he wonders how they got attached to his arms. "She's Pierre's grandmother and she used to live with him next door. But he travels a lot and she got to a point where she couldn't live on her own."

"Okay, but what does that have to do with you playing tile games with her?"

Banks huffs and lays his hands on the tabletop. "Contrary to what you might think of me, Kaitlyn, I'm not a monster. I help old ladies across the street and play games with them when they're in need of company. Jeez."

It's actually really sweet. My bottom lip wants to quiver or let out some oohs and aahs, but I firm it up. One sweet thing does not make a star athlete, or even a nice person. Although I consider myself a decent person, I've never gone to a home and played games with the elderly.

"Ohh! My favorite boy is here!" Beatrice lifts her bony arms in the air as the attendant pushes her to our table in a wheelchair. "Just don't tell Pierre." Banks hops up and gives the woman a hug before having a seat and positioning her chair between us.

Despite her obviously advanced age, Beatrice is dressed in black cigarette pants and a silk blouse. Diamonds flash from her earlobes and if I'm not mistaken, that's Chanel wafting in the air. I immediately like this woman, and when she glances down at my feet and tells me my heels are *trés chic*, we bond instantly. I've never played Mahjong, but Banks helps me pick up the rules and before long, over an hour has passed and if we don't leave soon, Banks will be late for practice.

I shoot out of my chair. "So sorry, Beatrice, but Banks is due at practice."

Banks groans, but cooperates, leaning down to hug Beatrice once again. "Let me go tell Judy we have to head out and she'll take you where you need to go."

She pats his head and whispers, "You're a good boy, Banks. My best days are when you visit."

I bite my lip, begging my tear ducts to cut this shit out. I can't be tearing up twice in one day. Next thing I know, pigs will be flying through Tampa's air space. Beatrice offers me a hug too, one I take because I can now see why Banks visits her on the regular. We exchange favorite clothing stores in the area and discuss brands. I hope to be just like Beatrice when I'm her age, still rocking the latest fashions and marching to the beat of my own drum. When our conversation dies down, I lean in closer. There's something I want to ask, and other than Olivia, I don't have a female in my life I feel comfortable asking. And Olivia would just tell me what I want to hear because she loves me.

"I envy how tight you and Banks are," I say quietly, trying to get the words just right. "I hope one day I have the same level of maternal instinct you do. Sometimes I wonder if I'm deficient in that department. If I'm somehow broken, destined to be the hockey player ball buster and that's it."

"Oh sweetheart," Beatrice rasps, sliding her bony hand on my arm and squeezing. "You don't give yourself enough credit. I'll let you in on a little secret. We have to kick ass in the world to get ahead, always outperforming the men to get the same level of recognition and less pay. You start to think that's all there is to you, but now you're the one limiting yourself. If you want to be a mother, then the maternal instincts are already there. Don't be afraid to lean into them when the time is right."

Her words bring relief to a worry that's been in the back of my brain. "I think I needed to hear that."

"Come back next week and I'll tell you again. And again. Until you believe it."

"Oh, I'll be back. Just consider me Banks's shadow."

Beatrice winks at me. "Such a pretty shadow."

Banks lets out a snort behind me and puts his hand on my back to escort me back to his truck. It's only when he shows up to practice without a second to spare, and I'm sitting in the bleachers watching, that I remember I didn't take even one picture back at the retirement home.

# Chapter Ten

Banks

The silence stretches between us on the drive from Bay Villages to the practice facility.

This is weird. No, maybe not weird...uncomfortable. No, it's weird *and* uncomfortable.

I'm not used to people being in my private business, and Beatrice is my private business. But with the way the two of them got along back there, it seems she's now Kaitlyn's business too. I think they even made a date for shopping while I was talking to Judy. Not that I would begrudge Beatrice a new friend, but Kaitlyn's already nosed her way into my relationship with Roman, and now she's living in Pierre's condo and making plans with my Mahjong partner? Enough, already!

"I think Beatrice is my new idol." Kaitlyn looks up from her phone and grins across the cab at me.

Okay, fine. So maybe I'm being petty. From what I've seen, Kaitlyn doesn't appear to have any friends apart from Roman and Olivia, so I *guess* I can share.

"She's really special, Banks. Thanks for introducing us."

Dammit.

"No problem. I know she enjoyed it."

It's hard to stay annoyed when her pleasure at hanging out with my surrogate grandma is so genuine. And when the conversation I overheard rears its head.

Kaitlyn would enthusiastically garrote me in my sleep if she knew I overheard her opening up to Beatrice about her insecurities. I could say it never occurred to me before that Kaitlyn Phillips even had a heart or emotions–apart from her passion for proving everyone wrong and making my life miserable. But that would be a lie. Every now and then I do think back to the engaging and captivating woman I met in that airport bar so long ago. That woman had a heart and emotions. She was also funny, flirtatious, and even self-effacing. So much so that I might have been half in love with her by the time we said our goodbyes.

But that's not the same woman in the truck with me right now. Is it?

I glance over to see her gazing out the window, a faint smile settled on her lips. The sun catches the caramel highlights in her hair, lending her a soft glow.

I try forming a mental picture of her with a gaggle of kids as I mull over the concern she expressed about being too much of a hard ass to be a good mom. With her fortieth around the corner, I guess it makes sense she's thinking about kids, but I never would have suspected she'd be anything but uber-confident about her abilities in any and all areas–including motherhood. I might have been wrong.

"Did you know she traveled the world as a flight attendant for Pan Am back in the day?" I ask. "And then she studied to be a paralegal."

Kaitlyn laughs gently, and the sound settles somewhere in my chest. "Now, why doesn't that surprise me?"

My lips spread in a responding grin, and I shove aside the last traces of weirdness and discomfort, allowing for the possibility that maybe Kaitlyn Phillips is human after all.

Olivia: Did you get a chance to check out the restaurant?

I pause on my way out the door to answer Olivia's text.

Me: Yeah. It's not gonna work.

Olivla: What? Kaitlyn's party is in three days!

Like she needs to tell me. With Olivia in North Carolina, I've been driving all over Tampa the last couple nights looking for the perfect place for my agent's 40th birthday dinner. No idea why I care, except that Kaitlyn will surely be critical of anything I have a hand in.

Me: It's not snooty enough for Kaitlyn. I switched it to another place you and she will both approve of. Promise.

Okay, fine. The place Olivia had chosen was all right, but when I envisioned Kaitlyn all dolled up and walking into the restaurant for her party, it wasn't... good enough. Now I've gone completely overboard and booked a private dining room at the most fancy-ass place I could find. And Olivia will never know that I forked up the price difference for the new spot.

> Olivia: You scared me for a minute there. I can trust you, right? You didn't book the play place at McDonald's, did you?

I grin at my phone.

> Me: Bite your tongue. I'm too big for the slide.

"What are you still doing here?" Speak of the devil. Kaitlyn stands in Pierre's doorway in body-hugging workout gear, a coffee mug the size of a gallon jug in her hand.

I shove my phone back in my pocket and raise both hands in surrender. "I'm going, I'm going." I make a concerted effort not to drop my eyes to the cleavage exposed by her sports bra, but it's no use.

"Please tell me you're not texting with puck bunnies."

Ha! If Olivia heard she was being referred to as a puck bunny, she'd lose her shit—which, for Olivia, would mean she'd glare real hard.

Kaitlyn swipes a hand across her sweat-dampened forehead, and the motion causes her to wince. It wouldn't surprise me in the least if she overdid it with her morning workout. She plays off the pain by nagging me. "I swear to god, Banks, if you're late for practice, I'll have your ass. Do I need to start driving you myself again?" She already banged on my wall and texted me twice this morning to make sure I was up and on my way.

"Please, no. Your taste in music makes my ears bleed. Don't you have other clients?" I turn to the elevator.

She calls after me, "Don't you worry about them. Focus on getting your ass to practice!"

I wave her off over my shoulder as my phone vibrates in

my pocket. As soon as the doors close, I pull it out to see a text from Eli and another from Olivia. I firm up this week's plans with Eli and text Olivia the details of the new restaurant.

The elevator doors open, but when I look up from my phone and move to step out, Kaitlyn is standing in my way, hand on her hip and a scowl directed at me.

"How did..." I trail off when I realize I'm still on my floor. I never pressed the button to the lobby, I guess. I click my phone off and go to return it to my pocket when Kaitlyn's hand strikes like a cobra and snatches it from my grip.

"Practice. Now." Did I just hear a tooth break?

When the doors close this time, I go for self-preservation and tap the button for the lobby.

"Oof!" I grunt as my chest connects with the ice and the breath is knocked from my lungs two hours later.

A pair of skates snowplows ice into my face and comes to an abrupt halt six inches from my nose. Pete Fornier's—otherwise known as Forns—stupid guffaw hits my ears. "First time on skates, Benny? Need a walker?" He skates away, yelling, "Roadie! Barzee! Come give the old man a hand!"

"Get to the locker room, Pete. I've got this one!"

Hell. Is that Kaitlyn's voice or have I actually died and joined the devil? I manage to roll to my back to find my agent staring down at me from behind the plexiglass with a look I've never seen from her—and never care to again.

Pity.

"Come on, hot shot," she beckons. "Practice is over."

I groan and pull myself to my feet as my teammates file off the ice. Practice was an absolute shitshow today, and the harder I tried to right the ship, the worse it got. I swear Roadie's skates had wings today, and the net was a magnet for every one of his pucks. Meanwhile, my stickwork was amateur at best, and I skated just like the newbie Forns accused me of being.

"I gotta fix my lateral pull around," I tell Kaitlyn, bending to retrieve my stick.

"You're not fixing anything in your state, Banks. Time for recovery."

I open my mouth to protest when Dave Wainwright, one of the assistant coaches, shouts from the bench, "Listen to your agent, Benny!"

Fuck. Looks like I'm outnumbered.

I exit the ice, eyes trained on my skates, but it's only seconds until a familiar pair of stilettos falls in step beside me. "I don't want to hear it," I preempt any forthcoming commentary on my play today. But instead of insulting me, I only feel the pressure of Kaitlyn's hand through the pads covering my back. Damn. This is worse than the chirping.

When I enter the locker room to peel off my sweaty gear, Kaitlyn pivots to talk to Roadie. I make quick work of changing into sweatpants and a tee before heading to a treatment room down the hall for some recovery work with my PT, Frannie. For a tiny woman, she's a beast at inflicting pain.

It's during a particularly unpleasant hammy stretch that Kaitlyn walks in—without knocking, I might add.

"Hey, Kaitlyn." Frannie's greeting is way too cheerful.

"Hi, Frannie. How's he holding up?"

I can't see Kaitlyn, since I'm doubled over with my ass pointed in her direction, but the blue pencil skirt from earlier is hard to forget.

"Just tight. He'll be all right. Wouldn't be surprised if some of it's mental," she remarks, like I'm a neurotic chihuahua on a vet's exam table.

I feel compelled to at least say, "I'm right here, you know."

Kaitlyn laughs and Frannie pushes on my shoulders until I grunt in pain at the increased stretch. "And now... you're done," my therapist declares. "You've earned a dip in the hot tub."

"Thank Christ," I mutter before straightening and then dropping my ass to the treatment table.

"See ya." Frannie exits, leaving me alone with Kaitlyn, who's standing with her arms crossed over her chest, assessing eyes on me.

"Maybe she's right." My agent steps closer. "Something stressing you out, Banks?"

Oh, no. She's not getting into my head. "Besides possibly being traded and having everyone talk shit about me? Nope. Can't think of a thing." But when her brow furrows and that horrible pity starts creeping back into her dark eyes, I nip that shit in the bud. "What's wrong with your shoulder?"

Her chin jerks back, surprise taking over. "Nothing. Why would you ask that?"

I push off the table and gesture to her right shoulder, the one that had her wincing this morning–the same one she's favoring now by carrying her bag on her left. "Rotator cuff?"

She steps back as I reach out to feel the joint, and I roll my eyes. "Relax. I'm not going to rip your arm off."

She scowls before allowing me to take her bag to set it on the floor beside her. I wait for her nod and cup her shoulder through the thin silk of her blouse. This one is black, and I don't fail to notice the swath of matching black lace peeking out from the spot where her bag shifted the fabric askew.

But as soon as I apply the smallest bit of pressure, she hisses in a breath on another wince.

I frown and loosen my grip. "Hey, you really are hurting. What happened?"

She shakes her head but doesn't pull away. "It's nothing. I probably just slept on it wrong." Her dismissal is so very Kaitlyn. It's also bullshit. And ever since that reminder the other day that she's not made *entirely* of ice, I've been keeping my eye out for more evidence. But she's giving nothing up.

"You're an awful liar." I move her so her back is to me and place both hands gently on either shoulder to compare them. "Well, it doesn't feel inflamed, but that doesn't mean much." When I take her elbow and begin rotating the shoulder joint, she flinches. "Are you taking anything? Seen a doctor? I can get Frannie back in here." Getting a mind of its own, my thumb glides back and forth over the silk covering her upper arm.

Kaitlyn turns to look at me over her shoulder, pulling in a sharp breath when she realizes how close her movement has brought our faces. She smells like flowers–the sweet kind–and the perfect cupid's bow of her upper lip draws my undivided attention. I wonder if her lips feel as soft as they look. Because there's no trace of ice anywhere in her expression or that mouth.

"We're supposed to be worrying about *your* body, not mine, you know." Her lips quirk the tiniest bit, and my gaze automatically drops from her mouth to skim down her body, only to find the outline of her hardened nipples through the silk of her blouse. With our current proximity and the temporary absence of her armor, I'm getting all kinds of dangerous ideas.

Acting entirely on impulse and not caring one bit about the consequences, I bend to whisper in her ear, "It's the strangest thing, but I'm suddenly feeling no pain," When her eyes drop to my mouth, I know it's absolutely on, so I press closer and lean in to drop a kiss on the hinge of her jaw.

"Oh, crap! Sorry!" Frannie's voice sounds from behind me.

Kaitlyn all but stumbles forward out of my arms, and I whip around to face my therapist. "Sorry for what?" I cover as best I can.

Kaitlyn interjects, "I think Frannie had better have a look at it, don't you think, Banks?"

Immediately catching on, I nod like a mad cuckoo bird at midnight, "Kaitlyn's got a shoulder thing going on. I think it might be the rotator cuff, but you'd know best."

Frannie's expression shifts to concern, and she steps directly to Kaitlyn. "Let me take a look, and we can get you to a doc for an official diagnosis."

Kaitlyn sends me wide eyes over Frannie's head as the therapist focuses on her shoulder, but instead of the regret I'm sure I'm supposed to be feeling, anticipation for a do-over is the only thing on my mind.

# Chapter Eleven

Kaitlyn

I shoot out of the elevator at breakneck speed, wanting to get to the safety of my condo more than I want my next cup of coffee. Living next to Banks suddenly seems like the worst decision I've ever made. What the hell was that moment in the PT room? For a split second there I felt like he was just Ben, the guy I fell for at the airport, and not Banks, my loathsome client. Aliens must have taken over my body. Or maybe I worked out too hard this morning, leaving myself dehydrated and hallucinating. Something must have been off. How else can I explain almost kissing my client?

"Kaitlyn! Wait!"

Banks's voice brings me to a halt. I mutter a string of curse words in my head before turning around. He's waiting for me outside his own door, arms crossed over the impressive chest that I've seen without a shirt too many times to count. So why is it distracting now? Okay, fine. It's always been distracting, but I can't seem to wrestle my thoughts into submission like usual.

"Banks. Hey," I say lamely, attempting an appreciative smile that isn't too friendly, but not cold either. It's a delicate balance I should be able to achieve effortlessly and yet, I find myself struggling. However, my shoulder isn't aching quite as badly as it usually is, and I have Banks to thank. Well, him and Frannie's magic fingers. "Frannie is..."

Banks flashes his guy-next-door smile at me and leans against his doorway. "Yeah, I know what you mean. I've asked her to marry me a few times after she's released some particularly painful muscle spasms."

I snort and shift my weight on my heels. "As your agent, I have to say that would be a bad idea." No worse than kissing his agent, but I refuse to bring that up.

Banks pushes off his doorway and strides toward me, all thick muscle and cocky handsomeness in his fresh polo shirt and jeans. "Don't worry, she turned me down and then dug into my muscle so hard I almost pissed my pants."

I grimace. Banks waves his hand between us, the tips of his ears burning red. "I'm not good at this sort of thing. Forget I said that last bit."

Warning bells clang in my brain. "What sort of thing?"

Banks leans in, his broad shoulders casting a shadow over me as he blocks out the overhead light in the hallway. His blue eyes practically sparkle in the low light as he stares at me. Oh shit. I can feel it happening again. The lightheadedness. The weird way my legs feel like they're going to give out.

The elevator pings and the doors slide open on our level, interrupting whatever this is.

"I need electrolytes."

"This thing between us..."

"Kaitlyn, my only daughter!"

All three of us speak at once. Me, Banks, and...my dad? I blink, staring around Banks's beefy arm to see my father limping off the elevator with a rolling suitcase held together by duct tape and old dreams.

Banks spins around and recovers quicker than I can, holding out his hand. "Mr. Phillips? It's nice to meet you. I'm Banks Bennett, center for the Florida Storm Chasers."

Dad eyes Banks like a sewer roach in the hallway of a fancy hotel. "Oh, great. You're one of them."

I close my eyes and pray for sanity, opening them to see Dad shake hands with Banks and then dismiss him as a lowly hockey player. He turns his bespectacled focus on me.

"Dad? What are you doing here?" I ask, maneuvering around Banks to give him a hug. He smacks my back like he always does, rattling my teeth. When I pull back, I take in the way he's combed his hair neatly and put on his best clothes. The collared shirt is pulling over his belly, straining the buttons, but the shirt has been pressed recently.

Dad scoffs like I've told a less than humorous joke. "It's my only daughter's birthday. Of course I'm going to fly in and see her. Especially when you didn't have time to visit me the last time you were in Georgia." Dad eyes Banks over my head. "You've been too busy with these figure skaters."

I can feel Banks bristling behind me. "They're hockey players, Dad. And wow!" I pump as much enthusiasm as I can into my voice, already rearranging my schedule in my head now that I have a shadow in the form of a slow, disgruntled ex-football player who plans to complain about everything for the next few days. Please let it only be days, not weeks. "How long are you here for?"

Dad shrugs. "I was thinking three days, but my schedule is open." He rubs his belly and winces. "Gosh, they don't even feed you on these airplanes anymore. The entire industry has gone to hell in a handbasket, don't you think? What's a man gotta pay to get a fucking sandwich?"

Banks cuts him off before he can get going, which is a bit of a mixed blessing. "I hear you on that. Grown men need more than a bag of pretzels to survive. How about we head out to Stone Antlers, the best steakhouse this side of the Gulf?"

Dad assesses Banks with renewed interest while I try to come up with a reason why Banks shouldn't accompany us. How awkward would that be? And why would he even want to?

"Oh, you don't have to–"

"Done! Here, Kaitlyn. Stow my bag and show me the way," Dad orders, a jovial smile on his face as he finds an ally in Banks. He shoves his suitcase in my direction and the two men step back over to the elevator to press the down button.

I roll my eyes skyward. So much for coming down to Florida to visit his only daughter. More like harass his daughter into taking him to all the best restaurants so he can feel like a big, important man again. By the time I get my door open and Dad's suitcase inside, the two most annoying men in the world are in the elevator and holding the door for me.

"Hurry up, Kaitlyn. I might die of hunger pangs with how slow you walk in those things. Haven't we discussed the damage to your foot structure?"

"I happen to think those heels look amazing on her," Banks says once the doors slide shut and we're locked in this metal tube together. "Plus, she swears she can run in them. For someone who scores goals on thin blades of metal, I think that's truly an art form."

My dad snorts and I give Banks a look that isn't quite thanks. Sure, he's sticking up for me, but he also invited himself along to this dinner with my dad. I'd rather run through a field of sharp nails in my bare feet without a coffee break than spend the next few hours trying to dodge topics of conversation between these two. Plus, isn't he just going to use all this information as the perfect opening to insult me later?

There's a brief argument about whose car to take, but Banks wins. Dad climbs into the front of his truck, leaving me to hoist myself into the back. Which is fine, but then that leaves me having to lean forward between their seats the whole way to the restaurant, trying to hear their conversation. Thankfully, they're only discussing the various levels of horsepower and the best cars on the market these days, which bores me silly.

Once we're seated at the darkly lit restaurant, the conversation isn't much better. Banks slides into the leather booth beside me, his thick watermelon-crushing thigh wedging against mine in the close quarters. He smells good too, a fact I quickly kick out of my brain to focus on what's most important: making sure Dad doesn't start reminiscing and telling Banks my entire life's story. My clients don't need to know about my personal life. Especially Banks, who will only use that information to get under my skin.

"A bottle of red. The best you got," Dad says as soon as our server comes to the table. "It's my girl's birthday week."

The server gives me a trained smile. "Happy birthday. Can I bring some bread to the table as well?"

"Yes, please and keep it coming!" Dad answers for us.

Banks shoots me a look, like he's enjoying my father and his gluttonous personality. I don't have time to glare back at him because Dad opens his mouth first.

"Did Kaitlyn tell you about the first time I took her to a football game?"

Banks leans his elbows on the table and gives his entire focus to my dad. "No, but I'd love to hear about it."

I push Banks out of my way and put my hands on Dad's. "We're about to eat. Maybe we can table that story for another time, huh?"

Dad huffs. "It's hilarious, Kaity-Bug."

Banks sounds like he swallowed his tongue at the insane nickname and I stomp on his foot under the table. He wheezes in pain. Dad carries on like my humiliation is second nature to him.

"She got so excited screaming for the Tigers she ended up puking right into her popcorn tub." Dad shakes his head, a faint smile gracing his aging face. "God, she loves a good match up. Does she ever puke while cheering for a hockey game?"

Banks pulls his elbows off the table and folds his hands in his lap. "No puking, but she bellows loudly. It's kind of endearing."

The server returns with our wine and pours three glasses. I take a healthy gulp and wonder if we can just order appetizers and leave. Dad takes care of that idea when he waves his hand in the air for her to come back and proceeds to list off a steak, two sides, an appetizer, and even dessert. Banks chuckles, and says to double that. I ask for a steak salad, dressing on the side.

"Kaitlyn, honey. You gotta start eating. You're way too thin, like your mother."

My shoulders pull up to my earlobes. Talking about my mother isn't a topic I'm comfortable with in front of Banks. Too many landmines of emotions.

Dad turns to Banks. "She's tenacious like her mother, but she keeps complaining that I gave her my typical midwesterner's corn-fed frame." Dad pats his belly where it pushes against the table. "I say she cares too much about what other people think. She should be happy with herself exactly like she is."

I nearly choke on my next sip of wine. "Oh really, Dad? Then why do you keep telling me to quit hockey and go back to the NFL? Or quit wearing stilettos? Or live in a house instead of a condo? You have plenty of opinions about me, none of them good." Well, holy shit. I don't normally go off like that on Dad, but apparently, I've been keeping that bottled up.

Dad waves me away like my outburst is a momentary blip of emotion. "I'm your father. Of course my opinion matters. It's all these other yahoos that don't." He points his thick finger at me, and I can see the wine has already loosened his tongue. "You should go back to the NFL because those are real men."

"Whoa there," Banks interjects, clearly offended but more diplomatic than me. "The real men comment aside, Kaitlyn is the best agent we have in hockey. Don't be trying to take her away to another sport."

Dad's eyebrows come together behind his eyeglasses. "Kaitlyn?"

My pride smarts at his obvious disbelief. Instead of raging at him, now I want to curl up in a ball and cry. Dear god, what is wrong with me? Normally I can handle Dad and all his bluster with ease. A warm palm lands on my thigh under the table and Banks gives my leg a friendly squeeze. For many reasons, I don't push him away, the most important one being that I need someone on my side for once. While I never thought it would be Banks defending me, it feels...nice. More than nice, if I'm being honest.

"How do you think the Tigers are going to handle their quarterback being traded?" Banks deftly moves the conversation to football and we're able to eat in peace. I mostly just toy with my salad, already calculating how many calories I consumed in wine alone. By the time we get up from the table, I'm a little unsteady on my heels.

As if he knows, Banks places his hand on my lower back and guides me out of the restaurant, only to stop short as a flash pops the second we emerge into the night. Banks instinctively puts his arm around my waist and turns us away from the photographer.

"Are you considering retirement, Bennett?" the man calls after us.

We're only a few steps down the sidewalk toward Banks's truck when I hear my father's voice ring out. And not from right behind us. Shit.

"I may not have a Super Bowl ring, but you'd think I could get invited to the Tiger's anniversary game. Name's Keith Phillips, former Tiger's tight end. You fellas want a picture for your paper?"

"Oh dear god," I mumble.

Banks stiffens and spins us around, marching right back to my dad. Banks carefully positions himself in front of my father while he addresses the photog. "Hey, I didn't catch your name."

The guy nearly bobbles his camera, but sticks his hand out for Banks to shake. "I'm Sergio."

The two men shake hands and Banks's smile isn't the one he gives me. This one is polished and oozing with charm. "Sergio, I'd like to introduce you to the best agent hockey has ever seen. Kaitlyn Phillips. Make sure you spell it with a K." He pushes me forward and I have no choice but to shake Sergio's hand. "Would you get our photo together with her father?"

Realizing he won't be the center of attention, Dad walks behind us to come up to my other side. With a grumble under his breath about no respect for elders, he gets in the shots. Banks keeps that smile in place while we pose for Sergio. When Sergio thanks us for our time, we head back for Banks's truck. Dad is walking ahead of us, talking nonstop about what the paparazzi were like during his short time in the NFL, even though no one is listening. I'm trying to wrap my head around Banks coming to my rescue more than once tonight.

Banks still has his arm around my waist as he leans down to talk quietly. "See, Kaitlyn? You don't have to plan everything with the paparazzi. You just gotta go with the flow and let things happen."

I scoff and Banks hoots with laughter. I'm not even mad enough at him to step away from his arm like I should. If anything, as my eyes fill with hot tears, I might snuggle closer.

# Chapter Twelve

Banks

"I guess all that time on your phone wasn't the distraction I feared it would be." Kaitlyn grins as she approaches from Alexi Barinov's direction. When I see Barzee staring at her ass, I glare and motion for him to knock it off. He smirks and heads to the locker room to dress for practice.

"O ye of little faith." I shake my head at her, adjusting my bag on my shoulder. If she doesn't stop distracting me, I'll be late onto the ice. Last night's game against the Blades was fan-fucking-tastic, and my efforts were rewarded with a goal and an assist. Not too shabby for a guy on the chopping block.

"Good god, are you picking up vocabulary from Beatrice now?" In contrast to the tone she'd normally use for such a comment, Kaitlyn's manner is purely teasing and, dare I say, friendly?

Today's pencil skirt is the color of wine–to match the heels–and it's taking more effort these last few days to keep my hands off. Ever since our encounter in the PT room and then that eye-opening dinner with her dad, I've been trying to get her alone, with no success.

Seeing her with her dad was like getting a peek at the great and powerful Oz behind the curtain. So much about her is clearer to me now, including the fact that the woman isn't used to having anyone in her corner. I swear, all it took was a couple truthful comments in her defense, and she was practically melting into me. I have to admit, I could get used to that.

But this isn't the place or time.

"Nah." I step closer than I probably should. "That woman cusses like a sailor," I lie, but it has Kaitlyn's lips widening into one of her beautiful smiles. I might be fucked. "Now, if you don't mind, I gotta run or I'll be late for practice, and my agent will have my ass."

I follow in Barzee's footsteps, glancing over my shoulder halfway to the locker room doors. My eyebrows spike when I see my agent's eyes trained on my rear end. Well, well, well.

"That's right, Banks! Show 'em who's boss!" I hear Kaitlyn's guttural howl from rinkside thirty minutes later as I catch a breakaway during a scrimmage and haul ass to face off with Drugov in his crease. I feint left, then flick the puck over Druggy's left shoulder with a backhand shot to the back of the net that has Druggy pounding his gloved fists on the ice and Kaitlyn losing her ever-loving mind rinkside. I hope she doesn't puke.

"Damn you, Benny." Druggy's eyes flick past my shoulder. "Where is *my* cheering section?" His glare doesn't hold much heat, despite his grumbling.

"Maybe you need a new agent," I suggest with a smug grin, gliding past him and rounding the goal to center ice once more. Glancing Kaitlyn's way, I see Roadie skating up to her, but her eyes never leave me. I send her a smile and hold her gaze until a puck comes whizzing past my nose.

"Yo! Benny! Can we get on with it, or do you need another

ten minutes to celebrate one measly goal in a scrimmage?" Danny "Dan-O" Bright, one of my wingers and our team captain, asks.

Roadie meets me at center ice, his usual stupid-ass grin absent. "Lucky shot, Bennet." If I'm not mistaken, somebody is butt hurt our agent is paying more attention to me today than him.

"Call it whatever you want, Roadie, but I don't see any points from you on the board."

The whistle sounds and we're off once more. I win the drop and pass to Dan-O who sails past one defender to send the puck off to our other winger, Rich Monkowski–known to all as Money, and for good reason. He gets caught up with a defender but manages to flick the puck my way before it's stolen. I get pressure from two directions and pass it back to Dan-O. Then, out of nowhere, my helmet crashes into plexiglass and a body slams me to the boards.

"What the fuck, Rhodes?!" I shout when I catch sight of a familiar hot-headed center over my shoulder. He rips his gloves off and comes at me again, but before I can do so much as hurl an insult, we're being pulled apart by our teammates and Coach is hauling ass in our direction.

Roadie is sent to the locker room with Dave to cool down, and I'm treated to the sight of Kaitlyn's spectacular ass in that pencil skirt as she stalks after them. I count myself lucky that I'm not on the receiving end of that ass-chewing, but it occurs to me that having my agent yelling *for* me instead of *at* me might become a problem in itself.

But it sure felt damn good.

> Kaitlyn: Don't get into any trouble tonight. I have plans, and I don't want to have to bail you out of jail.

I glance down from the mirror at the text as I finish tying my tie. Or attempting to. Why are these things such a pain in the ass? I whip the cursed thing from my neck and throw it in the corner of my bathroom before picking up the phone to type my reply. Open collar it is, I guess.

> Me: Uh, I think you meant to text Roadie instead of me.

I release myself from the collar's strangle-hold with my free hand and undo the top two buttons.

> Kaitlyn: Oh, believe me, my text to Bobby was way worse.

That has me grinning.

> Me: I plan on being a perfect gentleman at the strip club, as usual. Save your worry for your little boys.

When she doesn't reply right away, I shrug on my suit coat and assess my look for the evening. The last time I wore a suit was for a benefit the team sponsored, but I'm determined to get a reaction out of Kaitlyn. Especially since she's not expecting me at her little party tonight.

> Kaitlyn: Your sense of humor is unimpressive.

I can picture her aiming a tight-lipped frown at her phone, and it has me chuckling as I kick aside dirty laundry on my bedroom floor and head for the kitchen to fetch the bouquet of flowers I bought.

In addition to flowers, I called in a favor and got her dad a private tour of the Bucs stadium this afternoon so he'd have to meet us at the restaurant–and so Kaitlyn could have a break from him. No wonder she's such a hard ass. Growing up with that guy would make a bunny rabbit grow fangs and draw blood. How can Keith not see how brilliant and competent she is? He should be singing his daughter's praises from the rooftops instead of trash-talking her. One thing I can guarantee, though: there will be no belittling the birthday girl tonight.

Taking into account Kaitlyn's obsession with being early for everything–and adding in ten minutes for her to try and refuse both the flowers and my company as her evening's escort–I'm out the door and knocking on Pierre's moments later.

"Banks, I don't have time..." She swings open the door, her voice trailing off when she catches sight of the flowers. When her powers of speech don't immediately return, I let my eyes take in the beautiful goddess before me. If I thought pencil skirts showed off her body to its best advantage, I was an idiot. Because the sight of Kaitlyn in a slinky emerald dress–bare shoulders and collarbone begging for my lips– might actually kill me. She's breathtaking.

I extend the bouquet to her, and she takes it with limp fingers while her eyes skate down my frame and she stammers, "What are you... why are..."

I decide to put her out of her misery and step forward to

guide her into her apartment before closing the door behind us and announcing, "I'm your date for your birthday dinner. Well, not a date exactly, but when I say the word 'escort' out loud, it sounds like I'm a sex worker so..."

She's still not recovered from the shock, which has me wondering briefly if I should be insulted, but I brush it off and forge ahead. My hand drops to the small of her back as I turn her toward the kitchen, and when my fingers touch bare skin, my cock starts to thicken in my boxers. The fucking dress is backless, exposing acres of smooth skin that have my fingers and cock buzzing.

I clear my throat. "Let's get those flowers in some water. Do you have a vase?"

Kaitlyn spins around to face me again, her spine finally snapping straight in classic Kaitlyn style. "You can't be my date!"

"Okay." I shrug, reluctantly releasing her and prying the flowers from her newly tightened grip. "Then I'll be your sex worker. Vase?"

She shakes her head, absently replying, "I don't know. It's not my apartment."

I feign exasperation, if only to distract her, and go searching through Pierre's cupboards until I find a water pitcher. It will have to do. "I was told I had to remain celibate, but if you insist on escort, I can deal."

"You most certainly can't be that! How do you even know about tonight?"

I move to the sink to fill the pitcher, pausing to send her a fake glare over my shoulder. "About that, should I be offended you didn't invite me?"

She opens her mouth to reply and then closes it again as she approaches the counter across from me. It impedes my view of her lower half in that wet dream of a dress, but her face is arguably even more gorgeous. When she finally replies, there's caution in her tone. "You're my client, Banks."

Some crazy impulse has me wanting to tell her I'm more than that, but the worry lines etching themselves across her forehead still my tongue. This is her night. Her birthday. The least I can do is smooth the way for a carefree evening.

Plopping the bouquet into the filled pitcher, I slide it toward her and round the counter to get close again. "Olivia asked me to bring you." It's a half-truth, but it'll do.

"Oh." Her lips part as her eyes meet mine again. This is gonna be a long night if she keeps looking at me like that. But I resolved to be a gentleman, so I suck it up and crook my arm for her to take.

She nabs a wrap off a nearby chair and links her arm with mine. Then she sighs dramatically, returning the mood to casual and walking with me to the door. "I suppose it will save me the Uber fare."

I laugh and guide us to the elevator. And while I know she wants to keep our boundaries in place, I figure it's no sin to speak at least part of the truth. So I dip my chin to get a bit closer and murmur, "You look stunning, Kaitlyn with a K. Happy birthday."

# Chapter Thirteen

Kaitlyn

Banks's knee bumps mine for the thirty-sixth time tonight. How do I know? Because each and every touch sends a jolt right through my body, like his kneecap somehow wields lightning. Damn Olivia for putting him next to me at dinner. It was the flowers. Or maybe it was the way his gaze skimmed my body when he picked me up and all I could think about was finding out what his eyes would look like if I shimmied right out of this skintight dress.

"Don't even get me started on the mood swings," Olivia says to my right, leaning over the table to drop her voice so everyone else doesn't hear our conversation.

I sip my wine and try to pay attention to what she's saying as the servers clear our plates and prepare for dessert. Dad is at the opposite end of the table with Roman, who deftly guides my father to topics that don't include hockey all night long. I'll have to send Roman a personal thanks for keeping him occupied.

"It's not even that so much, even though tearing up at inopportune moments is annoying enough. It's this damn shoulder injury. I think the pain is causing my emotions to swing out of control. I literally stomped my foot so hard in a rage the other day, I snapped the heel off my stiletto!" Olivia nods as I list out the health concerns I've been dealing with recently. Shit. Maybe forty *is* old if I'm spending my birthday party recounting every ache and pain. "And then my cycle is all messed up, which makes me feel like I don't know my own body anymore."

Olivia grabs my forearm and whispers with wide eyes, "You might be dealing with perimenopause."

I choke on a sip of wine, and Banks looks over, his hand immediately coming to my back and singeing my bare skin with his touch. "Excuse me, what?" I manage to wheeze out, waving to Banks that I'm fine.

Olivia winces. "Sorry. I could have brought this up at a better time. Your birthday party is hardly the time to mention the dreaded M word."

I place my wine glass down and lean closer to her, hoping Banks can't hear us. The last thing I need is my client hearing about how I'm aging into irrelevance. Okay, fine. The last thing my ego needs is a hot hockey god hearing I might be shriveling up in my old age. I quite liked the way his eyes lit into a barely controlled fire the second he saw me in the dress I spent a small fortune on.

"Explain." I feel bad for snapping at my sweet friend, but along with my emotions, I can't seem to control my voice.

"Well, mood swings and even frozen shoulder are symptoms of perimenopause," she says with a pitying look. "And weight gain most definitely is. I got the belly fluff to prove it."

"But–" I shake my head. "I just turned forty today. I'm not old enough for that."

Shit, I haven't had a chance to find a husband or even a

suitable sperm donor to have a baby with yet. I can't be in perimenopause. I won't allow it.

Olivia shrugs. "All I'm saying is you should go to the doctor and get checked out. Demand blood tests. I have a really great doctor if you need one."

I nod at her, my brain already spinning with this news. Olivia can't possibly be right. I open my mouth to further dispute her hunch when the door to the private room of the restaurant opens and three servers arrive with a blazing cake held between them. The small table of guests at my party erupts into the happy birthday song and I smile through the awkward tradition. Banks shoots me a wink, singing louder than them all with a surprisingly good voice.

Looking around the table, I see my father in another pressed shirt filming the whole thing on his cell phone, my best friends Roman and Olivia smiling as they sing, and of course, Banks. My group of friends is not large, but I'm grateful just the same. I set aside the perimenopause conversation and focus on what's in front of me. The servers place the cake on the table and step back as the song ends.

"Make a wish!" Dad yells.

I lean over the cake, careful not to let my long hair get in the flames. I close my eyes and think of one thing I want more than anything else. Over the years this wish is normally about crushing Ed Presley and taking over the hockey world with my wizard-like agenting skills, but this year feels different. That wish doesn't grip me tight like it normally does. My thoughts skip to something that terrifies me, which is how I know it's exactly the right thing to wish for. I open my eyes and blow out the candles. My friends and family cheer and the servers hustle to cut the cake.

After eating my entire slice of chocolate goodness and not feeling one ounce of regret for the sugary calories, I lean back in my chair and groan. It's late and Banks has practice tomorrow. Dad is the first to scrape his chair back and head in my direction. He slaps Banks on the back first and thanks him for the tour. I frown, just now connecting the dots around my father's absence this afternoon. Banks got him out of my hair for me. A warm glow that's certainly not just from the excellent wine fills my body.

"Happy birthday, kiddo. I guess this means I'm officially old if I have a forty-year-old daughter," Dad says, pulling me into a slightly less violent hug than normal when I stand. "I'll call you tomorrow and see if we can have lunch before I fly home."

"Sounds good, Dad. Thanks for coming." And I actually mean it. He's a pain in my ass, but he's my dad.

Olivia and Roman say goodbye next and follow us out as we all leave the restaurant together. Thankfully no paparazzi are waiting for us, a small miracle considering Roman is one of Tampa's favorite celebrities, despite his recent retirement.

"Think about what I said," Olivia whispers in my ear. She lets go and turns to hug Banks. "And thank you for selecting the perfect restaurant."

"I didn't fuck it up?" Banks asks her with a cocky grin.

"Wait a second..." I mumble, confused. No one pays me any attention.

Olivia pats Banks's chest. "I humbly eat crow."

Roman hugs me quickly and then pulls Olivia away from Banks. "Quit feeling up the youngsters, honey."

Olivia snuggles into his side. "I only have eyes for you, Ice Bath King."

I roll my eyes and Banks shakes his head as the two lovebirds walk off to their car. "Do you think they'll ever quit?"

Banks chuckles, sliding his arm around my waist and turning me in the opposite direction. We walked here since our condos are only three blocks away. "I hope not. They're my reason for thinking relationships might actually still work these days."

I ignore the way my ears perk up, listening to him talk about the topic of love. Down, girl. This one is a client, I remind myself. Besides, Banks is as annoying as a pair of thong underwear that slides up where it doesn't belong. "What's this about picking the restaurant?"

Banks inhales and won't look at me, guiding me along the sidewalk and around a questionable pile of take-home boxes someone didn't bother to put in the trash can. "Olivia may have asked for some help with the party planning."

My eyeballs prickle with heat and I beg them to get their shit together. Now is not the time to cry, no matter how touched I am that Banks helped plan my party. "May have? Or did?"

"It's not a big deal, Killer Kaitlyn." Banks tries to lighten the mood with the nickname, or maybe he's just always ready with a joke. Either way it just makes me appreciate him more, which makes my eyes water more, which makes me even more irritated that Olivia might be right about the hormones thing.

And that's the excuse I'm sticking with for turning right there on the sidewalk three buildings down from our condos and throwing my arms around Banks's neck. I'm *hugging* him.

"Thank you, Ben," I manage to say with a wobbly voice that's so fucking embarrassing I can't lift my head from his chest and look him in the eye. I try not to think about the way his solid body feels against mine, his arms banded tight around my waist. I beg myself not to inhale his scent and lock it away in my memory bank, but I do. I stand right there on the street and fucking *melt* into his embrace.

Banks sways us side to side once, then twice. And then his hands leave my waist and I assume he's pulling back from the awkward hug his agent threw at him without his consent. But he's not. He's cupping my face with his hands and looking down at me with something damn near close to affection. My lip wobbles, because I clearly have no control over my emotions any longer, and I'm altogether too unsteady to be balancing on thin heels with alcohol sliding through my veins. Banks's gaze drops to my lips and time freezes. The sounds of the cars and people out on the street fade and suddenly it's just me and Banks and a whole lot of heat between us that I've been trying to ignore.

His head blocks out the light from the nearby streetlamp, his descent slow, giving me time to object. But I don't. Before I can will myself to come up with an entire list of reasons why this is a bad idea, his lips are on mine, steady, warm, and most definitely the best thing I've ever wished for on my birthday.

His mouth parts mine and with a vibration coming from the back of his throat, he nips at my bottom lip before his tongue swipes away the sting. My hands fly to clutch his arms, my nails biting into his shirt. I want to pull him closer and climb him like a tree until I can get so close that I imbue myself with his heat. His tongue sweeps inside and now it's me making the noises, my head chanting for more, more, please god, more.

Something wet hits my forehead and we jolt apart, staring at each other with wide eyes. Another drop hits my face and I look up to see dark clouds above dumping moisture.

"Shit," Banks says, grabbing my hand and lacing our fingers together before racing for our condo building. I have to run to keep up, yelping as the rain pelts my face, and maybe it's the wine or maybe it's all the sugar I consumed tonight, but it strikes me as hilarious that it took forty years on this earth to finally get kissed in the rain.

My laugh rings out, and Banks looks back and joins in. "Damn, you really can sprint in those heels!"

He gets a hand on the door and pulls me through to the safety of the lobby. We're out of breath and still laughing. The moment feels light and happy and exactly what I needed when faced with turning a whole decade older. Banks sobers first, his eyes holding that same heat from earlier. I can feel his gaze touching every wet inch of me.

"Look at you," he says softly, squeezing my hand.

I look up and catch sight of us in the reflection of the mirrored elevator doors. Raindrops sit like jewels in my dark hair. My dress is plastered to my body, my nipples indecently outlined. And our hands. Still laced together.

In public. Where anyone could have seen us.

And just like that, all the laughter and lightheartedness of the evening vanishes.

# Chapter Fourteen

Banks

Kaitlyn is quiet on the elevator ride up to our condos, and I wonder if she too is focusing all her attention on begging my dick to behave himself. It's been too long since I got laid, and I'm not fucking this up just because I'm past due for some action. Kaitlyn doesn't deserve me acting like an unhinged feral animal—even if it's taking everything I have to keep from ripping that dress off her body and taking her on the elevator floor. I gotta keep it classy for this woman. Because Kaitlyn Phillips is all class.

A younger me might have walked her to her door and said something douchey like, "Let's get you out of those wet clothes," but I'm not that idiot anymore. I'm also coming to realize there's so much more to Kaitlyn than the ballbuster I knew her to be all these years, and I can't help but think we could actually be something more than agent and client together. I don't know exactly what, but *something*.

I guide her down the hall, my thumb tracing circles on the

backs of her fingers. "You want to come in for one more birthday toast?" I may have had a couple bottles of pinot noir delivered last week just in case I decided to suddenly become a wine guy.

But when we come to a stop outside my door and I turn to her, it's clear wine is not on the menu–nor is anything else for that matter. She pulls her hand from mine and takes a step back, unwittingly providing me an even better view of her body in that plastered-on dress. Nearly tearing my ocular muscles apart, my eyes behave and scan her face instead, as her brow wrinkles and her mouth turns down.

"Banks," she begins, and it takes effort not to interrupt and ask her to call me Ben again like she did on the street. "This can't happen." Her finger wags back and forth between us, and as if she's just realized how exposed she is in her dress, she pulls her wrap snugly around her. "I'm your agent. Not only would this be career suicide for me, it wouldn't do you any favors either." Her spine straightens. "We need to focus on the contract and your optics. We're lucky nobody saw us down there."

Unwilling to give up, I close the distance between us again and bring a hand up to cup the soft skin at her jaw. Her eyes close, and I suppress a groan. She's trying to kill me. "It could be our little secret," I whisper, barely able to restrain myself from taking another taste of her sweet lips.

Again, she steps back, blinking as her head shakes almost violently. "No. This is not going to happen. We got carried away–the dinner, the wine, my birthday..." She throws a hand out. "The rain! It could happen to anyone." I decide not to point out that the rain is what interrupted our kiss, not what caused it. She ties the front of her wrap in a knot with restless fingers and forces a smile. "Thank you so much for tonight. It really was wonderful." Then she turns and walks to her door.

And I let her go.

It goes without saying I need a beer after that, but the bitter liquid masks the lingering taste of Kaitlyn on my lips, so I dump it down the sink and decide to hit the hay early. Won't my agent be impressed when I'm up with the roosters in the morning. Back to business as usual.

My suit and shirt go onto an armchair in the corner where my cleaning lady, Greta, will find them, and I flick the covers back to settle in before grabbing the TV remote. It's early enough that I catch the end of a college basketball game, but it's not enthralling enough to keep my mind off my tempting neighbor.

I get her point, but not only are we two potentially consenting adults, we live next door to one another. Nobody would have to know. It's just sex. And, besides, she won't be my agent forever. It seems crazy to deny ourselves. Or maybe I'm kidding myself that she wants me as badly as I want her.

Kaitlyn has fought tooth and nail to establish herself–in an industry and sport dominated by men, no less–so I understand that she wants to keep things simple. For both of our sakes. That doesn't change the fact that the kiss on the street tonight might have been the best of my life.

I grunt my frustration to the empty room and flick off the TV. The remote clatters to the nightstand and I bark at my home system to shut off the lights. This is gonna be a long night.

To make matters worse, not five minutes later,I hear a cat meowing–which is particularly odd seeing as I don't own a cat. Still, I turn the lights back on to make sure one didn't find its way inside my condo when I wasn't looking. Weirder things have happened in Florida. But, no, there's no cat.

I go to settle back in, and there it goes again. And now that I'm paying closer attention, I can pinpoint the direction of the sound as coming from the wall behind my headboard. Shit. I've heard about cats getting into the space between walls when people repair drywall. The only problem with that is there are only two condos on this floor, and neither Pierre or I have been moonlighting as drywall repairmen. Which means either Kaitlyn is an undercover bleeding heart and adopted one or...

It's not a cat.

The latter is confirmed two seconds later by the very distinct sound of a female voice moaning my name. Which, in turn, has me going hard as a steel fucking pipe in my boxers.

I'm absolutely unashamed to admit my ear is flush to the shared wall a millisecond later as a mewling Kaitlyn pants out my name again, this time following it up with several desperate whimpers.

Holy fuck is that hot.

This not being my first day owning a cock, that bastard is fisted in my hand in no time flat.

My eyes close as I envision a naked Kaitlyn spread out on her bed, thighs splayed, the fingers of one hand stroking her clit while the other teases those nipples that nearly caused me to go blind earlier. Is she really masturbating to thoughts of me? That might be the hottest thing I've ever considered in my entire life.

When I hear more panting, my imagination shifts to the feel of Kaitlyn's lithe body under me in my bed as I finally get to caress all of that silky skin with my fingertips. She shivers under my touch, so I retrace every inch with my lips, warming her with my hot breath and soft whispers of praise against her skin.

Her sweet sighs and aroused gasps make me harder still, and even though I know this is all in my head, I swear I can feel her beneath me—those long legs wrapping me up tight and letting me feel how hot and wet and ready she is. I can even smell her floral perfume mixing with a hint of her perspiration, but they're replaced by the scent of her desire as I slide farther down her body to the promised land.

I continue to stroke myself, gritting my teeth and groaning into my pillow now so real-life Kaitlyn won't hear me. She's quieted down, but in my mind she's still giving me those mewling sounds as her back arches at my touch. My tongue traces a line down from her navel to her bare mound and lower still as I settle between her thighs and get my first taste of her hot center.

All the blood in my body rushes down to my cock as I imagine delving my tongue into her wet heat and teasing her clit on each upstroke. She's soaked, and she tastes fucking delicious. When she bucks and squirms, I hold her thighs in place and suck her clit into my mouth. I'm rewarded by her crying out my name and spearing her fingers through my hair in a silent plea to continue.

I stroke myself faster, using my pre-cum to lubricate as my fist pumps over and over until my entire pelvis tightens and the familiar rush races across my back and into my balls. And then I'm coming all over myself like a teenager, my face buried in my pillow as I groan out Kaitlyn's name and continue to jerk until the very last drop of cum is drained.

A minute later, I'm still sucking wind, my chest heaving against the mattress and the sticky wetness under me making me curse myself. The last time I lost control like that was... hell, I can't even remember, it's been so long.

The one thing I know for sure is this attraction to Kaitlyn isn't going to go away, and based on what I heard tonight, she's got it just as bad for me.

I guess we'll have to see how long she can hold out because there's no way in hell I'm making myself scarce now.

# Chapter Fifteen

Kaitlyn

My assistant's text comes as I'm trying to glide the black liner on my top eyelid. Being forty has made me wish to rock a cat eye in some bid to stay relevant. Or maybe I'm just trying to put on the full professional armor before I have to see Banks again. The right eye looks like I'm a makeup artist but the left one is making me look like a kindergartener drew on my face.

Bella: Ed just signed Grayson.

The black eyeliner slides toward my temple before I remember to pull it away from my face. "Shit!"

Grayson, a fourteen-year-old already turning heads as a freshman in high school, was supposed to be my newest hockey client. Ed Fucking Presley must have gotten to him while I've been here in Tampa babysitting Banks. I pick up the phone to text Ed a death threat, but think better of it. Barely.

My hands are shaking as I look up at myself in the mirror,

ignoring the hideous black eyeliner ruining my makeup and turning my head this way and that, sure I spot a gray hair slipping through my strands. A few seconds later, I get my fingers on the hair that has betrayed me and I yank it from my scalp. Of course, it stings and now my eyes are watering, which triggers my mouth to release a string of expletives born from a gut boiling with rage. I wonder just how bald I'm going to be if I keep plucking out every single gray hair that shows itself. I stomp my foot like a petulant child.

I've gone from a calm morning to rage in two-point-two seconds flat. I'm a fucking basket case.

So I do what any rational woman does when faced with insurmountable odds: I wipe my eyeliner from my temple, create the perfect cat eye on my left side like a badass, and then pick up my phone to dial the first gynecologist that I see on a search list in Tampa, Florida. I'm still not convinced Olivia's right, but until I can prove her wrong, I'll wonder. At this point, I'm almost hoping it's perimenopause and not me losing my goddamn mind. My therapy bill is already up there with my grocery expenses every month.

"Gulf Coast Gynecology, can I help you?" a pleasant woman says in my ear.

"Hi, yes, I'm looking to evaluate if I'm in perimenopause." I don't beat around the bush. I can feel my remaining eggs shriveling as we speak.

The woman chuckles. "It's your lucky day."

"Is it though?" I ask wryly, thinking about Ed Presley besting me.

"Well, I can't speak for winning the lottery, but I just got off the phone with a last minute cancellation for this afternoon at two. You want it?"

I look at the desk set up in the primary bedroom. I'd have time to make the calls I need to make, but not enough time to make Banks's practice. Probably for the best, given what happened between us last night. Besides, I can't have Banks starring in any more of my late night solo pleasure sessions. Distance sounds like just the thing we need.

"I'll take it." I give her all my information and hang up. Switching to my text messages, I tap one out to Banks.

Me: I won't be able to make your practice today. Behave yourself.

"We'll test your hormone levels and run some other blood tests just to rule anything else out, but based on your symptoms, I suspect your friend is right."

The doctor stands up from the swiveling stool and tucks her auburn hair behind her ear like the appointment is over. Congrats, your baby making machinery is on death's door, have a nice fucking day.

"But–" I peel my legs off the paper examination table and hop up, some of it trailing me like toilet paper stuck to my shoe. Panic has my voice shaking. "I just turned forty yesterday! How is that possible? Aren't I supposed to be, like, fifty or something?"

The doctor smiles calmly, probably used to seeing hormone swings in action. "Listen, the average age of menopause in America is fifty-one, which gives you a normal range of forty-five to fifty-five. Considering perimenopausal symptoms can happen seven to ten years before you hit menopause, that puts normal perimenopause starting as early as thirty-five."

The math is blowing my mind. But it makes sense. The mood swings, the frozen shoulder, the extra weight gain around the middle. Turning forty is well within the window of possibility. It all adds up to perimenopause. My new curse word.

"But I still want to have babies."

The smile fades into something that looks like pity. "Then you better get pregnant sooner rather than later." She taps a few keys on her computer. "I'll send someone in to draw your blood and we'll be in touch." And with that, she's gone, on to the next patient.

I realize my jaw is open when my tongue starts to dry out. I snap my mouth shut and sit back down on the examination table to wait for the nurse, shoulders slumped. My stomach has swooped so low I'm not sure it's still inside my body. All the dreams of pink bows on a smooth baby head and blue onesies climbing out of cribs flash before my eyes. Did I wait too long? Should I have sacrificed my career for babies? I shake my head, unwilling to go down the road of regrets. What's done is done. All I can do is make a plan for my future. The nurse comes in and draws several vials of blood while my thoughts swirl. All through getting dressed and heading back to the condo, I shift gears into formulating a plan. This is where I shine. I can normally plan my ass off with one hand behind my back and blindfolded, but today, I come up empty.

All I can do is heat up some milk, pour in a generous scoop of hot cocoa mix, sit on my couch in my comfiest sweats, and cry. It's easy to blame Broderick, thinking I wasted precious time on a man who didn't want to have a family. Or to blame my failing body for not having another ten years of fertile eggs in me. But somewhere between the first box of tissues and the second, I stop the useless blame game and I take stock of where I'm at.

I'm forty, I'm successful professionally, and I have a ticking time bomb of a womb. With one last sniffle, I wipe my nose and take a sip of my now cold cocoa. A loud banging on my front door has the cocoa sloshing over onto my sweats. I bite back a curse.

"Kaitlyn?"

It's Banks. I sigh and put my cup down on the art deco coffee table in front of me. I catch sight of myself in the mirror in the foyer, grimacing. "Hold on a second," I say through the door, fully intending to not let him in when I look so hideous, but he beats his fist on my door again, vibrating the whole wall.

"Open the damn door, Kaitlyn."

My mood shifts again and I'm pissed he's basically breaking my door down. I swing it open, ready to give him a piece of my mind, when he lunges through the doorway and sweeps me into his arms. The anger bleeds out as I rest my cheek on his chest, the thump of his heart a metronome of comfort. His arms band around me like a steel cage, holding me up exactly when I'm unsure of what my body is capable of.

My breaths come slower and I stay in his arms, wanting just a few more moments of bliss before I step back and face my reality. Banks shifts his head and kisses the top of mine. It's the sweetness that breaks my heart wide open.

"Please don't cry, Kaitlyn," he whispers. "I can't stand to hear you cry. Whatever happened yesterday doesn't matter. I just want to be your friend, okay?"

And just like that, my mouth is curving upward. I don't know how he does it, but the egotistical man can pull me out of a bad mood with a simple sentence. And a hug. Damn, does Banks give good hugs.

I pull back just enough to look up at him, one eyebrow

raised. "I'm not crying over you, jackass." For an insult, it lacks heat. Banks cracks a smile, his big hand landing on the back of my head and pushing me back down to his chest.

"Thank fuck," he mutters, rocking me side to side.

I poke him in the ribs and he finally lets go enough that I'm standing on my own two feet. He keeps his hands on my arms though, as if he's not sure I won't go right back to crying. "I'm good, I promise. What are you even doing here?"

He was supposed to go out with the team after practice today, a scheduled team bonding I'd told him was a good idea. He needs to be an example for the younger guys. A mentor on and off the ice. Negotiations won't wait, and I need him looking like a leader and a choir boy.

"I, uh, didn't sleep well last night," he answers, letting my arms go and avoiding my gaze. "Figured I'd catch a late nap, but then somebody was weeping and gnashing their teeth next door."

I put my hands on my hips and give him a look that would make a houseplant wither on the spot. "I wasn't weeping."

His gaze swings back up to mine. "Could have fooled me. Plus you used up all the tissues in Tampa so don't bother claiming nothing's wrong." He tips his head to my left where I'm sure he has a clear view over my shoulder of my used tissue pile.

I sigh and walk back to the couch, scooping up the pile and tossing it into the trash can before sitting again. Banks joins me, dropping down a few inches away, still studying my face. Pretty sure my cat eyes look more like a litter box right now.

"Are you going to tell me or am I going to have to pry it out of you with whiskey shots and threats to strip if you don't start talking?"

I tilt my head, my brain momentarily getting stuck on the

mental image of Banks stripping for me. *No, bad brain.* "I'm old," I blurt into the silence.

"No shit. I was at your fortieth birthday party yesterday."

I backhand his arm, and he fakes like it hurt. "You're supposed to say, no you're not, Kaitlyn," I finish in a falsetto voice that makes him grimace.

"I'm only eighteen months behind you. Of course, I don't think you're old. Though there's nothing wrong with a hot cougar." His impish grin, along with the exaggerated eyebrow wiggle, is actually making me feel better.

"I went to a doctor's appointment today."

Banks drops the grin and grabs my hand. "Everything okay?"

I shrug, but clutch his hand. I don't have it in me to make up a lie for why I was crying. "Sure, if being told you're peri-menopausal is good news."

He shifts uncomfortably. "I'm sorry, I don't know if that's something to celebrate or something to mourn." His gaze traces over the tear tracks on my cheeks. "Clearly something to mourn. Got it."

"It just means my ovaries are giving out, which isn't necessarily a bad thing. Every woman will go through it."

"Should we take your ovaries out back and shoot 'em?"

I give him a half hearted smile. I appreciate him trying to cheer me up, but this is going to take some time to wrap my head around. In the meantime, I accept his offer of friendship and tell him the truth. "I just wanted to have at least one baby, but now that's looking like it won't happen."

Banks jolts, but then covers it up by throwing his arm around my shoulders and pulling me into his side. "Want to know the best way to work through some mental gymnastics?"

I tilt my head against his shoulder to look up at him. He's unfairly handsome. "Yes, please."

"Video games. And I have a bazillion over at my place." He kisses the top of my head again, pulls his arm from around me, and stands. "Come on, Killer Kaitlyn. Come slay me on the screen. You'll feel better, I promise."

He holds out his hand and I take it, letting him tug me over to his place where we play video games until way past my bedtime.

And he's right. I do feel better.

# Chapter Sixteen

Banks

I'm officially fucked, and not in the good way.

Not only did I reassure Kaitlyn that I'm on board with the friend-zone plan–*again*–but she proved last night that she's a hell of a lot of fun to hang out with. And she could totally smoke Eli at Warlords, which pleases me to no end. I'll have to get those two together one of these days.

Except I can't because Kaitlyn is only here to get me my contract and then she'll be back in Atlanta or flying around the country to see her clients and chase down new ones, all while pursuing her mission to bury Ed Presley. And I'll be just as busy nine months of the year.

But now I'm stuck with not only a constant hard-on for this woman, but... feelings too.

I couldn't help it. First, that kiss, and then the woman cried–and confided in me. And, by the way, she's the only person I've ever met who's maybe even more beautiful when she cries. How is that even possible?

When I woke up yesterday morning, I thought I heard her cursing through the wall, but I couldn't be sure. All I know is my skin felt itchy and I was restless as hell. Her text didn't help, and I even knocked on her door, but I either missed her or she was avoiding me. I spent all practice scanning the arena for her face every few minutes, earning myself sore ribs from a mid-ice collision with Barzee and then the boards. It had him giving me the side eye the rest of practice.

I pushed too hard in the weight room, ignoring Frannie's scolding, but by then I was too keyed up to do what I should have. It was a no-brainer to blow off the guys and take my sore, exhausted ass home to check on my neighbor.

And, despite how I'm feeling right now, I'm glad I did. It felt good to be useful, especially when I was rewarded with several of her smiles for my efforts—not to mention a fun evening sparring on the PlayStation. I could really get used to that.

Scalding water sprays over my back as I press my palms into the shower wall, dead-ass tired, even more sore than yesterday, and trying not to get a hard-on thinking of Kaitlyn. As I said, I'm officially fucked.

I groan and switch off the tap before opening the glass door to snatch a towel from the rack. I dry myself off as I force my brain to tonight's road game against the Devils. That's what I should really be thinking about. Their D is world-class, and it's gonna take every trick we've got up our sleeves to come out on top. The fan is no match for the steam, so I use my towel to wipe the mirror down, tossing it on the sink as I open the door to my bedroom.

And then I freeze.

"My eyes!" Kaitlyn shrieks, slapping both hands over her face and bringing one of my t-shirts with them. What is she doing with my shirt? And what is she doing in my bedroom?! Did I pass out in the shower?

No, that can't be it. If this were a dream, Kaitlyn would obviously be naked–although today's red skirt and black stilettos do come in a close second now that I think about it.

She shifts her stance on my bedroom rug and parts two fingers, only to gasp and cover up again. "Can you please put that thing away?"

A smirk settles on my lips and I cross my arms over my chest, resting a shoulder against the door jamb and doing absolutely nothing to cover myself. "Are you smelling my shirt?" I can't help messing with her.

She gasps in indignation and tosses the tee to the floor, momentarily forgetting that it was helping to shield her eyes. "Dammit!" She growls her frustration and whips around, giving me a prime view of her lush backside and hips as they flair out from her slim waist. My fingers twitch.

"Last I checked, this was *my* condo. And I don't recall extending an invitation this morning," I respond. "Not that you aren't welcome."

Did she just stomp her foot? "I thought you were still sleeping and were going to be late for the airport! The last thing we need is you missing a team flight."

My grin widens. "Well, as you can see, I'm already showered and on my way. But you still haven't explained how you got into my condo."

She ignores that, instead throwing her arms out and asking, "How do you live like this? You have the bedroom of a frat boy. I'm pretty sure there's old pizza under your bed."

"Should I be flattered you got on your hands and knees for me? Maybe we should make this even. I showed you mine; now you show me yours. It's only fair." I shrug and try not to let my dick get hard at the thought. A glance around the room shows my laundry and shoes strewn across the floor and my bed unmade (although I did change the sheets the night of her birthday, so at least they're clean). It's not so bad.

"You wish, hot shot," Kaitlyn scoffs, and I have to bite the inside of my cheek to keep from responding that I heard her doing a little "wishing" herself just the other night.

Since she's clearly not going to budge and be the bigger person, it's up to me. I move to my dresser for a pair of boxers and step into them. "You can turn around now. I'm decent." I don't try keeping the verbal eyeroll out of my voice.

She turns, and I can see her jaw tighten in self-admonishment when her eyes drop directly to my crotch. My smile is impossible to bite back as I add, "I have a flight to catch. Wanna enlighten me?"

Finally giving in, she props her hands on her hips and confesses, "I had a copy of your key made the day after I moved in." She ignores my raised brow. "It was inevitable that I'd need it to either wake you from a nap or evict a puck bunny at one point or another." When I open my mouth to protest the puck bunny part–the nap part being entirely plausible–she raises a hand and cuts me off. "I've been texting you for an hour."

Hmm. I guess I lost track of time in the shower. "For your information, I don't live like a frat boy. My cleaning lady, Greta, is coming later today–and how many frat boys do you know who own an espresso maker?" I nab a fresh T-shirt from the next drawer down and pull it over my head. "Coffee may not be its own religion to me like it is to you, but I've become more discerning since my twenties–especially since someone horrified me with a story about airline coffee a few years back."

Kaitlyn's lips twitch before she gives in and sends me an actual grin. My heart thumps hard knowing she remembers that afternoon at the airport as well as I do. "Get dressed and meet me in your living room. We need to talk strategy before you leave for Tennessee."

"Now, *this* is the kind of hockey I can get behind," Eli drops his backpack on the wood floor next to the air hockey table I had delivered this morning. It's only a rental, but it does sort of complete the living room, I must admit.

"It's a start," I reply, heading back to the kitchen to stock the fridge with the beer that was delivered too. I won't be drinking any since I have Eli, but I'm sure the pissants will help themselves as soon as they get here.

I grimace. Not pissants, Bennet. *Teammates.*

Kaitlyn is determined to turn me into a mentor to her boys Bobby, Pete, and Alexi even if it kills all of us. And I'm not exactly in a position to refuse. But if I'm doing this, it's going to happen *my* way, not hers. Before I left town for this latest string of away games, she informed me I'd be inviting the younger players over to my condo for "quality bonding time," which is a phrase no man has ever used to invite the guys over for beers.

But since I was in a good mood from the shower after-show, I nodded along as she outlined her party plan and offered to script a pep talk for me to deliver sometime after the goal sharing but most definitely before the trust fall exercise. Needless to say, we're not doing any of that shit.

It's not like I haven't mentored anyone before; I always take on the odd college or high school hockey player in the offseason. But the difference is those kids come into it already respecting the hell out of me. The Three Ass-kateers love nothing more than to show me up and point out how old I am.

Roman is much better at this crap, so I called up my old team captain and best friend and asked for advice. He didn't hold back, telling me to get over myself and put my thirty-three years of experience to good use (I was a late bloomer and didn't start playing hockey till I was five). "They already respect you; they just need to know you respect them too."

Roman's words hit home, so I'm feeling oddly optimistic about this afternoon with the younger generation. And since I thought Eli might get a kick out of hanging with some more pro athletes, I asked Denise if he could join in.

"Can we get wings today?" Eli asks over the mechanical dings and tinny cheers from the air hockey table as he tries it out.

I close the fridge and frown at him. "I wish you'd told me earlier. I already ordered you a salad." He's not fooled for a second.

A knock sounds at my door, and I pivot that way to let the pis–*teammates* in, but the knocking turns to incessant pounding in the two-point-three seconds it takes me to get there. "Jesus," I mutter.

"See, I told you it wasn't a trap," Pete Fornier says as he barrels past me and into my condo. He's followed closely by Alexi Baranov and Bobby Rhodes.

"I didn't say it was a trap," Roadie protests, at least pausing to give me a chin lift in greeting. "Yo, Benny, what's up?" Then he turns back to Forns. "I said for *you* to shut *your* trap."

Forns scowls at him before heading directly to my refrigerator, as predicted.

Barzee stops at the air hockey table. "Who are you?" he asks Eli with all the manners of his twenty-three years.

Eli hooks a thumb my way and doesn't miss a beat. "His lawyer."

Roadie guffaws and follows Forns to the kitchen while Barzee challenges Eli to a game. The two immediately square off, and I fetch a soda while resisting the urge to throw these asshats off my veranda and reminding myself this is all part of a bigger plan.

Forty-five minutes later, Eli is at my kitchen table on his tenth hotwing and Barzee and Forns are locked in a tie-breaking round of cornhole (yes, I had cornhole delivered to my condo too) while Roadie and I hang on opposite couches eating pizza.

"Nice pad, Benny," Roadie says, surveying the large living area. "My place is a shithole compared to this."

Not to brag too much, but my place *is* pretty sweet. The giant open living and dining space is edged on one side by floor-to-ceiling windows and a massive wraparound veranda with views of the Gulf. The other side tapers to a hallway leading to two spacious bedrooms and a home gym. "Believe me, my old place was nothing to write home about either." I toss my half-eaten slice back onto my plate on the coffee table. "I felt like it didn't matter, being on the road so much."

"Exactly. I mean, it's not like I've got a wife and kids to take care of or anything. It's essentially just a crash pad for the offseason. I've got better places to spend my money." His grin tells me I probably don't want to know.

"I hear you." I hesitate to continue, but then decide to anyway. "My therapist said something that kind of made sense to me, though." When he doesn't immediately laugh or even scoff, I continue, "If your head is a mess, then living in chaos is only kicking yourself in the ass." When Roadie raises a brow at me, I shrug. "I may be paraphrasing."

He doesn't look like he's buying it, so I try again, leaning forward to rest my elbows on my knees. "Basically, I was stressed the hell out with a bad season and a nagging hip injury–this was back in 2016–and she started talking about 'safe spaces,' which had me looking at her about the same way you're looking at me right now." Roadie huffs out a laugh, running his hands through his dirty blond mop of hair and relaxing back into the couch cushions. I take this as an invitation to keep talking. "She asked if I felt relaxed at home, and I realized I really didn't. I hated my apartment and put exactly zero effort into it–hell, I only picked it because it was close to practice." The chagrined expression on his face tells me he might currently be living at my old address. "And she was right–she even had me calculate the number of nights I was home, and it was more than I thought."

I take a swig of my soda and notice Forns and Barzee have stopped chirping at each other and started eavesdropping. "So I took her advice and got this place with a killer view and lots of space. I furnish it with comfortable shit I like, and I've got a cleaning lady who keeps it respectable and fills my fridge with good food so I'm not eating takeout every night. She even makes me home made lasagna once a month, man."

"I fuckin' love lasagna," Forns announces as he drapes himself on the arm of my couch. At my glare and its accompanying gesture to the kid at my kitchen table, he corrects himself. "Uh, I mean I *freakin'* love lasagna."

"You got any right now?" Barzee asks, attempting to shove Roadie off the couch to take his seat but jumping back up again with an, "Ow! What the hell is that?" He reaches between two of the cushions and pulls out the offending object. All three men examine it before turning to me in perfect sync.

Shit.

I consider blowing them off and lying, but saving face is not the point of today's gathering. I need to be real with these guys if we're going to get anywhere.

I feel the tips of my ears turn red. "Knitting is extremely relaxing. Something about the repetitive movements is incredibly soothing."

Silence. Utter silence.

It's finally broken when Forns laughs and reaches for a slice. "He's fu–messing with you guys."

It's the perfect out if I want to change my mind, but I don't, so I shake my head and dig my index finger into the honeycomb afghan draped over the back of my couch. "I'm not messing with you. See this masterpiece? That's all me, baby."

The pizza slice drops from Fornier's fingers and their gazes all shift to the buttery soft blanket. Roadie reaches out a tentative hand to touch it before his eyebrows spike in surprise. "Damn, that's soft." He yanks it from its place and buries both hands in it. "Dude, you gotta feel this thing," he beckons Barzee.

"It's like a fluffy cloud," Barzee agrees, and pretty soon all three of them are feeling up my afghan like a two-dollar street walker.

"Now that you mention it," Forns says, looking my way. "I may have been feeling a bit stressed out lately. Coach has been riding my crossover pretty damn hard."

I resist a grin. Barely. "You want me to show you how to knit? It's pretty easy once you get the hang of it."

# Chapter Seventeen

Kaitlyn

I can hear the party happening next door, but I stay in my condo, feverishly working on emails and researching what I'll need for the next round of contract negotiations for all my other players. Besides my ridiculous workload, Banks needs alone time with the younger guys without me breathing down his neck.

Okay fine, I'm also hiding.

So would you if you'd seen what I saw a few days ago. It's imprinted in my head like some kind of dick pic gone oh so very right. I walked into Banks's bedroom and the door opened, steam billowing out like I'd landed myself a front row seat on the set of Grey's Anatomy. McSteamy–I mean, Banks–walked out naked as the day he was born, his fingers combing through his thick wet hair. My gaze shot south immediately and who could blame me? When there's a baseball bat swinging in the room, you look. For safety, of course. Not because I was both curious and momentarily stunned by the length, girth, and coloring of the most perfect dick I've ever had the pleasure to see.

I'm his agent, goddammit. I'm above all that. Sadly, I wished I was actually below and around all that perfectness. Which is why I slapped my hands to my face to cover my eyes. My eyelids weren't closing like they should have. I felt like that cartoon with toothpicks holding my eyes open so I could see every last second of the show. The fucker didn't even had the decency to cover himself, not that two hands would have been capable of it while it was lengthening and lifting like that.

Hoooooly fuck. With my back turned, I had the horrifying–yet completely tantalizing–thought that Banks's dick very much liked me back. Which was why I lined my spine with steel and forced myself to remain utterly professional. Dropping to my knees in front of the world's most perfect dick to get a closer look is not in my job description, no matter how much I felt like doing it.

So when my ears prick as the party goes suspiciously silent next door, I wonder if they've gotten themselves into trouble I won't be able to get them out of. Reluctantly, I put on my big girl agent pants and go over there. I let myself in, expecting to see a puck bunny or a drinking game or something that will make me so angry I can finally forget what Banks is packing under that hockey uniform.

Instead, I find four professional hockey players and one teen boy sitting on the couches in the living room, focused on a project in each of their hands while Banks calmly calls out directions. The boys don't even lift their heads to see me approach. They're too busy...*knitting*.

My jaw drops and I suddenly wonder if perimenopause can cause hallucinations. Banks looks up momentarily, shooting me a wink before telling the boys to hold the yarn tightly.

"Fu-freak!" Bobby whines. "I dropped my stitch faster than that puck bunny with my name tattooed on her ass."

I turn to Bobby, ready to ask a thousand questions about this woman he never told me about. If it can affect his image, I need to know about it. But none of the boys are paying me any attention. It's like I'm not even in the room.

"Here," Banks reaches over with a crochet hook like this is a common problem. "Just hook the yarn from behind and pull it through. Like this."

My head is swiveling like I'm at a tennis match. When I demanded Banks host the younger guys for some bonding time, I never envisioned a knitting circle. Moving surreptitiously, I pull my cell phone from my pocket, snapping pictures like I've found some species of animal far, far away from their natural habitat and it has to be documented to be believed.

"Okay, now that we've all casted on, we'll start the most basic of stitches called a purl stitch," Banks instructs, holding his knitting project out so everyone can see. Holy shit, that blanket is already three feet long and at least four feet wide. How long has Banks been a knitter? The guys are all quiet for a bit, copying Banks's every move.

"Dude, I just knitted an asshole, not a row," Pete whines, holding up his yarn masterpiece.

Huh. It does kind of look like an asshole, if assholes were bright purple and fuzzy.

"Your tension's too tight. Quit knitting at the tips of the needles and give yourself some extra yarn. Finesse the purl stitch, don't force it."

"Purl stitches?" Alexi makes a face but attempts to do the same motion Banks is demonstrating. "How about a pearl necklace? I can make that."

The three younger players crack up laughing before Banks

clears his throat and darts wide eyes in the teen's direction. "Dude," Banks chastises.

Alexi coughs, his cheeks turning red. "I mean, my mom would like it if I made her a pearl necklace out of yarn."

The teen frowns back at him. "You know I'm not five, right?"

Banks lets go of his knitting needles long enough to rub his eyes. "Jesus. Your mom is never letting you come over again."

As if she was summoned, there's a knock on the door behind me. Banks makes eye contact and I put my phone away long enough to answer it. A beautiful woman stands there in a suit I immediately wish I owned.

"I love your shoes," she says as a way of greeting.

"I covet your suit," I answer back, motioning her in.

"Thanks. I assume my son didn't burn down the place?" She stops short, catching sight of the men on the couches. "Umm..."

"No fires. But I think he's learning to knit. Hope you want handmade slippers for Christmas." I stick out my hand. "I'm Kaitlyn Phillips, Banks's agent."

She smiles at me, shaking my hand. "I've heard good things about you, Kaitlyn. Take good care of Banks. He's special."

That's genuine warmth and affection I see on her face before she steps into the living room to collect her son. I meet him too before he leaves, with promises to hang out next time he's over. Eli even challenges me to a Warlord battle, which I promptly accept. No teenager is going to beat me. I'll have to practice every day before then, but I'm sure Banks won't mind if I borrow his PlayStation.

The boys leave shortly after, taking their knitting needles and yarn projects with them. Bobby looks like his brain has exploded. "I think I like knitting," he says in a stupor as he gives me a quick hug goodbye. Banks glares at the back of his head and nearly pushes him out the door. Alexi and Pete confirm a date two weeks from now when they plan to get together again.

When the door finally closes behind the last of them, I turn slowly and eye Banks. He looks over at me sheepishly. I may be his agent, but I'm a woman first, and he looks good enough to eat with his well worn jeans, fitted T-shirt, and yarn dust on his chest. I scan his apartment, seeing zero evidence that he did any of the team building exercises I wrote down for him.

"That looks like it went well." And it does. That scene on the couch looked like Banks had done things his way and it had turned out perfectly. I underestimated him yet again and he proved me wrong. I wonder how many more things I got wrong about Banks.

He stacks dirty paper plates with the remnants of the pizza and wings he ordered. I move past him to the kitchen, grabbing a trash bag and holding it out. We move around his condo, collecting trash and straightening things up while he tells me all about it.

"It was, dare I say, nice?" He puts down the bag, tying the ends together before standing straight and dusting his hands off. "Thank you, Kaitlyn. For pushing me to do that. Those guys are still pissants, but they're *my* pissants, you know?"

I'm so proud of him I could burst. He hasn't been late to practice in several weeks. He's volunteering at the retirement center on his own time. He mentors Eli, and now he's taken the younger players under his wing. He even stood up to my own father just to protect my feelings. He helped plan my birthday party for crap's sake. He's literally nothing like I thought he was. He's exactly who I thought Ben was all those years ago.

"I have a confession," I blurt out.

Banks tilts his head and steps closer. His blue eyes spark with humor and I suddenly realize that I've become accustomed to seeing those royal blue pools every day. I fucking *missed* him when he was on the road this week. I had time and distance to do a lot of thinking. I have regret running through my veins from waiting so long to have a baby. I can't have yet another thing I regret not doing. "Do tell."

I run my tongue across my lips, then take the leap, telling a little white lie. "I got a Tigers tattoo."

Those eyes no longer hold humor. They hold heat. The kind that crackles and snaps because it's burning so hot. In the blink of an eye, he's closer, heat pumping off his chest in the narrow space between us. I tilt my head back and boldly hold his gaze. Because there's something I've learned about myself over the years. Just like my athletes, when I want something, I go after it. I don't wait for it to fall in my lap and I don't hem and haw back and forth, unable to make a decision. When I'm in, I'm all in. And the raw truth is that I'm so fucking in to Banks.

"Guess where it is."

His gaze drops to my lips and then shoots back up to my eyes. "I thought you told me that if you ever got a tattoo I'd be the last one to know."

"That was back when I didn't like you."

I don't miss the subtle tilt to his lips. "Does that mean you like me now?"

Putting my hand in the center of his chest, I decide it's time I allowed myself to have some fun. Time I took my eye off the puck and let myself be a hot-blooded woman. "Guess, Banks. For every wrong guess I'll lose an article of clothing."

His pupils blow wide and suddenly he's breathing like he just finished a breakaway sprint on the ice. "You know this is like backward strip poker, right?"

I grin. "You gonna complain about my rules or are you going to play?"

"Big toe," he barks out, making me laugh.

"That's a horrible guess."

"Rules are rules, Killer Kaitlyn. Lose the damn shirt."

I unbutton my blouse slowly, enjoying the way his gaze follows my every move. I feel powerful under his attention. This big man with all the athletic prowess of a Greek god is at my mercy. When I get the blouse open and let it slip down my arms to pool on the floor, leaving me in a black lacy bra, Banks swallows so hard I hear it in the silence of his condo.

"Earlobe," is his next guess, this time with a voice that sounds strangled.

I kick off one stiletto.

"Pinky finger."

I kick off the other stiletto.

Banks narrows his eyes. "Collarbone."

I roll my eyes. He can see that my collarbone doesn't have a tattoo, but I'm having too much fun drawing this out to point out the obvious cheating. I unbutton my jeans and wiggle them over my hips and down my legs to kick them off. Banks's jaw goes slack as he stares at my matching black panties.

"Got another guess?" I ask, popping one hip out and hoping he can't see that extra weight I've put on recently.

His gaze flies back to my face and he looks like he's in pain. "As much as I'm already kicking my ass for asking this, I thought we weren't supposed to do this?"

I shrug one shoulder. "I can keep a secret, can you?"

Banks leans down to sit on the back of the couch, immediately standing again and howling in pain. He throws a knitting needle across the room and rubs his backside. I roll my lips in and try not to laugh. God, he's funny. And sweet. And loyal. And possesses all the body parts that would make for the kind of night I desperately need.

"No one knows about Eli or my girl, Beatrice, right?" he finally answers.

"Then get over here and find that tattoo."

Banks takes one giant step forward, his hands cupping my face. "You have one last chance to say no."

I stare right into his eyes. "Kiss me, Ben," I whisper.

And he does.

# Chapter Eighteen

Banks

It's time to face the truth.

Since the day I met Kaitlyn Phillips at the Atlanta airport ten years ago, I've compared every single woman I've met to her. Even after she stuck that dagger in my heart rinkside and did nothing but glare at me or insult me since, I haven't been able to help it. Kaitlyn with a K from the airport has always been my gold standard, the one nobody else could ever compare to.

So, you could argue I've set myself up for disappointment by placing her up so high on that lofty pedestal... but you'd be wrong. Just like her humor, vivacity, and intelligence have proven to be better than I could have imagined, the woman's beauty as she tells me to kiss her far surpasses any of my fantasies about her. And there have been a lot.

The first touch of our lips takes me right back to the sidewalk down the street where we kissed on her birthday. Desire shoots directly from my lips down to my cock, which is already testing the confines of my jeans after that fuck-hot striptease. I need to rein myself in or this has a chance of being over before it even begins. But her mouth is so soft and sweet, and when she flicks her tongue against mine, I'm done for.

Gone is any possibility of slow exploration or savoring, and Kaitlyn is obviously of the same mind because the second my palm slides over her sweet ass to the back of her thigh, she does a little hop and locks her legs behind my back. My hands instinctively support her, one on each perfect ass cheek as I pull her in tight without breaking our kiss. Even through my T-shirt and the lace of her panties, I can feel the heat from her pussy, and it makes me groan into her mouth.

She smiles against my lips and murmurs, "You're like a giant sequoia." Her comment makes me laugh, but the need to keep tasting her wins out, and my tongue sweeps past her lips again. Her legs flex as she tightens around me, and I decide it's time to take this party horizontal. I'm impressed with myself when I manage to maneuver us blindly from the living room, down the hall, and into my bedroom without knocking at least one of us unconscious.

Kaitlyn isn't a person to do anything in half measures. I already know this about her. But I still find myself pleasantly surprised by how fully and openly she's giving herself into this... whatever it is between us. I can't think about that now. The only thing I'm allowing myself to think about is how fucking hot this woman is and how fast I can get a taste of *all* of her.

I lower her to the bed and nip her bottom lip before untangling her legs from around me and going up on my knees to enjoy the view. But she follows me up, foiling my plan and gripping the bottom of my T-shirt to yank it off me. I reach a hand behind my back and pull it off myself to save time and get back to surveying her delectable body.

She gets distracted running her nails over my pecs, so I put both hands on her shoulders and press her back into the bed. "Stay."

Her glare has no effect at all and quickly fades when I thumb her nipples through her bra. My mouth waters. She's fucking gorgeous with her silky black hair spread around her face and across my sheets like an ornate crown. The late afternoon sun slanting through my windows illuminates her heated skin, and my entire body trembles in anticipation as I scan from her molten eyes to her swollen lips, past her delicate collarbone and across her black-lace-covered breasts where her tight nipples press against my thumbs. She's not wiry or cut; just soft and smooth with curves in all my favorite places.

"Beautiful." I inch down the bed and bend at the waist to drop a kiss on the skin just above her panties, causing her to shiver. So I do it again, this time tracing my tongue along the edge of the garment. Kaitlyn moans and drives her fingers through my hair, so I take it as encouragement and hook the sides of the lace with my fingers to ease the panties down her thighs. I almost swallow my tongue when I feel and see how wet she is for me already. If I didn't think she'd have me arrested, I'd steal her panties to keep with me at all times.

I tilt my head up just enough so my chin rests on her bare mound and I get her eyes. "Dripping." I know my expression is self-satisfied, but I can't help it.

Kaitlyn inhales, her lust-drunk eyes and hoarse tone belying her words as she replies, "I see the lack of blood to your brain has reduced you to single word sentences."

My only response is a short chuckle before I duck my chin again and yank her thighs apart. Her ensuing gasp shifts to a deep moan as I drag my tongue from ass to clit in one long, slow swipe, stopping to suck that bundle of nerves into my mouth when I'm done. Kaitlyn's back arches right off the bed and she grinds her pussy into my mouth.

Fuck. Yes.

My tongue swirls around her clit before I release it to start all over again. Before long, her thighs are over my shoulders and I'm tongue fucking her sweet pussy. My fingers dig into both ass cheeks to hold her steady as she rolls her hips and grinds the heels of her feet into my back just below my shoulder blades. I'm going to have bruises there tomorrow, and I couldn't give a flying fuck. Especially when she yanks my hair hard, locks all of her muscles, and comes on my tongue with the same mewling and chanting of my name as the night I heard her through the wall.

My cock throbs so painfully, I have to take one hand from her ass to pull my jeans and boxers down to offer some relief, not that it helps much. I thrust my tongue into her one last time as she starts coming down, then suck her clit, showing no mercy as she cries out and pounds her heels into my back so hard it almost feels like I just got slammed into the boards. I fist my dick to keep from coming undone and surge up in one move to nestle my hips between her thighs and bite the velvety skin of her throat.

Her hips roll up, and then she's got me wrapped up in those long legs again, shifting so the head of my cock is right at the entrance to her wet, still-pulsing pussy. "Ben," she says my name like it's a plea and rolls her hips again. It's all the invitation I need, so I thrust forward in one hard, long stroke and fill her.

She sucks in a breath and I groan into her neck as her slick tightness envelops me. It's the best goddamn thing I've ever felt in my entire life, hands down. I draw my hips back only a couple inches before surging right back in. I don't want to lose her heat for even the brief time it would take to fully withdraw. But Kaitlyn has other ideas.

"Again," she moans, scoring her fingernails down my back and reaching for my ass to assist me. I'll do anything she asks, so I pull out almost fully and thrust back in, every one of the nerve endings in my cock clamoring for more. She meets me with another roll of her hips, and we start moving as one, surging against each other stroke for stroke, pull for pull.

When Kaitlyn breathlessly keens, "Oh god, you feel so good, Ben," I almost lose it and have to shift all my focus–what there is of it left–onto hockey. The mental image of Druggy's ugly mug blocking my puck in practice helps the tiniest bit, but I know it's not enough to stem my body's urgent need to spill into Kaitlyn and drain myself dry at the altar of her bare, hot pussy.

I glide the tip of my tongue along the edge of her jaw until my mouth finds hers again, but when our tongues begin to match the rhythm of the rest of our bodies, I have to pull out for a quick breather. You'd think I killed her cat and danced on the carcass, however, based on her reaction.

"You bastard!" she cries. "What the hell are you doing?!" Her hands go for my junk, but I back out of reach just in time.

"Making this last longer than a five-minute major. Your pussy is damn greedy, woman." She narrows her eyes, but before she can utter a comeback, I go in for another kiss and use the distraction to undo the clasp on her bra. Her breasts spill out, each a perfect handful, just like I knew they'd be. But if I thought I was in control of this show, I'm proven wrong when Kaitlyn throws her hips to the side, banding my torso with her arms at the same time and flipping me over.

Okay, I'll admit I let her do it, but my reward is the fuck-hot sight of Kaitlyn Phillips straddling my hips, her loose midnight hair spilling over her shoulders as she looks down at me with pure carnal intent and a satisfied smirk. She rises to her knees without a word and reaches for my cock, teasing the tip with a swipe of her thumb before nestling it against her entrance again. The world stops when she lowers her hips and fills herself with me, her head dropping back on a loud moan.

My hands can't decide if they want to feel the weight of

her gorgeous breasts or hold her hips in place while I thrust up into her like a madman until we both pass out from exhaustion. I decide on a compromise, exploring the silken skin of her breast with one hand while the other caresses her from torso to thigh and back again while she sets a new rhythm. She's an absolute goddess perched on my cock, fucking herself as she mewls and groans with each movement of our hips.

When she picks up speed, I know there's not a lot of time left, and I need her to come one more time. So I drop the hand from her breast to skim along the sweat-dampened skin of her belly and beyond, finally finding my prize. I circle my thumb over her swollen clit and she gasps before working my cock even harder with that dream of a pussy. Her juices coat my fingers, and I can feel the heat of them dripping onto my balls, which has the countdown clock starting. With each pinch and swirl of her clit with my thumb, I get another sound of pleasure from Kaitlyn, and pretty soon I feel the familiar electricity shoot down my spine and up from my balls to my cock.

"Oh, fuck!" We both shout as our orgasms hit us at the same time. Kaitlyn loses track of her rhythm, but I've got us covered, thrusting up into her like my life depends on it while sweat beads on every inch of my skin and I come into her tight heat. I don't still until every last tremor has left my body. All I can say is thank god nobody else lives on this floor of the building.

Kaitlyn collapses onto my chest, her sweat melding with mine as we both gasp for breath. I manage to wrap my arms around her, but she's too spent to move any muscle beyond her mouth. "I think you killed me with your giant sequoia," she pants into my neck.

My chest starts shaking with laughter, but I'm still catching my breath so it almost feels like I'm dying. Which is actually fine since this is one-hundred-percent the way I want to go when it happens. Kaitlyn manages to pat my chest with a limp hand, and I capture it in mine when she eventually pulls up to a sitting position again. Her expression is as unguarded as I've ever seen as she gazes down at me. I couldn't stop my smile if I tried.

It may sound crazy, but something happened just now between us—and the mind-blowing sex is only part of it. I feel irrevocably connected to this woman, and the look on her face tells me I'm not alone. I curl at the waist to reach up and kiss her, my palm cupping her cheek and our lips settling against one another's in a touch I can only describe as tender.

I have the overwhelming urge to pull her down to the bed and curl my body around hers so I can bury my face in her hair and feel the beat of her heart under my palm. To just lie here on my bed and... *cuddle*?

Huh, I never would have pegged myself as a cuddler, but here I am. The notion has me grinning against Kaitlyn's lips. "Let me take care of this condom and..." my voice trails off before my chin jerks back and my heart begins banging against my chest wall.

Kaitlyn's drowsy, sated look takes a couple seconds longer to drop before it's replaced with the same one of horror I'm likely wearing.

Motherfucking fuck. I didn't wear a condom.

# Chapter Nineteen

Kaitlyn

I'm staring down at the base of Banks's bare penis where it is still lodged inside of me as I sprawl on his lap, practically in a sex-coma. My eyelids blink but my brain is having trouble untangling the many problems here. I've never had sex without a condom before. Never been so far gone for a guy that I lost all control and did something so fucking stupid like forget protection. Banks and I stare each other down, two sets of eyes wide and unseeing. All that pleasure, all that rightness that felt like being wrapped in the coziest of soft blankets in the middle of a snow storm fizzles right before my eyes.

Worse than condom-gate? I just slept with a *client*.

"Shit!" I scramble off his lap, sucking in a breath when my core contracts and my whole body lets out a shiver of delayed pleasure as he slides out of me. I turn and run naked, yes, I fucking *run*, to his bathroom, slamming the door shut behind me as I trip over my feet getting to the toilet paper. No amount of frantic wiping will clear away the potential consequences of forgetting a condom, but I can't bear the feel of him dripping down my thighs either. I squeeze my eyes shut and try to count out the days since my last period.

"Kaitlyn," Banks's deep voice says from the other side of the door. "Don't freak out, okay? I can send someone discreet to get something from the pharmacy. I swear I'm clean. I haven't been with anyone..." he trails off and even my heart beat pauses, waiting for his next words. "Huh, well, in over a year actually."

I swing open the door in disbelief, my eyeballs and brain disobeying the gravity of the situation and taking a joyride down the length of his naked body and deciding a round two is in order because what's done is done and we might as well do it again for good measure. But there's nothing good about what we did here. Except, looking deep into Banks's concerned eyes again, there is a kernel of goodness.

Reaching out, Banks takes my hand, tugging me into his chest and wrapping me in his solid arms. My face burrows between his pecs, and despite the wrongness of sleeping with a client, I breathe him in like I can't get enough of him. I breathe him in like he's just Ben and I'm just a woman at the airport, no ties to his profession and nothing better to do than flirt with a handsome man.

"I haven't been with anyone since Broderick, so all good here," I mumble into his chest. "And it's super late in my cycle so I doubt my geriatric egg has swallowed your swimmer."

"I'd ask about this asshole, Broderick, but we're still naked and I have a strict policy of not talking about ex-boyfriends when my dick can hear, so that'll have to wait for another time. And your eggs aren't geriatric. They're just seasoned." Banks says to the top of my head.

We stay in the embrace for long minutes, and despite the situation and the lack of clothing, it's not uncomfortable. That's the thing with Banks. Everything with him is so damn comfortable. And happy. And so full of life, I can't help but like the guy. Everything I thought about him was wrong. And if life was different, maybe we'd stand a chance.

But back in the real world, the world beyond the walls of this condo, I'm his agent. He's my client. And *this* can't happen.

With all kinds of regret pinging around in my chest, I step back from Banks. "I'm not freaking out. Promise. But you have a game tomorrow and need your beauty sleep, so I'm going to go." I'm already walking out of his bedroom to find my clothes scattered on the floor where I stripped out of them just an hour earlier. I feel Banks following me.

"Are you saying I'm ugly?" he teases, slipping back into our easy dynamic. Though there's a hardness to his voice that can't be masked.

"Hideous," I reply, pulling on my shirt and stepping into my jeans. There's no hope of putting the stilettos back on with how wobbly I am on my legs, so I scoop them up in my hands and march to the door. "That's why it's been a year since you slept with a woman. You practically had dust on your balls, Bennet."

I hear him make a noise like I physically hit him. "Killer Kaitlyn strikes again."

With one hand on the knob, I turn back to him, refusing to look south of his chin and summoning my job duties as his agent. "Make sure you drink some electrolytes so you're not dehydrated tomorrow."

Banks mutters my name and reaches for me, but I duck out the door and close it behind me before he can touch me. If he touches me, I'll forget once again that being his agent is all I'm allowed to be. The walk of shame is short and for that I'm grateful. Once in my own condo, I strip again and get into the shower, letting the pelt of waterdrops wash away every trace of Banks. When even the memory of the slide of his hands over my skin is erased by the sting of hot water, I flip the valve off.

Stepping out, I find my comfiest pajamas and pull them on. I'll regret tying my wet hair in a messy bun on top of my head tomorrow morning when no amount of flat-ironing can save it, but I do it anyway, opting for the easiest route to bedtime. I need to fall asleep where my thoughts won't race and my heart won't squeeze so tightly at the image of Banks's face when I left his condo.

A loud knock on my door makes my chin drop to my chest in defeat. I should have expected Banks wouldn't let me have the last word. When he calls my name and bangs on the door again, I take a deep breath and walk over to it. I pop it open, but don't let him in. I already let him in way too far.

He looks delectable in gray sweatpants and a T-shirt with a video game character on it that only he or Eli would know. His thick hair looks like he's been running his fingers through it. His big puppy dog eyes meet mine and I can feel my steely resolve starting to wane.

"Please. Don't do this. Don't revert back to Killer Kaitlyn, the best damn hockey agent out there."

"I have to," I interrupt. "Or do you not care anymore about being able to play next year?"

He leans his shoulder against the door frame, so close I can still smell us on him. "I just mean you're so much more than my agent. We can still be us here, behind closed doors."

I'm already shaking my head. There's no way I can keep Banks a dirty secret, despite what I carelessly promised. Or pretend I don't have feelings when we're out in public. I'm a damn good agent, not an actress.

He puts his hand on my elbow. "Then we push pause. Get through the negotiations and then reassess things after you're no longer my agent."

I search his face, latching onto that solution so fervently I wonder how long Banks has been more than just a client in my heart and I failed to notice. Just...push pause. We could do that.

But then my eyes fill with tears and I'm doing math in my head that just isn't mathing. Two glaring problems are shouting in my brain as loudly as those people who talk on the phone while walking on the treadmill at the gym, and I can't simply sweep them away. First, I can't date Banks even after I'm done being his agent. It would be professional suicide to date a hockey player. Even if I wasn't his agent. No one would ever take me seriously again.

And second, I don't have time to have an affair with Banks, no matter how tempted I am. I want to have a baby. I need to find a fertility doctor, select a sperm donor, and shoot needles into my ass so I can be fertile enough to get pregnant with the help of modern medicine. Banks would hate every bit of that. He once told me that Drugov's daughter puked on him the first time he held her and he's never understood why humans procreate just so they can get shit on by a tiny, sticky, loud mouthed human with zero ability to take care of itself. If I had an affair with Banks, I'd have to push off trying to have a baby, and I don't have enough eggs left to wait any longer.

"Kaitlyn," he breathes, pulling me into his chest. "Please don't cry. It kills me when you cry."

I don't put my arms around him, but I do use his shirt to collect my tears. My whole body trembles with the sobs that are now wracking through me. I want Banks and I want to be the best damn hockey agent that ever lived and I want my own precious baby in my arms. I want it all but I can't have any of it if I take what Banks is offering. Exploring a relationship with him would forever taint my career and it would delay any babies, maybe to the point of missing my fertile window in life altogether. And it's not even a sure thing that we wouldn't be clawing each other's eyes out after a solid month of dating, making the sacrifice of my other dreams for nothing.

Banks kisses the top of my head and I have to squeeze my eyes shut to stop the flow of tears. "Please tell me we can push pause," he whispers.

With one last inhale of his scent, I push away from him and grip the doorknob to keep me upright. His gaze sweeps over my tear-streaked face and he looks like he might cry with me.

"I'm sorry, Banks, but I can't push pause."

He shakes his head, refusing my refusal. "Why not?"

"Because a hockey agent can't date a hockey player, and I need a baby daddy. STAT."

Banks's jaw drops open and I count to ten before he snaps it shut again. He makes a noise in the back of his throat, like he's trying to swallow a scream but is only half successful. With accusing eyes, he spins away from me and marches halfway down the hall to his condo before he spins back around and points at me angrily. Words fail him, so he shoves both hands in his hair and pulls, stalking back to his door and disappearing inside.

"See?" I tell the empty hallway. "That went as well as I expected."

# Chapter Twenty

Banks

"Get a move on, Benny!" Roadie slaps the backs of my skates with his stick, and I blink to attention, only to see I'm blocking his way to the ice for warm-ups. The arena is already half-filled with a noisy home crowd, so it's a wonder I spaced it like that, although I've been preoccupied all damn day. I give Roadie a nod and haul ass to the ice. Tonight is going to be a struggle; I can already feel it.

After stewing for hours about Kaitlyn last night, I overslept this morning and almost missed the team meeting. For once, she didn't bang on my wall, something I'm taking as a bad sign. To make things worse, my rhythm was off during drills in the morning skate, and my racing mind kept me from nodding off during my usual game-day nap. I just can't stop thinking about how quickly the best evening of my life turned into such a nightmare.

What kind of asshole forgets to wear a fucking condom? I acted exactly like the juvenile Kaitlyn accused me of being all these years. No wonder she gave me the Heisman on any chance of a relationship between us. How can she trust me to take care of her when I can't even remember to protect her during sex? She's all class, and I'm all ass. Maybe it's time for a tattoo so I don't forget.

But I know she felt the connection between us like I did—that feeling that we're almost inevitable. I saw it in her eyes, in the tears on her cheeks. But she's determined to deny it since it would mean giving up some of that damn control that defines her. She doesn't know that it's in those moments when she lets her guard down that she's the most beautiful.

I drop to the ice for a hip stretch, grinding my teeth at the memory of her throwing that baby daddy gauntlet down. I know exactly why she did it—to scare me off. She apparently forgot she told me weeks ago that her ovaries have given up the ghost—another occasion when she almost killed me with those tears. But I'm the guy who's faced off at center ice with some of the biggest badasses out there. She thinks she can frighten me with the mention of a mini-human? Ha! If that's something she'd want down the road, there are lots of ways to make it happen. I'm just pissed she thought I'd be so easy to get rid of.

After a couple more stretches, I get to my feet again and start taking my frustrations out on a few pucks. The air in the arena begins to electrify, aided by music from the sound system and the excited chatter of the crowd. It's time to set everything else aside and focus on the game.

But as the team files off the ice for last-minute prep in the locker room, I spot Kaitlyn in a seat to the left of our bench. She's been avoiding me all day, and if her nose buried in her phone is any indication, she intends to continue doing so. I barely resist the urge to bang on the glass to get a rise out of her, instead continuing on my way to the locker room.

"Fuck!" Roadie slams his bare fist into the side of his stall three hours later, followed immediately with another shout of, "Shit. That hurt!" He pulls his hand to his chest and cradles it.

I should probably offer some words of encouragement—or at least check to make sure our second-line center didn't just break his hand—but I'm feeling just as shitty after that brutal loss. A loss I'm partly to blame for.

Despite my determination to leave all distractions aside and do my damn job, I ended up shooting myself in the foot by glancing Kaitlyn's way during a line change in the first period. Rule number one of hockey is to keep your eyes on the ice, and I fucked it up almost immediately.

In the past, I've been able to easily regroup if I catch sight of Kaitlyn during a game, but this time it was impossible because the second my eyes landed on her, Ed fucking Presley lowered his oily ass into the empty seat next to her—the one she keeps for colleagues, guests, and prospective clients. And from the look on Kaitlyn's face, Ed hadn't been issued any such invitation.

With every glance their way, my temper flared hotter and hotter as I imagined the bullshit vitriol spewing from Ed's spittle-coated lips. Kaitlyn was visibly uncomfortable, and if I thought it wouldn't end my career on the spot, I would have jumped the bench and tackled that asshole to the ground right there in the seats. The sleazebag doesn't appear to have learned the lesson I tried to impart at our last meeting. There are just some lines you shouldn't cross.

Suffice it to say, my focus was shit after that. I missed a cue from Dan-O, I caused a minor for too many men on the ice, and I didn't score a single goal—not even the gift the Fury's goalie handed me in the third period.

If I were Sam Macalby, I'd trade all our asses, starting with mine. The media room is going to be torture tonight, and I don't envy Dan-O since, as captain, he can't escape an appearance. I, on the other hand, will be making myself scarce.

Druggy has his head bent, talking to his agent a couple stalls over, and I can feel it the moment Kaitlyn enters the locker room, even though my back is turned. I glance over my shoulder to see her poking at Roadie's hand, and the scowl she sends him would normally have me smiling if I weren't so pissed.

I do what I should have done for the last two and a half hours and ignore her, heading for the showers. I won't do either of us any good by starting a conversation while stuck under this cloud. When I emerge from the locker room thirty minutes later, my mood hasn't improved, even if my appearance has. I've been following Kaitlyn's advice and have reverted to the custom of wearing a suit on game days to better reflect my commitment to... something or other I can't remember.

I spot her in the hall outside medical and stalk her way, completely ignoring my better judgment.

"You made me play terribly!" I accuse her like some lunatic, complete with an index finger to her face.

She barely glances up from her phone, only cocking a hip in her tight suit and muttering, "Bobby is in with Doc after his temper tantrum. I'm already dealing with one child tonight; you don't need to make it two."

In an attempt to regain some of my dignity, I change course. "What in the hell was Ed doing sitting next to you? Did he say something to upset you?"

This has her finally lifting her eyes to meet mine, if only for a brief second. "I can take care of Ed. You worry about your wrist shots. They lacked even a hint of precision."

When her gaze drops back down to her phone, I lose my cool once again and snatch it from her hands.

"Hey! Give that back!" She lunges for the device, but I easily pull it out of reach, holding it over my head while I turn the screen so I can see it. For the second time in twenty-four hours, I'm left speechless. "Don't look at that. It's private," Kaitlyn scolds as she starts to climb my body before stepping back and straightening her suit—she clearly forgot where we were for a moment.

I swallow hard and glare down at her. "What the actual fuck, Kaitlyn?"

Her eyes dart around the hall, which is now teeming with players, families, and staff, before she pulls me by my jacket sleeve to an empty alcove under the stands. I willingly follow since she's not getting away from me without a damn good explanation for why in the hell she's scrolling through a dating app when we just fucked last night.

As soon as we gain some privacy, I shake the phone at her. "Are you seriously trolling for a fuckboy after last night?"

Her responding scowl at my crassness beats even the one she delivered to Rhodes in the locker room. "Don't be an asshole." She sighs before continuing, "And I'm not trolling for anything. I'm researching sperm donors."

My eyes attempt to jump from my skull as they bounce from the woman before me to her phone and back. "A sperm donor? Why?"

"The usual reasons," she responds with an eye roll, attempting and failing again to regain possession of her phone.

I look at the screen again, making a closer inspection this time. On it is the profile picture of some dark-haired guy with a goatee, identified only by the number 472. He looks like a douchebag.

"But you said the doctor told you you were...probably closed for business."

Kaitlyn shakes her head at my furrowed brow. "Not yet. At least, hopefully not. Modern science might pull off a miracle."

I inhale and let that sit for a minute. Shit. She was being straight up last night about her urgent need for that baby daddy. "So...you're looking for some perfect guy to fill the turkey baster?" If I'm not mistaken, things just got way more complicated.

Her eyes close, giving me the distinct impression she's drawing on her last traces of patience. "Yes, however, now I'll never be able to cook a turkey again for the rest of my life, so thanks for that."

I raise a skeptical eyebrow. "I'll bet you six million dollars you've never cooked a turkey."

"That's not the point."

I decide to let her have her way—for now—and turn the phone's screen to her. "If you're looking for Mr. Perfect, this guy ain't it, I can tell you that much."

Kaitlyn frowns. "What's wrong with him? He's six feet tall and has a PhD in astrophysics."

"Yeah? And I'm sure his mommy is real proud," I scoff. "He's a douchebag."

Her jaw drops and she lunges for the phone yet again, but I'm already swiping through the next guys on her list.

"Narcissist." Swipe.

"Virgin." Swipe.

"Mommy issues." Swipe.

"Nose picker." Swipe.

The next one actually has me wincing. "That chin! Do

you *want* people thinking you slept with Jay Leno?" I glance in disbelief at Kaitlyn as I swipe again.

I turn the phone this time, needing some explanation as to her shitty taste in baby daddies. "Seriously? This guy?" I shake my head in disgust. "He's a redhead. You can't have a baby with a redhead."

"And why not?" Her arms are crossed haughtily over her chest now.

"Uh, sunburn for one." Duh. "And do you know all the nicknames kids have for redheads? Your baby will be mocked —and he'll never get laid."

"You're being ridiculous."

"*I'm* being ridiculous? *You're* the one being ridiculous!" I snap, finally lowering the phone and allowing her to take it from my fingers.

"And why is it ridiculous wanting to grab hold of my last chance at having a baby?" Her voice is strangled, her eyes beginning to shimmer with tears that will undoubtedly have me on my knees in seconds.

But I'm too worked up to be gentle just yet, so I shout, "It's not the having a baby part that's ridiculous! It's choosing someone other than *me* to be the *father*!"

Fuck. Did I just say that?

# Chapter Twenty-One

Kaitlyn

Well aware of prying eyes and elephant ears, I shove his wall of a chest and hiss, "Lower your fucking voice, Bennet." When he only stares me down harder, his lungs heaving like he's still on the ice in the middle of a game, I address his ridiculous suggestion. Offer? Whatever the hell that outburst was.

"Why would I consider *you* as the father of my baby?" I ask, honestly at a loss. To be fair, he looks like a GQ model touched by the perfecting hand of AI in that suit, so our baby would be gorgeous, but other than that, I come up empty for other reasons. And believe me, I considered it. After condom-gate, I thought long and hard about Banks being my baby's father, and while the idea makes my insides melt into a puddle of baby drool, I know it wouldn't work. My career would be tanked forever and I'm not so sure Banks, with his newly acquired ability to wake up to an alarm clock like an adult, is up for the eighteen year commitment of being a baby daddy.

Banks is a perpetual bachelor and we fight like feral cats.

He hates babies and using vacuums. Pretty sure having a baby requires you to vacuum at least three times a day. At least that's what TikTok told me last night when I couldn't sleep and searched the hashtag singlemomlife.

He rears back, horrified. "Why *wouldn't* you is the better question."

Is he for real? "Well, for one, you're still a damn baby yourself."

Okay, fine, he's actually turned out to be way more responsible than I gave him credit for, but simply putting your dirty socks in the hamper isn't enough maturity to be thinking about fathering a baby. That's a whole other level of responsibility.

"I am not," he snaps testily. I lift an eyebrow at his childish response and he huffs. "Listen, I'm a professional athlete so our kid would be athletically inclined. I *almost* graduated from college so our kid would be reasonably intelligent. And don't forget I have pretty blue eyes, a discerning taste in gourmet cheeses, and..." he leans in to whisper, "a sequoia between the legs."

I roll my eyes, refusing to acknowledge the butterflies that take flight when he's that close and talking about his admittedly stunning cock. "You're good with Eli. I can admit that you'd make a good dad...for *someone*. That someone not being my child."

My eyes sting suspiciously at the sudden vision of him and Eli on the couch playing a video game and giving each other crap while snuggled together like they can't bear to be apart. Shit. Now is not the time to have one of my hormonal mood swings. I hear the door open around the corner and Bobby chatting with the team doctor. I need to get back out there and do my job. I drill Banks's chest with my fingernail.

"Can we get back to the reason I'm even here? I need to get your contract negotiated. All the rest of this," I flutter my hand through the air between us, "can wait." I meant all the arguing, but when hope lights like the flick of a Bic lighter in Banks's eyes, I know I've said the wrong thing.

"I do like a challenge." He shoots me a determined grin and walks away.

I roll my eyes heavenward and beg for patience. Instead of finding even a scrap of it, I have to deal with Bobby's bruised knuckles and Pete's temper tantrum about the ref sending him to the penalty box. By the time I make it back to my condo and sink into a hot bathtub, I've almost forgotten about Ed's impromptu visit during the game.

My phone, resting on the edge of the tub, pings with a new message. I sweep away the mountain of bubbles and open it. I immediately regret letting Ed disturb my bathtime.

*You take things too personally. Just because I scooped your hockey kid? That's business, sweetheart. If you can't hang with the big boys, maybe you shouldn't be an agent. Emotional females aren't really made for this cutthroat business.*

"You motherfucking asshole," I mutter, sitting upright and sloshing water over the edge of the tub. And just like that, I'm enraged, semi-seriously thinking of ways to off Ed Presley. At the very least, I use some creative curse words to describe various parts of his anatomy.

Ed sought me out tonight at the game, not the other way around. Just to taunt me about signing the kid I was already in talks with. The only reason this business is cutthroat is because of assholes like Ed Presley who think about himself first and foremost. That poor kid he signed probably has no idea that he's just a dollar sign to his shiny new agent. Ed will use him when he needs to inflate his already out of control ego and then dump him when he isn't useful any longer. No help building a sustainable career, just money in Ed's bank account. Ed Presley is what is wrong with the world of agenting these days.

Relaxing bath ruined, I rinse off and wrap a towel around me. I hear Banks's door slam down the hall. Just the thought of the hurt in his eyes when I said he wouldn't make a good dad to my child has my heart squeezing and my eyes burning, rage forgotten.

Emotional female much? Fuck. Maybe Ed is right. Maybe these hormones have finally fucked me over enough that I can't control my emotions. Maybe I'm not a good agent if I can't even keep my feelings on lockdown around one extremely annoying hockey player. Killer Kaitlyn has yet again morphed into Kitten Kaitlyn, a weak, mewling pushover whose claws haven't grown in. I slip into silky pajamas and slide into bed, ready to tune out the world and scroll mindlessly through sperm donors on my phone until my eyes get heavy.

That's when the phone rings, the single word *Dad* scrolling across the top. Not feeling like being a glutton for further punishment tonight, I try to let it ring through to voicemail, but then bobble the phone as I pull a blanket over my lap and end up answering the damn thing.

"Hello?" Dad bellows from my lap. "Kaitlyn?"

Silently cursing, I put the phone to my ear. "Hey, Dad..."

"Hey, Kaity-Bug. I was thinking about you tonight."

"Oh yeah?" It's nice to know someone is thinking about you, especially when it's someone like Keith Phillips. Emotion is up there with flossing his teeth. He simply doesn't do it.

"Yeah. The Tigers played over the weekend and the camera guy panned to a dad with his whole torso painted in orange stripes, but then his kid stole the show by choosing that moment to puke all over his hot dog. Can you believe that? It was just like when you threw up in your popcorn!"

I let my head fall back against the headboard with a thump. "That's...really great, Dad."

He uses another ten minutes to describe the scene in

excruciating detail while my brain wanders. I spent my entire youth being coached not to cry. According to Dad, the only acceptable emotions are happiness and determination. A hearty bellow when competing in sports or trying to lift the bar during bench press is perfectly acceptable. But tearing up over a commercial? Might as well strap me in a straightjacket. I mean, I successfully own my own business in a world full of Ed Presleys which should be proof enough that I have my emotions on lock down. So how did I get here, sleeping with my client and swinging through a hundred emotions every other hour of the day?

"Can I ask you something about Mom?" It's out of my mouth before I can think twice.

Dad's chatter instantly ceases. He grunts and I rush to fill the awkward silence.

"Did she want to get pregnant with me?" Mom died a week after she gave birth to me, a rare infection they didn't catch in time. Dad had already been on the injured list when Mom was pregnant with me, but when she died, the story was, he quit the NFL altogether to raise me. I learned early on that asking questions about my mother led to a display of one of the "unacceptable" emotions and Dad withdrew from the world for a few days. But a girl needs to know about her own mother. Especially when she wants to become a mother herself.

"What brought this on all of a sudden?

"I don't know. I guess my fortieth got me thinking about motherhood."

"Of course she wanted to get pregnant with you, Kaitlyn," Dad grumbles. "You were the light of her world."

The tears don't even burn this time, they just slide down my cheeks silently. "Yeah?"

"Yeah. Your mom would have been the perfect mother. Instead you got stuck with me, kid."

"You weren't so bad, Dad," I whisper, then clear my throat. "You got me through school and you got me my first client, remember?"

Dad huffs. "Yeah, and look at you now. Running around with fucking figure skaters."

"Dad," I sigh.

"Yeah, yeah. Hockey players. Whatever. All I know is that you'd make a good mother too, Kaitlyn. If that's what you want. Just don't make the same mistake I did."

I frowned. "Quit the NFL?"

"No. I got so involved in your mother, I took my focus off the game. That's how I broke my leg. I kept looking up in the stands at your mother. God, she glowed pregnant with you. That fucker just plowed right into me, snapping my leg. Then you were born and your mom died right after. I could have come back from the injury, but I was distracted by grief that time. Love is all well and good, but don't let it steal your focus. Keep your eye on the ball and keep pushing forward. You hear me, Kaity-bug?"

I'm not sure if Dad thinks we're in a huddle and I'm in need of a pep talk but his words do sink in. I have been letting Banks distract me from my job. Question is...am I actually going to take advice from Keith Phillips about love and life?

"Thanks, Dad, but I gotta go."

"That's right. Early to bed and up early for a workout. You make me proud, Phillips!"

We hang up and not even scrolling sperm donors sounds good right now. I've got too many competing thoughts spinning in my brain. What am I going to do about Banks and these pesky feelings I can't seem to tamp down? Can I really find a suitable sperm donor and raise a baby on my own while juggling a career? And last but certainly not least, what substance can I buy to poison Ed Presley without alerting the authorities?

# Chapter Twenty-Two

Banks

"Baby," I mutter through gritted teeth as I dig deep for my last few leg-press reps. "I'll show her who the baby is." Wait. That makes no sense. The weights land with a loud clang, and I nab a towel to wipe the sweat from my face. I know having a baby is huge, but if it's something Kaitlyn's got her heart set on, then she's not doing this with anyone but me. I'm thirty-eight and one of my favorite people to hang with is a twelve-year-old; it's not like I've never thought about it. I just need to convince her we can work together and that I'll be a kick-ass dad.

"Who are you talking to?" Druggy asks from the leg extension station next to me.

"Nobody." I frown at him, and he raises a brow.

"Quitting already?" He grunts as his lower legs lift the bar, making his giant quads bulge. "Without effort, you will not pull a fish out of the pond."

I've gotten pretty good over the last decade at interpreting the many sayings my teammate brought with him from Kazakhstan, and this one is no different. "I'm not quitting. I'm thinking."

"Try not to hurt yourself," he responds, continuing to count his reps.

I stand to head for the free weights but then pause to face Druggy again. "How's Ayana? You talk to her lately?"

His eyes light as they only do at the mention of his daughter. "She tells me she has only A's on her report card." Fatherly pride infuses his words. The girl is seven now, and she's destined to be a heartbreaker.

"Did you... uh... adjust pretty easily to fatherhood when she was born?" Niko and his ex, Peyton, didn't plan on having Ayana as far as I know, but shit happens when your cock gets involved.

"I loved every minute of it. Why do you think I will not stop seeking custody?" Druggy doesn't talk about it a lot, but he and Peyton have been fighting a pretty nasty custody battle, one which Peyton continues to win.

"So you think you can make it work, even with all the traveling and late nights?" When he pauses his movements to glare at me, I throw both palms toward him. "I'm not suggesting you can't. I'm just curious."

Still not quite losing the sternness in his expression, he responds from behind his beard, "Why do you ask me these questions? Did you get someone pregnant?"

"No!" I insist, adding on the silent *not yet*. "I'm just making conversation."

It takes another few seconds for him to shift focus back to his workout. "Children are always a blessing. Life takes on new meaning when you have a child."

I only nod because what do I know? But I can't help picturing a little girl in hockey skates with Kaitlyn's gorgeous hair and eyes and my killer slapshot. I resist the urge to toss my sweat-dampened towel at my teammate (time to cut out that immature shit if I'm going to be a dad) and move to the free weights for some bicep curls. I need to make a new game plan to speed things up on this contract and win Kaitlyn over.

First on the list? Play the part of the choir boy like she wants.

Second, don't let my future baby mama distract me from the game.

And third, make Ed Presley wish he'd never been born.

I know the last one might accomplish nothing except pissing Kaitlyn off, but it's on the list if she approves or not. A guy has got to have standards.

The rest of my workout flies by while I flesh out the specifics of my plan and then move to the showers. I'm walking out to my truck while sending a text to get things in motion when my phone rings.

"Hey," I greet my mom as I slide my sunglasses in place.

"Hi, sweetie. We caught the game last night. I just wanted to make sure everything's okay." She's my own personal cheering section whether I bite it hard or score a hat trick, so this tells me I sucked even worse than I imagined last night.

"Yeah, I'm fine. Just a bad vibe on the ice, that's all. We play them again next week, so we'll turn it around."

"It's just that you seemed... distracted. Anything you want to talk about?"

Uh, yeah, Ma. My career is circling the drain, and I might be in love with my new agent who I used to hate but am now trying to convince to have a baby with me. No biggie. "Nope. Not that I can think of."

"Any chance you can come visit soon? Travis and Dad just put up a new shed out back, and they're putting a pool table in, if you can believe that. The darn thing even has air conditioning." I don't know why my brother pays a mortgage on his own place when he spends all his time at our parents' house.

"Ma, you know the season is too busy with travel and games. Why don't you guys come down here? I'll put you up at a swanky hotel and get the whole VIP treatment for you like last time." Ma acted like she'd been crowned Queen of Florida last October when the usher led them to the VIP lounge.

"I suppose we could do that—if it's not too much trouble, that is. I just feel bad that we haven't seen you since the fall. I told your dad we shouldn't have taken that romantic Christmas cruise."

I hit the unlock button and fold myself into the driver's seat of my truck while holding back a smile. "What? And miss sharing your anniversary dinner with Trav?" At least I can claim my hectic schedule as the reason I've never been married. Travis has no excuse, apart from being the ultimate mama's boy. All the more reason to have a kid—it's not like Ma's going to get a grandkid from my brother. "Take a look at the schedule and give me some dates that'll work for you, okay?"

"All right, Ben. I miss your face, sweetie." There's a little crack in her voice that almost does me in, so I change the subject.

We chat for another few minutes about Dad's retirement plans and Ma's book club, and by the time I hang up and get back to my condo, my text has been answered.

Me: I've got a few women I want you guys to meet. You free on Saturday after the team meeting?

Roadie: Depends. Are they single?

Forns: Are they hot?

Barzee: Are they over twenty-one? Kaitlyn says that's my cut-off age.

Me: Single, of age, and probably a little
classier than you're used to. Definitely hot.

I grin down at my phone as I hit send and enter the elevator.

Barzee: I'm in.

Roadie: Same.

Forns: Ditto. Classy might be refreshing.

Excellent. Phase one is officially in motion.

"My favorite boy!" Beatrice exclaims as the orderly wheels her into the social room at Bay Villages Saturday afternoon. Her hair is extra full today, and I notice she used a heavier hand on her makeup too. The woman does like to preen.

I bend to drop a kiss on her cheek. "You get more gorgeous every time I see you."

"The girls are beside themselves," she whispers in my ear. "I hope your friends don't mind if they get a little handsy."

I straighten again with a chuckle. "They'll love it." A glance to the boys reveals them all standing in various poses of discomfort against the wall by the entrance. It took until we walked through the doors for them to get wise to my plan, but, honestly, they should have known something was up when I insisted on driving us all in my truck. "Guys! Come on over." I command.

Forns peels himself from the wall first, shooting me a wicked glare as he nears. "You're going to pay for this, Benny," he mutters under his breath.

I drop a hand on his shoulder. "Pete, this is my friend, Beatrice. And this..." I gesture to a woman seated at a table to my right. "Is Marjorie. Marjorie, this is Pete. He'll be your Mahjong partner today."

Forns's head snaps my way. "Her what?" But before I can do more than smile, Marjorie stands and grabs his hand.

"Don't worry, handsome. I'll break you in easy."

Forns swallows hard and sends a panicked look over his shoulder as she leads him away. Beatrice cackles, and I introduce Barzee and Roadie to their partners, Nina and Yolanda.

"You know I like them a bit older, man, but this is taking things a little far, don't you think?" Roadie asks through gritted teeth as I push Beatrice's chair in. I just clap him on the shoulder.

"I'll explain the rules to the newbies," Nina pronounces, patting Barzee on the knee and tugging on the sleeves of her blouse. It looks like one of Kaitlyn's silk numbers and fits almost as well. These women came prepared.

"My, you're tall, aren't you?" Yolanda stares up at Roadie, pink lighting her cheeks at his classic good looks.

He loses the attitude and grins down at her. "You should see my brothers. They're all over six-four."

This has his partner putting a hand to her chest. "God bless your mother." Roadie laughs and takes a seat next to her.

It doesn't take long for the guys to get over themselves and get the hang of the game. Before long, their competitive streaks take over and they're chirping at each other, the women joining in with a few insults I'm not sure I've ever heard before.

We all play a few rounds, tournament style, until it's down to Forns and Marjorie against Beatrice and me for the title. When they lose, Marjorie takes a hands-on approach with Pete, delivering a spanking that I swear has the guy blushing. Beatrice and I take a victory lap around the social room to the cheers of a dozen or so residents while the boys reluctantly submit to defeat.

Then it's picture time. The women don't need to be asked twice to buddy up with their partners and strike a few poses as the press photographer I called yesterday snaps a few photos. He even gets one of Beatrice kissing me on the cheek, and I ask him to send it to me.

Goodbye hugs and promises to return for a rematch are exchanged, and we head on out into the Florida winter sunshine and back to my truck.

"Next time, Yolanda and I are kicking your asses," Roadie vows.

"Not a chance. Nina and I have got it in the bag," Barzee counters, putting Roadie in a headlock while he fights to get free.

Forns scoffs and opens the passenger door. "These guys are delusional. Marjorie and I would have won if your girlfriend hadn't cheated."

"You're a bad loser, Fornier." I point at him. "Beatrice is an angel. She'd never cheat."

I start the car and turn the radio to my favorite classic rock station, feeling a definite lift to my spirits after that adventure. Besides winning and giving the residents a good time, the best part about the afternoon is that it will knock Kaitlyn's socks off when she sees the pics online in the morning.

Maybe letting people into my business isn't as bad as I thought it would be.

<h1 style="text-align:center">Chapter Twenty-Three</h1>

Kaitlyn

Two days later and I am still riding a high off those pictures in the newspaper. Banks gave me a very public reason for the Storm Chasers to keep him on at least another season or two. Those pictures went viral on social media, leading to a new hashtag #hattricksandoldchicks that made me shake my head at people's ingenuity. Add in a win on the road yesterday, with Banks outshooting everyone else on the team and scoring the game winning point, and I am sitting in the perfect position to continue negotiating his contract next week. Ed might have gotten the ball rolling, but I'm going to bring home the win.

Banks isn't due home until after midnight tonight, and while I would prefer to celebrate with him, it's for the best that I'm alone. The last thing I need is another moment between us where we forget all about the lines in the sand and why we can't cross them. Putting on tennis shoes that have barely seen the outside world, I leave the condo on foot, headed for the local wine shop I found a few weeks ago. While I peruse the selection of Pinot Noirs, I recall the article I read earlier today when I typed "peri menopause" into my search bar. A horrifyingly long list of dos and don'ts pulled up. Chief among them? No alcohol. And considering I want to get pregnant the moment I find the perfect sperm donor, I should get used to living the dry life. I leave the wine shop determined to find a healthy substitute.

Which is how I land at Fermentation Friends, a little hole in the wall shop a half mile away that has a selection of house-made kombuchas that promise alcohol free imbibing and good gut bacteria to boot. I'm not sure if my gut needs more bacteria but the girl with the septum piercing behind the bar assures me it does. She gives me several free samples and that seals the deal. It's fizzy and tasty without tomorrow's regret. I buy a quart of both the lemon ginger and the mint lime mojito in these cute little glass jars. Despite paying double what I would have for a bottle of wine, I thank her and head back to the condo.

The lemon ginger kombucha goes down perfectly with the leftover pasta I have for dinner. I'm just going over the last of the material to present at the negotiation when I pop open the mint mojito. The top flies off and hits the wall, which makes me yelp in surprise. I didn't expect it to have that much fizzle. My stomach lets out a gurgle, but I ignore it in favor of this mocktail that tastes remarkably like the real thing.

I'm halfway through that quart when my stomach lets out more than a gurgle. It's officially an SOS that I can't ignore. I put a hand to my stomach and then double over when my stomach kicks back. I jump to my feet and run to the guest bathroom since it's closer. With a moan, I sit on the toilet and ponder my life choices while all the good gut bacteria engage in a battle to the death with bad gut bacteria in my belly. Sweat dots my brow, but the gurgling hasn't abated. I've made a massive error somewhere but I'm unclear what it is.

"Alexa, how much kombucha is too much?" I call out, my voice strained.

The little machine in the living room picks up my voice and answers in that overly cheerful tone, "A serving size of kombucha is six to eight ounces. Overconsumption of the fermented drink can lead to stomach upset."

My stomach rips out a noise that would scare a lesser woman, agreeing with Alexa. "Shit. Alexa, how many ounces are in a quart?"

Her answer has me doing math in my head that can't be right. I didn't have six to eight ounces. I had a quart and a half, which is forty-eight ounces. Forty-fucking-eight ounces! Dear god, I've over bacteria'd myself to the point of death. Nothing's coming out of me and I can't determine if that's good or bad, so with a quick pep talk, I force myself off the toilet. My legs quiver and even that hurts my stomach. Heeding the belch that seems to come straight from the pit of hell, I crouch back down, contents from meals three weeks ago coming up and out into the toilet. By the time I'm heaving up ghosts from the past but thankfully no more actual stomach content, I end up crawling out of the bathroom, a moan emanating from me with each inch of ground I cover. Do I call poison control? Do I just lay down and die?

I choose door number two, slumping to my side right there in the middle of the living room and panting like a dog, hoping this next wave will pass before I puke up a vital organ. Fermentation Friends, my ass. No friend has ever done me dirty like this. I swear I'm in and out of consciousness, dreaming of little spiky bacteria sword fighting in a dark cave, when arms come around me, lifting me off the hard ground.

"Kaitlyn?"

Ah, that's cute. One of the bacteria must be Banks. He sounds just like him.

"Slay the bad bugs!" I cheer with my eyes closed, delirious from pain.

"Kaitlyn! Baby, talk to me. What happened?" Banks the bacteria's voice has gotten louder. He rubs his sword across my face and then he's talking again, this time barking out words that make no sense. I'm lifted again so I let out a playful "whee" only to groan when that hurts my stomach. Everything's jostling and then I'm covered in something warm. I whimper myself to sleep.

I wake to a bright light in my left eye. I moan at the source of the light but it just switches to my other eye. It takes me a dozen blinks before I can see clearly again. I'm laying on a hard bed in a room with curtains for walls. A stressed out guy in green scrubs is talking to Banks, who's holding my hand while he stands next to the bed.

"We'll pump her full of electrolytes just to be safe. Normally a little food poisoning passes on its own, but we don't know for sure how much she threw up and that bottle you brought in looks like it was brewed in a back alley."

"Thanks, doc." Banks shakes his hand and the man leaves. It takes me that long to realize they're talking about me and this is not a dream. More like a nightmare.

"Banks?" My voice comes out in a whisper.

He immediately sinks down to my level and tosses me a grin. "Hey, sport. Glad to see you conscious. I'm a little late with the advice, but never buy kombucha from the hippie place on 23rd, only buy from the legit ferment place on 22nd."

The door opens again and a woman comes in, wheeling an IV pole behind her. "We're going to get you hooked up and feeling good as new by morning."

I look back to Banks and burst out crying, to my horror. Banks climbs on the bed with me and cradles me to his chest.

"Ssh, it's okay, Kaitlyn. You won't even feel it." The woman takes my arm and I let her, focusing on Banks and the feel of his solid length against me. Why does this man make everything feel like it's going to be okay? "Did I tell you I did a press conference after the game tonight? Talked all about my plans to play a few more years when they asked me about retirement. Hopefully the GM will see the interview."

He keeps talking, regaling me with a play-by-play of the whole game. I know he's trying to distract me from the IV in my arm, but needles don't bother me. I let him comfort me because I can't tell him the real reason I burst out crying. I felt like I was actually dying earlier tonight and all I could think about was wanting Banks by my side. I can't tell him that I think about him all the time, or that I relive those moments in his bed every single day, or how I try daily to find a solution to us being able to be seen together. I treasure waking him up every morning with a pounding on the adjoining wall. I want to whisper good night to him every evening when I lay my head on my pillow. I'm embarrassed for having poisoned myself with a fizzy drink and yet he doesn't make me feel ridiculous at all.

I have it bad for Banks Bennet and tonight, I'm too wrung out to push him away like I know I should.

He insists on carrying me out of the ER as the sun starts coming up the following morning. I'm beyond exhausted, but thankfully not in pain. Laying my head on his solid shoulder, I think my good gut bacteria has finally won the fight and settled down. Banks drives us home in his truck and carries me into my condo, even when I fuss about people seeing us.

"Kaitlyn. You spent the night in the ER. I found you unconscious on your floor. I'm not letting you fucking walk."

There's a firmness to his jaw that tells me he won't bend on the issue. And secretly I love the feel of his arms around me.

He puts me straight to bed, gathering the covers around me like I'm a kid who needs to be tucked in. He sits on the edge of the bed and stares down at me. The lines around his eyes are deeper than normal. He looks as exhausted as I feel.

I put my hand on his bicep. "Thank you," I say simply when what I want to say is *thank you for taking care of me and being sweet instead of giving me a hardass pep talk about sucking it up and the game must go on like my dad always did when I was sick as a kid. Thank you for killing Killer Kaitlyn with kindness.*

He leans down and kisses my forehead, his lips lingering a few seconds too long to be strictly friendly. Then he stands up, walks around the bed, and unbuttons his shirt before pulling it down his arms.

"What are you doing?" It's not quite a shriek, but it's close.

"I'm tired, Kaitlyn." He toes off his shoes and shoves his slacks to the ground, leaving him in boxers and half-staff erection that has my poor abused insides perking up. "Scoot over."

And then he's in the bed with me, laying on top of the covers and spooning me. I want to object but can't find the harm in two tired friends taking a nap together. Before I know it the exhaustion wins out and we've both fallen asleep. Blessedly, I don't dream of a bacterial civil war.

I wake a few hours later to Banks whistling in my kitchen. I glance at the time and sit up, groaning when my abs protest the movement. They feel like I did a thousand sit ups yesterday. Who knew vomiting is a superior workout?

"Kaitlyn?" Banks calls out and then his tousled head appears in my doorway. "Oh good. You're up. How do you feel?" He comes into the room and I have to turn away from the gray sweatpants slung low on his hips, his entire delicious torso on display.

"Better," I squeak.

He sits on the side of the bed and feels my forehead. "You look better. No pain or nausea? The doctor said to go back in if you still felt anything later today."

I shake my head and straighten my spine. I can look at a half naked grown man without becoming a simpering female. I look into his concerned blue eyes and just about melt into a puddle. "No, I'm fine."

He smiles and it's too much. I have to look away or I'll jump on this man and beg him to sleep with me. To keep me like a dirty little secret that could explode my career.

"I actually came over last night to give you this." He picks up a cardboard box from the floor that wasn't there last night, stuffed with books, lotions, bottles of supplements, and even an infrared heating pad.

"What's all that?"

Banks looks down at his hands, his one knee bobbing up and down. "Just some things I put together for you. I read up about the perimenopause symptoms you're feeling and they suggested this lotion for your shoulder, the heating pad for aches and pain. This perimenopause book hit the New York Times best sellers list for like twelve weeks in a row so I figured it might have more good advice."

His gesture, along with everything he did for me last night, hits me right in the chest. And the eyes. Tears blur my vision. I could blame it on the hormones, but I'm starting to understand that it's so much more than that. Things I'm unwilling to acknowledge yet.

"Thank you," I say again, knowing the words aren't enough.

Banks nods his head once and then stands, backing up.

"I'll go make some toast for breakfast. Hopefully your stomach can handle that."

"Aren't you going to be late for practice?" I ask, the mother hen habit too strong to turn off, even now.

Banks grins. "Coach gave us a late start today because of how well we played in the game. Fear not Killer Kaitlyn. Our plan for world domination is still in place."

# Chapter Twenty-Four

Banks

"That's a lie," Kaitlyn accuses as she reaches for another handful of popcorn.

I lean back into my couch cushions and toss both hands up. "I swear on my mother's grave."

Her nose wrinkles, and I know I'm a goner because even that turns me on. "You said your mother is coming to town next month."

It's intermission between the second and third period of the Stingers–Blades game. Kaitlyn's got a client on the Blades, so I suggested we watch together at my place. Normally I'd be surprised by both my invitation and her quick acceptance of it, but ever since the day at the hospital, there's been a shift between us. I'm just not clear on exactly what it means.

Kaitlyn hasn't brought up the sperm donor thing, and she's not avoiding me—or calling me names. I've even caught her watching me when she thinks I'm not paying attention, and she can't hide her body's reaction when I brush against her or put a casual hand on her arm or back. But the wall isn't completely down, so I'm not pushing my luck by bringing up the elephant in the room. Even if I want nothing more than to pick things up where we left off that night in my bedroom.

No, I'm biding my time. I'll win her over eventually, so there's no real hurry. In the meantime, I'm enjoying spending time with her and working on our plan to get my contract re-upped. The unexpected popularity of hockey players challenging old women to table games has given me a boost in both the media and in the upper offices at team headquarters. As have the handful of podcasts I've been on, an appearance at a youth hockey clinic Kaitlyn set up, and the current winning streak of the Storm Chasers. I even posted a short video from the weight room on my Instagram this afternoon, which earned me one of Kaitlyn's smiles. To top that off, Ed has quieted down—it's been two weeks since I heard any trash talk through the grapevine—so I'm feeling confident.

Kaitlyn sits on the other end of the couch wearing a pair of yoga pants and an oversized sweater, her bare feet tucked under her and her hair gathered haphazardly on top of her head. She's intentionally put space between us, but that's okay. For now.

"It's a figure of speech." I wave her objection off. "But I promise I'm being straight with you. He sprained his elbow just the way I said. It was the highlight of my week." Okay, that's an exaggeration. Forns is out for a couple games with a bum elbow, an injury he sustained in the locker room yesterday when he tried vaulting himself off his stall's bench and onto Druggy's back and missed.

"That son-of-a-bitch!" Kaitlyn smacks the arm of the couch. "He told me Monkowski tripped over his own skates on the ice and took him out."

"I might have lied to my agent too if I'd been that big of an asshat."

She shoves the entire handful of popcorn in her mouth in frustration and unearths her phone from somewhere inside that enormous sweater. Her words are garbled as she fires off a text. "He's going to pay for this. Tomorrow is now officially leg day, and his ass is in the weight room at six a.m."

I grin and take a sip of my beer as the TV switches from a commercial and back to the game. The Blades manage to eke out a victory in the last couple minutes, so Kaitlyn is pleased with the outcome. She stands to take the popcorn bowl to the kitchen and toss out her seltzer can. No more kombucha for her.

She scared the shit out of me when I found her drifting in and out of consciousness on the floor of Pierre's condo last week. I'd just arrived home from the airport and heard whimpering from behind the door, but there was no answer to my knocking. So I rifled through my junk drawer in a panic to find my neighbor's spare key and let myself in. Even now, recalling the mental image of Kaitlyn sprawled on the rug hits me like a punch to the solar plexus.

"Hey," I call over my shoulder. "Eli's got a talent show at school Thursday night. Since there's no game, I told him I'd be there. You wanna come?"

"What's his talent?"

"Last I heard, he was trying to decide between a stand-up comedy act and a psychic reading."

I hear her snort from the kitchen. "Oh, I'm there." When she comes back to the couch, she drops onto the middle cushion, her knee brushing mine in the process. "You never told me how you and Eli got together." When I give her the side eye in response, she laughs and pats my arm. "Don't worry. I'm not planting pictures of a child in the media. I'm genuinely curious."

"You'd better not." When she puts two fingers in the air in a classic Boy Scouts oath, I continue, "It was a few years ago during the off season." I shrug. "Niko had his daughter for a couple weeks, and we all went to a baseball game. I don't know. I guess seeing a wide-eyed kid at her first professional baseball game with her dad made me think there are a lot of kids out there who don't get to do shit like that but would probably love to. So I figured it might be fun."

"You know you two are adorable together, right?" Her eyes soften as they turn my way, and I like that a lot.

"It's my ultimate goal in life to be called adorable, so thank you," I deadpan, turning her grin into a full-blown smile.

"I always wanted a sibling, you know." She rests her elbow on the back of the couch and props her cheek on it. "I even tried buying one for my dad for Christmas one year."

"Interesting. I never would have pegged you for a human trafficker." This gets me a smack on the arm.

"Shut up. I was five. I thought you could order a baby like you could order a pizza. Turns out you can't. My pre-school teacher convinced me he would prefer a '#1 Dad' coffee mug instead."

"I've got a younger brother. Believe me, they're not all they're cracked up to be. They follow you around like dogs and always smell like lawn clippings for some reason."

"That doesn't sound so bad." Her tone is wistful, so I don't even try to argue.

"No, it's really not." I wonder if she's thinking about the baby she wants to have. She'd make a great mom. Her kid would never go to school without a box of freshly sharpened pencils. "What was your mom like?"

She shakes her head. "She died a week after I was born, so I never knew her."

"Damn. I'm sorry." I take her hand without thinking, and she doesn't pull it back. A childhood without my parents and my brother is unfathomable, even if I know it's the reality for a lot of people.

"My dad did his best. And, hey, I probably wouldn't have become the ass-kicking agent-to-the-stars you see before you if it hadn't been for him." She lifts her chin as her lips curve, clearly trying to shake off the serious mood. She doesn't quite succeed, so I squeeze her hand and decide maybe it's time for at least part of that elephant to get a mention.

"You're gonna make a great mom."

Her eyes immediately shine with gathering tears. "You think so?"

"I know so. Look at how you've whipped all us assholes into shape. A kid will be a breeze after that."

She smiles and ducks her chin into her chest, and the uncharacteristic coyness of the gesture has something shifting in my chest. "In a dream world, I'd have two kids so they'd each have a sibling. But I'm afraid my ovaries will only have time for one—if things work out, that is."

"I want two kids too," I respond, telling her the truth. "But I'd settle for one. There's enough rugrats between all the Storm Chasers that the kid wouldn't be starved for playmates."

"Yeah?" She lifts her chin, her eyes going soft again, her voice almost breathy. Is that hope I hear? Damn, please let it be.

Jesus, I'm turning sappy.

The ringing of Kaitlyn's phone breaks the moment, and she pulls her hand from mine to grab it. After a glance at the screen, she puts it to her ear. "Hey, Bella." I watch her play with a strand of hair that's come loose from its band. "Yes, I'm still meeting Macalby tomorrow to talk terms in person on Bennet's contract, so I'll need those files." She stands from the couch and steps clear of the coffee table to start pacing as she talks to her assistant. "Fornier's is in the bag already, but he just got himself on my shit list. So help me god, if he fucks with the sweet deal I got him, I'm going to murder him."

Gone is the vulnerable Kaitlyn from moments ago, and in her place is the ball-busting, take-no-prisoners agent who's going to save my ass.

Honestly, I can't decide which one I like more. Which is fine since I have the benefit of enjoying both—for a very long time to come if things go my way.

Kaitlyn

"Look, we've sat across this same table before so you know I don't like to beat around the bush."

I nod at Sam Macalby, General Manager for the Florida Storm Chasers, knowing exactly the type of negotiator I'm up against. Two of his lawyers flank him in their flashy suits, and my own agency's lawyer sits next to me. I'm doing some grandstanding myself with the high end leather laptop bag that cost almost as much as my car back home in Georgia. My hair was blown out professionally this morning and I'm wearing my best suit, the one with the red pinstripe that matches the sole of my favorite stilettos and makes me feel like a badass.

"I remember. Which means you already have a number in your head. Why don't we start there."

Sam flashes me a smile like he knows I'm skipping ahead to a foregone conclusion of them not trading Banks, and while he gives me credit for being a pushy broad, he's not quite ready to throw a number out on the table.

"Frankly, when the season started, I was set on letting Bennet be traded for a rising rookie. Bennet's always been phenomenal on the ice, but a problem off it, and everyone knows he's not getting any younger. However, Bowman has informed me that he's changed his ways this season. Stepped up as a leader." Sam huffs, his lips curving into a tight smile. "My own mother bought a shirt with the hashtag #hattricksandoldchicks emblazoned on it, which I found out is because of Bennet."

I tilt my head. "Add in upward of twenty-three minutes of ice time per game and I think we can agree that age hasn't been a factor."

"Yet," Sam adds, letting the word hang between us.

"Listen. You just lost LaFontaine. You lose Bennet and suddenly you have a young team without half its backbone. Bright makes a good captain but he hasn't been here long enough to fill LaFontaine's or Bennet's shoes. Most of the newbies are scared shitless of Drugov, and Monkowski has a rep issue worse than anyone's.

One of Macalby's lawyers jumps in. "Do you foresee an issue with clause 2e?"

I credit the years of negotiating with sharky lawyers for the way my face stays neutral. He's referring, of course, to the clause in the standard player's contract that requires conduct befitting the league. Sam's lawyer is either testing me and my preparation for this negotiation and training in general or he still has some questions regarding Banks's personal life.

"Absolutely not," I answer without moving a muscle. "Unless you consider Mahjong with seniors unbefitting the league."

Sam chuckles as I knew he would. The lawyer writes something on his yellow legal pad, but doesn't respond. Sam pulls a sheet of paper out of his desk drawer to lay it on the table and stabs it with his thick finger.

"Here's our offer: no trade, one year, one million, no signing bonus. We have to make room for some rookies." He slides the sheet to my side of the table but I don't reach for it or even look at it. My heart sinks. Their initial offer is worse than I thought it would be. Banks is holding out for two years and two million a year, a stretch from this piddly offer.

"He's currently finishing a six year contract for four-point-five per year with a two million signing bonus. Ice time is right up there with your fresh starters, he played in all but one of the eighty-two games last season, recording 26 goals and 47 assists for 73 points." I tap my knuckles on the table. "This is insulting."

Sam spreads his beefy hands. "This is a start, Ms. Phillips."

"Correction. This is a *rough* start, Mr. Macalby. The fans will back me up when they vote Bennet into the All-Star game and you'll look like a fool for letting him go as a free agent."

Sam concedes. "The All-Star development could affect things, for sure."

I stand and my lawyer stands with me. "I'll take this to my client and see you the day after tomorrow. I hope whatever insanity has taken over you is temporary."

Sam smiles despite himself. I saunter out of the room, making sure the panic I feel in my chest doesn't show in my pace or my facial expression. Only much later, when I'm alone in my condo, do I let out the breath I've been holding and yell at the walls.

I knew this negotiation wasn't going to be easy. After all, Ed Presley started the ball rolling months ago, most likely doing the bare minimum to present Banks in a good light. I'm coming in at the end, trying to button up a troubled player who lost another agent and only has a few more years before his body gives up. But it's Banks. Sweet Banks who bought me a fucking neck fan so I never break a sweat when my hormones get the best of me. The guy who's a machine on the ice and an absolute sweetheart off it.

I had such high hopes this deal would be over and done with quickly so I could head back home where my actual life is. I can't stay here next door to Banks forever, spending all our time together instead of furthering my career or choosing a baby daddy for my last decaying egg. Flopping onto my couch and kicking off my heels, I lean my head back and stare up at the ceiling. I couldn't even scroll through the sperm donor site last night without pitting the statistics against Banks. Why am I comparing all possible baby daddies to Banks like he's some sort of measuring stick? I need to get back to my real life in Atlanta so I can get my head together.

The numbers are blurring as I recalculate each player's salaries, trying to determine how much wiggle room in the cap the GM has for Banks's contract. A headache's brewing after an hour of staring at papers scattered over my rug as I make a list of reasons why my numbers are reasonable and Sam's are bullshit. The television is on and the newscasters are discussing the upcoming hurricane season like they're excited to see what damage Mother Nature can inflict upon the area. I'm so focused on the contracts I don't even hear the chatter anymore. Then my phone starts pinging with notifications. After six pings in a row, I shove the pen in my bun and take a look. Bella's name flashes across the screen with a call and I answer.

"Do not kill the messenger, K, but click on the link I'm sending you." Then she hangs up on me.

Nerves flare to life as I wait for her text to come through. I groan when I see it's one of the tabloids that likes to find professional athletes in compromising situations. I swear to god, if Pete's gotten himself into more trouble, I'm going to strangle that kid. I click on the link and my jaw drops open at the photo on display.

It's a hotel room, blurred out areas over the body of a naked blond woman as she lays provocatively in bed curled up with a man who is fast asleep. The man? None other than fucking Banks Bennet. My face goes hot and all I see is red. There's no time for irrational anger though, not when the media has a picture of my client in a compromising position. A client who is already teetering on the edge of being a free agent without a team next season. I put a cool hand to my cheeks and then torture myself by zooming in on the picture. The woman is exquisite and there's no doubt that's Banks with his gorgeous physique and his perfectly ruffled dark hair.

The room itself is a disaster. Empty champagne bottles litter the nightstands. A framed print on the far wall hangs off kilter. And there, right on the floor by the bed is a hotel makeup mirror with what looks like three powdery white lines.

"Fuck!" I drop the phone to my lap and try to breathe past the panic that burns as hot as that incriminating photo. Maybe it's just a puck bunny. Totally expected of a single hockey player. But drugs? Banks can get kicked out of the league for that shit. The lawyer asked me today to confirm that Banks wouldn't be engaged in behavior unbecoming of the league and I was so confident in my answer. Of all the rotten timing...

I close my eyes and take deep inhales, identifying jealousy along with the panic. Banks and I aren't dating. Never have, never will, but even so, it hurts to see him with another woman. Did it happen his last road trip? When I went out of town for four days to Atlanta? Before or after we slept together? God, I'm such an idiot for believing it had been almost a year since he'd been with a woman. Now I have to call my obgyn back and get scheduled for an STI test. I'm so mad I could punch a hole in my wall, but Pierre seemed like a nice guy and I don't want to damage his condo.

Something niggles at the back of my brain, trying to poke through the panic and anger. Something doesn't add up. My eyes fly open and I stare at the television, eyes unseeing. Wait. Something is definitely off about that picture. I grab my phone and unlock the screen to zoom in on it again. It takes me a couple minutes, but when I find it, I leap to my feet and immediately call Bella back.

"It's bad, huh?" she answers.

"No. Yes!" I snap, brain spinning. "It's from three years ago, Bella. Look at Banks's sideburns. Remember all the guys growing out those ridiculous pork chops during their playoff run? This photo was taken three years ago when they made it all the way to the finals."

"Oof," she replies. "Those sideburns were so gross."

"Hockey players and their stupid superstitions, right? Remember Bobby called me daily to cry about not being able to grow his out?"

Bella snorts in my ear. "It was quite unfortunate because then all the NARPs started doing it too and they looked like pathetic Wolverines."

"NARPs?"

"You know. Non athletic regular people."

I squeeze my eyes shut and try to zero in on the matter at hand so we can figure this out. "Focus, Bella. Don't they drug test them all season long? Why would Banks risk his career when he's a seasoned player? Why is the photo being leaked now? Who leaked it?"

"Ohh..." her voice trails off, just as confused as me. My phone buzzes against my ear and I pull it away to see the screen. "Hey, Bella, it's Banks on the other line."

She hangs up without another word and I answer Banks's call. He doesn't bother with a hello. "I have no idea where that picture came from, Kaitlyn." He sounds panicked. As he should be. "I don't even know who that woman is. I've never, ever used drugs. It's gotta be a staged pic or Photoshopped or something. And it's from a while ago at that."

My heart squeezes in my chest, but I ignore it to focus on what this means to his career. "I know."

"Wait. You know?"

I pace my condo. "Well, the timeline at least. Your sideburns gave it away."

His exhale is one of utter relief. I quickly disabuse him of the belief that the worst is over.

"But that won't matter to the GM. He'll only care that it's bad press, old pic or not. Drugs, Banks. They won't overlook that."

Banks curses as if he pulled the phone away, then he's back. "You have to believe me, Kaitlyn. I have never done drugs in my whole fucking life. I can't prove it, but I think Ed has something to do with this. When I fired him–because, make no mistake, I fired *him*, not the other way around like he made it seem–he threatened he had dirt on me. I figured he was bluffing."

I halt my pacing, senses tingling. "You think Ed...?"

There's a long pause. "I swear I've never seen that woman before. On my family's honor, I swear it. Something's not right here."

I wrap my head around the idea of believing Banks. He's done some stupid shit, but jeopardizing his career over a random woman and drugs while on the road playing hockey, just doesn't sound like the Banks I've come to know. Somehow, someway Ed leaked that picture to ruin this deal. I know the man hates me, but this is a step too far. He can try to take me down professionally, but to ruin Banks's career in the process is unspeakable. Immoral. Might even be illegal. If I can prove Ed's behind the picture, Ed could lose his certification with the league.

"Don't breathe a word to anyone, Banks. This is going to be a PR nightmare. Let me handle this."

"I'm not sure I can promise that," he growls before hanging up.

Banks

I'm halfway to the airport, intent on flying to Atlanta to confront Ed, when a text from Kaitlyn comes through.

> Kaitlyn: We got off the phone an hour ago. I've been listening for you next door, and you're not here yet. Promise me you're on your way and not doing something crazy that will hurt your career.

"Shit!" I pound my fist on the steering wheel and start arguing with myself. Confronting Ed isn't crazy, given what I suspect he's done. But this affects Kaitlyn too, and I can't forget that.

> Kaitlyn: We'll figure this out. I promise! Come home.

She's waiting for me. That thought never sucks, even in the middle of a clusterfuck like this.

I get off at the next exit and steer my way back toward the condo building, letting the silence settle around me. I want to believe Ed couldn't stoop that low, but his threats from our last sit-down in December ring in my ears.

*"You don't want to go, Benny. Not over something so trivial." Ed sat on the edge of my couch, his toupee leaning more off kilter than normal. I didn't intend to let him in after our blowup the day before, but he bolted past me the second I turned the knob.*

*Trivial? He calls what he's doing trivial? He's gone too far this time. "I not only want to, I'm already gone," I announced, purposely remaining standing so he wouldn't get too comfortable.*

*"After everything I've done for you? I'm the best agent out there, and everybody knows it." He scoffed and relaxed back into the cushions.*

*"Maybe ten years ago, but the fact that you still believe that tells me you're even more out of touch than I thought." The guy is a delusional pig.*

*"You're going to regret it."*

*I crossed my arms. "I'll take my chances."*

*His jaw ticked as he watched me for a moment before leaning forward again. "No, I mean I'm going to make you regret it."*

*"Are you threatening me?" I took a step closer. It was time for him to leave.*

*"If that's how you want to look at it."*

*"Go ahead. You ain't got shit on me."*

*And that's when he smiled—the oily kind that made me want to rearrange his face. "Oh, that's where you're wrong, Benny. I walk out that door, and your career is over. I'll see to it."*

*"Go fuck yourself, Ed. And get out of my house."*

I thought he was bluffing, but...

"Goddammit!" My shout ricochets off the windows of my truck, and I pull over with a jerk of the steering wheel. The second the tires squeal to a stop, I snatch my phone from the dashboard mount and flip to the picture from the news article again.

Chicago. I knew it!

There's a print on the wall showing the Chicago skyline with the city's name in block letters above it. I remember that night. It was three years ago during the playoffs, and Ed and I were in the middle of a rough patch. I was sick with a virus and had run myself ragged on the ice to take Chicago out of the running. Adrenaline can kick the flu's ass when you need it to, but as soon as the mission was accomplished, I went back to the hotel and passed out. I didn't even celebrate with the team.

But before I passed out, I took nighttime cold medicine that Ed gave me.

That fucker! He actually staged this shit? What kind of Machiavellian mindwarp does it take to devise something so twisted?

The rest of the drive home is a blur, and the second my feet hit the carpeted hallway of my floor, Kaitlyn's door opens.

"There you are!"

"I know what happened." I don't bother with hellos, instead closing the space between us and filling her in on what I figured out.

"That's... I mean, I knew he was an asshole, but that's just *beyond.*"

I open my condo door and hold it for her to go ahead of me. "What are we going to do? I mean, this could be career-ending."

"Until the team PR department arranges a meeting, we're going to keep our mouths shut; that's what we're going to do." When I try to interject, she puts her hand up between us.

"Public relations 101. 'No comment' is your friend. You acknowledging it in public will only draw more attention, and that's the last thing we want." She crosses her arms and sighs. "Negotiations... didn't go so well this morning as it is."

I drop my bag on the floor near the kitchen and grab two water bottles from the fridge. "What does that mean?" I ask as I hand her a bottle. She accepts it absently, her eyes never leaving my face.

"They offered one million for one year. No signing bonus."

"And the hits just keep on coming." I whip the cap from my water at the kitchen wall. I need a two-year contract, without question.

"If you think we're settling for that, you don't know me very well," she reassures. "A trade isn't on the table anymore, so we can check one thing off."

"You sure about that after this whole cocaine thing?"

"The *alleged* cocaine thing. Like I said, let's wait for the PR department."

"Kaitlyn, Ed is a legend in the league. He's got his nose so far up everyone's asses, they'll never believe me."

"You leave that to me. The only thing I need you to do is behave like a goddamn angel for the next couple weeks while I get negotiations back on track. All-Star votes come in the day after tomorrow, and I'm so confident of your chances, I already scheduled another meeting with Macalby."

"At least one of us is feeling optimistic." Macalby has to know his offer would piss me off.

"Hey," Kaitlyn says, her voice having lost its fire as she walks toward me. "It's going to be okay." She reaches out for my hand and I close my fingers around hers. "Now that I know the real Banks Bennet, I won't rest until the world knows him too."

"Kaitlyn, I..."

Her phone dings with two successive notifications before I can finish–not that I really know what I was going to say anyway. She glances at the phone in her hand and curses.

"What now?"

"Nothing."

Her phone is angled so I can see the screen, and the name Ed Presley jumps out at me from her messaging app. I can feel the blood rushing to my skin's surface, and I snatch the phone from her hand.

> Ed: Just saw the news. I always say trash belongs with trash.

"What the actual..." I begin, but the words die on my tongue when I see this isn't the first message of this kind she's gotten from my former agent and her former boss.

Kaitlyn scrambles for her phone, but I easily hold her off as I continue to scroll through one vile message after another.

"That's private, Banks!"

My anger isn't cooling anytime soon. "Why didn't you tell me he's been harassing you?!"

"Because it's none of your business!" she shouts through gritted teeth.

I gawk at her. "None of my business?"

"I'm your agent. It's part of my job to decide what you do and don't need to know. This is a definite don't."

"He's got it out for you, Kaitlyn," I state the obvious, but it's even worse than I already knew.

"He's an asshole. I think we've established that. Why do you think I want to shove my victories in his face so badly?"

I let her have her phone back, and she scowls at me before dipping her chin to scroll to another text thread. "Bella needs me to send some files, so I have to get back to work."

"Kaitlyn." I stop her with a hand to her shoulder, and she turns back. "You need to be careful with this maniac."

She straightens her spine in Killer Kaitlyn mode and gives me a reassuring smile. "I'm a big girl, Banks. I've dealt with Ed Presleys before. Just worry about keeping your nose clean, and I'll talk to you in the morning."

Since I know I'll get nowhere now, I muster a half smile of my own. "It's too early."

"What?"

I tap a finger to the side of my nose. "Keep my nose clean? You're going to have to give it a few years before that will be funny."

She goes up on tiptoes and kisses my cheek before closing the door behind her.

I'm too keyed up to sleep, so I do the only thing I can think of to ease my mind. I turn on a game and grab my yarn. By the time I've completed the third row of black, gold, and white hat for my mom to wear to games, my heart rate has slowed enough for me to not be in danger of cardiac arrest.

Ed has always had it out for Kaitlyn. I know this. In fact, it used to amuse me when I thought I hated her. But I always assumed it was professional competition—with an extra dose of misogyny on Ed's end, of course. People talk shit all the time, especially in professional sports, and Ed always took it too far. It's how I ended up firing him, in fact. I just never thought he meant his trash talk so literally until this stunt with the photo. And now I find out about these texts to Kaitlyn?

Kaitlyn is in his crosshairs now because of me.

This woman has worked her ass off for almost two decades to get where she is now. She has fought tooth and nail against a system that didn't want her to have a seat at the table to begin with, and she is fantastic at what she does. She has always put her players first, even above her plans to have a kid, it seems. No way can Ed Presley be allowed to touch her.

What's to stop him from doing more underhanded shit to not only end her career, but possibly do something even worse? He's shown what he's capable of, and he's got to be stopped.

And I'm thinking I'm the only one who can do it.

If we wait for the head office to address this developing story in public, we'll have to toe whatever line they decide on. And it would be in their best interest to sweep this shit under the rug and turn a blind eye to Ed's antics. Which means the only way to stop Ed from hurting Kaitlyn–or anyone else in his orbit–is to nail his ass to the wall for everyone to see.

It might be career suicide, and it will definitely piss Kaitlyn off, but she'd stick her neck out for any of us if we needed it. Despite her determination and reassurances, my contract is probably dead in the water already. But it's not too late to bring Ed down with me.

It looks like I'm about to call my first press conference.

# Chapter Twenty-Seven

Kaitlyn

> Me: I know you leaked that picture, Presley.
> Keep your nose out of my business.
> Whatever petty grievances you have about
> me, you need to stand down with this shit
> about Banks.

The reply back is almost instantaneous.

> Ed: I had nothing to do with your client
> being a loser. Just sad to see my protege
> becoming a loser right alongside him.

I scoff out loud, the secretary outside of the public relations office for the Storm Chasers giving me a wary look. I was never Ed's protégé and we both know it. I was his lackey, at best.

> Me: You better hope I don't find evidence to
> prove you leaked that picture on purpose.

Ed: You better hope I don't find evidence of your own misconduct and the NHLPA kicks you out.

I don't have a chance to respond to that thinly veiled threat because a door opens and the lead attorney for the PR team waves me inside the meeting room. I move quickly, knowing I need to face down this PR nightmare for Banks and get to my meeting with the GM. Damage control has never been my favorite, but that's what I'm doing today: fixing everything that's gone awry due to that damn picture.

"I think we can all agree that the picture doesn't look good," the director says from the leather executive chair at the head of the table. There's more suits around this table than in Banks's whole closet.

"Agreed," I say quickly. "But it's also not damning evidence."

The director tilts his head. "Pretty sure that's not powdered sugar on the mirror, Ms. Phillips."

"I'm sure it's not either, but we don't know for a fact. Nor is there evidence of my client using whatever that substance is."

The lawyer cuts in. "The league will take a look at all the evidence. What we need to do is make sure this doesn't reflect poorly on the Storm Chasers as a whole."

"Understood. And Bennet is willing to help out in whatever way he can." If they want him to make a statement, he'll make a statement. Donate money to drug rehabilitation programs? No problem. Be the spokesman for an afterschool special? Consider it done.

"I'm glad to hear that," the director says, steepling his hands in front of his face. "We're putting together a plan as we speak and will need to meet with you both tomorrow morning to go over it. I'll warn you now, Benny won't like it."

I nod, swallowing hard. "We'll be there."

The next meeting goes just as poorly. Sam and his lawyers are grilling me on everything to do with that picture and I'm defending Banks as best I can under the circumstances.

"Honestly, a trade might be the best thing for everyone," Sam finally admits.

My phone vibrates for the sixth time from inside my leather bag. I dig my hand in, disappointed by how things are going and irritated that whomever is texting or calling can't take a hint. I don't have time for distractions while my client's career is circling the drain.

Except when I hazard a glance at the screen of my phone, it's good news. I pull the phone into my lap and read the full text from Bella. When I raise my head, I know I can stop the hemorrhaging of these negotiations.

"You probably shouldn't trade Bennet just yet. He just got chosen by hockey fans to be in the All-Star game. The public loves him."

Sam's lips tug into a reluctant smile while he huffs. "I swear that kid has nine lives."

I grin. "Damn right. And he plans to play every single one of those lives for the Florida Storm Chasers."

Sam waves his hand. "Give it to me. What does he want?"

I slide a piece of paper across the table with our own terms clearly stated: two years at two million each, plus an upfront signing bonus.

Sam doesn't even look at it. He just tucks the paper into his briefcase and stands. I follow suit, shaking his hand and walking out. The All-Star pick is exactly what we needed to turn this thing around. I can feel the momentum turning. If we can just kill the picture in the press, we can get the public to forget about it. They'll see Banks in the All-Star game, absolutely crushing it, and we'll have ourselves a beautiful contract extension. I can practically taste the victory.

I rush home, wanting to tell Banks the good news, but Olivia calls me as I'm flying out of the elevator on our floor.

"Hey Olivia!" I tuck the phone between my ear and shoulder, marching straight to Banks's door and knocking.

"Hey, lady. I saw the picture. Oof. Roman already tried to call Banks. Is everything okay?"

When Banks doesn't answer the door, I fumble through my bag to find the key to his condo. "Define okay." I chuckle. "Actually, it was looking bad, but he just got chosen for the All-Star game so I think he'll be good in the long term. Now I just have to get Ed to leave him alone long enough to get a contract extension signed."

"Ed? Ed Presley? What does that greasy guy have to do with it?" Olivia is not a fan of the man either. "Wait, hold on. Roman wants me to put you on speaker."

I wait until Roman calls out my name. "Yo, Kaitlyn! How's our boy doing?"

I repeat myself, letting Roman know that things are on track again. I finally get the key in the door and open it, letting myself into Banks's condo. I dump my bag at the door and kick off my heels. Banks isn't here and that makes me nervous. He should have been back from practice already. The man doesn't miss a naptime for anything.

"I'm pretty sure Ed Presley leaked the photo to hurt us both. You got any dirt on the guy?"

Roman hisses. "Sadly, no. That guy is an icon in the

hockey world. All the young kids want to sign with him, thinking he's their ticket to stardom. I never liked the guy though. Seemed shady."

I tell them about a few of the things Ed has said or done to me when I worked for him. Roman is hopping mad. "Man, I heard a few rumors about that asshole, but I dismissed them, thinking it was way too outlandish to be true, but now I'm not so sure."

Sitting on Banks's couch, I get a bad feeling in the pit of my stomach. "What rumors?"

"Well, I don't recall the details, but it was something to do with Ed blackmailing one of his high profile clients to get him to behave."

I nearly drop the phone. "Blackmail? That's terrible. And pretty damn close to what I think he did with Banks, except Banks followed through on leaving Ed. Do you recall who the rumor was about?"

"Nah, sorry, but I can ask around. Carefully. Kaitlyn, I don't know. This sounds dangerous. Maybe we should let the PR team sort things out. Ed's the number one agent in the league for the past two decades with all kinds of influence over GMs and high profile clients. You'd be David, going after Goliath."

I lick my chapped lips and consider the alternative. "I think I may have to. Ed isn't going to back off anytime soon. Besides, didn't David win in that story?"

I have an idea, one I can't say to Olivia and Roman yet. I don't want to get their hopes up, but Roman mentioning the word blackmail got the wheels in my brain turning. Maybe I can prove the photo was staged, taking the heat off Banks and pinning it on Ed where it belongs.

"Most important is extending Banks's career, right?" Olivia asks, getting to the heart of the matter.

I nod, even though they can't see me. "I just need Banks to

lay low. Negotiations are back on track and this photo debacle will blow over if he keeps quiet and plays his heart out in the All-Star game."

"I'll try calling Banks again. I'll keep telling him to lay low until he's sick of me," Roman laughs.

"That would be great, Roman. Thank–"

"Shit. Wait. Banks is on TV," Roman barks.

"What?" I snap, lunging for the remote on the coffee table and clicking on the television to see my client having a press conference. Without me.

As a throng of reporters shout questions at him, I feel all that momentum from this morning dying a quick death. If this is Banks laying low, I'd hate to see him trying to draw a crowd.

# Chapter Twenty-Eight

Banks

Fuck. Why did I think this was a good idea again?

"You about ready, Bennet?" the woman from a local TV station asks as I blink at the gathered reporters and rethink my life choices.

There are only supposed to be a handful here—enough to cause a ruckus but not be a drama queen about it. But more of them keep showing up, telling me someone has a big mouth. Oh well, maybe it's for the best. I had hoped to control this a little bit, but more reports on Ed's bullshit is a good thing, right?

As soon as I see the sports reporter from The Sentinel step onto the grass, I nod, take a deep breath, and step forward into the circle of waiting microphones and cameras.

"Strange way to announce a retirement, don't you think?" one jagoff asks, but I ignore him.

"Thanks for showing up today." I clear my throat and try to continue, but another guy cuts me off.

"What do you have to say about the cocaine in that photo that dropped this week?"

"Shut up and let the man speak," Barry from The Sentinel snaps at him, and the guy thankfully shuts his trap so I can continue.

"As I'm sure you're all aware, a not-so-flattering photo of me was leaked to the media earlier this week. I wanted to come forward to address it so we can all be clear. I am a well-paid, hardworking professional athlete who takes this sport extremely seriously. Never have I used cocaine or any other illegal substance in all my years as an employee of the Florida Storm Chasers or any other team. I love hockey too much to do something that stupid."

"How do you explain that photo?"

"Who is the woman?"

"Where are Coach Bowman and the team reps? Why are we doing this at a public park?"

I hold a hand up to halt further questions. "I'll answer all your questions as soon as I finish my statement." When they quiet down, I go on. "The photo in question was taken three years ago in a Chicago hotel during the playoffs."

"The sideburns," a woman says, and I nod. Yeah, those pork chops weren't exactly the best look, but you never want to be the guy who brings bad luck by shaving.

"Regardless of the date, at no time would it be acceptable —to me personally or to the Storm Chasers franchise—for me to be in a room where illegal drugs are being abused. Which is why this photo was a complete setup."

They all start talking at once, and I wave my hands in a quiet-the-fuck-down gesture.

Here goes nothing. "Some of you may know a man by the name of Ed Presley of the King Agency."

More murmuring, but at least they're not shouting over me this time.

"Until recently, I retained Mr. Presley's services as my sports agent. In mid-December, after increasing concerns about his ethics, I released him as my agent. At that time, he used threatening language to warn me he intended to ruin my career." All it takes to quiet them down this time is a glare. "At the time the photo in question was taken, I was ill with the flu and had taken nighttime cold medicine given to me by my agent, Ed Presley. I fell asleep in the hotel room by myself and woke up the same way. Mr. Presley had a key to my room, and I had recently expressed some dissatisfaction with his services. It is my belief that Mr. Presley orchestrated and staged an incriminating photo to keep as insurance and to use against me should I fire him."

"This is a little far-fetched, isn't it?" the guy from Sporting Tampa asks, and I certainly can't fault him.

"I understand this may be hard to believe," I respond.

"Sounds like a he-said, he-said," the podcast guy says.

"I'm aware how it might look. I'm taking a big risk putting this out there with no hard evidence to back my claim. But I suspect I'm not the only person Ed Presley has tried this with, and I'm hoping by speaking up, someone else might feel that they can come forward as well. I'm not done playing professional hockey, and I won't allow a spiteful bully to play god with my life or the lives of anyone else who stands in his way."

My heart continues its drum solo in my chest as I take a few questions and hope to hell this paves the way for someone to come forward. It's my only shot to make this plan work and keep Kaitlyn safe—and hopefully my career as well.

After a half-dozen more questions, it's time to wrap this shit up, so I hold out both hands and raise my voice. "That's it for today, guys. But I need to say one more thing before I go." My jaw goes tight, and I have to force it open as I stare into the cameras and envision Ed's smug face behind them. "This is a message for Ed Presley. There's a reason you don't see the arena behind me or anyone standing at my side, and that's intentional. This is all *me*. So if you've got a problem with it, you come at *me* and not anybody else, you got that?"

Two hours later, I step out of the elevator and brace like I'm expecting a live grenade to roll across the carpet and land at my feet. I stopped to see Beatrice after the press conference while I waited for the first story to hit the internet. It was closely followed by two more and a call from the Storm Chaser's head office that I didn't pick up. By now I'm confident Kaitlyn knows what I did.

Against her explicit instructions.

When the hallway remains clear, I walk to my condo door and let myself in with a tired sigh.

"You want to tell me what the actual fuck that was?" My elbow jabs the door with an audible *thwack* as I almost jump out of my skin at the sound of Kaitlyn's voice.

"Jesus! I think you just gave me a permanent heart condition." I claw at my chest and frown at her where she sits perched on my couch, back as straight as a nun's ruler and expression just as stern.

"Exactly what part of 'let me handle it' was unclear?" Her tone could slice right through six inches of ice. Her entire demeanor stands in stark contrast to her relaxed appearance. This last week or so, she's been showing up at my place in casual clothes with no makeup and her hair up in messy topknots. It's a side of her few people get to glimpse, I'm guessing, and I love the fact that I'm one of the few.

"I know—" I begin, but she cuts me off.

"No. You *don't* know. If you *knew*, you would have kept your mouth *shut* like I instructed, and you would have played the part of hockey's good little golden boy while I negotiated the kick-ass contract I promised."

I can feel my nostrils flare. "What? So I'm a child now?"

"Did you ever *stop* being one?"

"Listen, Kaitlyn—"

"No, *you* listen, hot shot." She jabs the air with a red-tipped index finger. "I had it handled. I had Macalby just where I wanted him. You had a spot on the All-Star team. I would have figured out how to spin that photo or make it go away."

"Ed's not going to lie down that easily," I insist, stepping away from the door and dropping my keys on the entryway table.

"And going off half-cocked like that was supposed to help how? I'm your agent, Banks. It's my job to keep you from hurting yourself, but you made it impossible for me to do my job."

"I couldn't let you be involved and draw Ed's anger." No fucking way. That was the whole point.

She shoots to her feet. "It's my job!"

"It's not your job to lay your career on the line for me!" That guy is unhinged, so who knows how far he might go?

"Oh, please." Her fingers dig into her hips as she throws a death glare my way. "I can handle Ed Presley. What I *can't* handle is my new client being suspended for violating his current contract—and seeing all my hard work on his extension go down the drain. Talk about a career killer! You just managed to ruin my reputation worse than Ed Presley ever could. And all for what? Vengeance against some asshole?"

Suspension? Well, shit.

"What are you talking about? They're suspending me for the cocaine?"

"Not for that. Although you've now made it impossible for that photo to disappear quietly into the night." Her lips firm as she exhales sharply through her nose. I'd be unsurprised to see fire shooting from her nostrils at this point.

"You're suspended for misrepresenting the franchise," she clarifies. "Two games, pending an investigation. Imagine if every player called their own press conference to hurl unproven claims against assholes. It would be mayhem! There would be lawsuits left and right. They're pissed, Banks. The head office runs the narrative. Always. A fact I could have impressed upon you had you thought to clue me in about your plans."

"I knew you wouldn't let me do it."

"So, naturally, you thought you knew best." This time she huffs out a mirthless laugh. "I should have listened to my instincts from the beginning and never taken you on."

"I'm sorry." I take a step closer but halt when she puts a hand up. "But it's more than Ed just pissing me off, and you know it. If he's doing this to me, imagine what he's doing to other people! Imagine what he could do to you! The head office would have swept my claims under the rug. They don't want a fight with Ed and his clients if they can avoid it. Path of least resistance, Kaitlyn."

She watches me for several long moments.

"Kaitlyn." I have to break the silence, but I regret it immediately when she speaks her next words.

"You're a great hockey player, Benny, but you should stay on the ice and let other people do what they're great at off it." She sweeps past me to the door. Benny? She *never* calls me that.

I spear frustrated fingers through my hair and turn to follow her. "Where are you going? We need to talk about this."

"To Atlanta," she says without even a backward glance.

Adrenaline spikes in my lower back. "Don't confront Ed, Kaitlyn! Just stay here."

She finally turns in the open doorway, and her expression hits me like a punch to the gut. "I'm not going to confront Ed. I'm going home. Tell Pierre he can keep my wine. It's a bitch to pack in a suitcase."

The door clicks quietly closed—too quiet to fittingly punctuate the momentous nature of Kaitlyn Phillips walking out of my life.

# Chapter Twenty-Nine

Kaitlyn

The number of times my father talked right over me or disregarded my feelings over the years is too high to keep track. I've come to expect that from him, a constant disappointment that I chalk up to being my dad and thinking he knows better. I thought Banks was a better man than that, but this stunt with the press conference shows he doesn't believe in me either. He doesn't listen, doesn't believe in my abilities, doesn't trust me to do what's necessary to keep his career on track. No wonder he and my father got along so well.

My condo in Atlanta is downright depressing and the late spring thunderstorm casting the whole city in ominous shades isn't helping. In my quest to build a career soaring over Ed Presley, I forgot to build a home. The gray walls and boring furniture almost look like this is company housing. No personality whatsoever. I could use a knitted throw blanket on my sofa in a riot of colors right about now. Of course, that just makes me think of Banks again and my cheeks burn with both fury and hurt.

I'd be pissed if Bobby or Alexi or Pete disregarded my professional advice, but I wouldn't be hurt. No, that added component is because I let myself have feelings for Banks. I broke my number one rule and caught feelings for a client. Because that thought is simply too crazy to think about, I focus on the anger.

I'm mid-rant while pacing my condo when my phone rings. I almost don't answer because I've been fielding so many calls from the media, but it could be the GM or even the Storm Chaser's PR team and I haven't officially told them I'm done with Banks. My resignation will be yet another blow to Banks's public image and therefore his chances of getting his contract extended. For some reason, I can't make myself place that call quite yet. Thankfully it's not anyone I'm trying to avoid.

"Hey, Roman." I plop down on my sofa and frown at the uncomfortable furniture. Why the hell did I buy this thing?

"What the hell, Kaitlyn?" Roman snaps, all pleasantries brushed aside. "Banks said you dropped him?"

I rub my fingertips across my forehead as I close my eyes, trying to ease the headache that's been brewing since I saw Banks standing before a bunch of reporters on television. I desperately need to get some sleep, but I have a feeling that dreamland is going to escape me for many nights to come.

"Listen, Roman. I don't need you lecturing me. That man ignored everything I told him to do. I had Sam ready to listen to my proposal and Banks went and held a press conference without me, getting his ass suspended. I can't work with someone like that. No, I *won't* work with someone like that."

Roman huffs. "You knew what he was like when you agreed to help him."

I cut him off. "Yeah, I did and I distinctly remember

saying it was a bad idea. Or did you selectively forget that part?"

Roman is silent for a moment. When he starts talking again, it's with a much calmer tone. "I don't think you understand the situation. I'd hoped Banks would tell you, but it looks like that hasn't happened."

My eyes fly open. "What are you talking about?" I can't handle any more surprises right now.

"The whole reason Banks left Presley was because he overheard Ed talking on the phone about the possibility of having someone follow you. He wanted dirt on you so he could get you kicked out of hockey."

"What?" I jump off the sofa.

"Apparently Ed had always talked horrifically about you, which is why Banks and Ed got into it all the time. Banks would defend you and Ed would get pissed and question his loyalty. Thinking about having someone follow your every move was the last straw. Banks yelled at Ed about going too far and it spiraled from there."

I'm stunned. Absolutely speechless as I try to comprehend this news. That whole time I was giving Banks shit for being dropped by his agent and he'd actually left him because he was defending me. I feel like an ass. A scared ass, because apparently, someone might be following me.

"Shit," I mutter, my head bowing. Guilt twists my ribs until I'm not sure I can take a full breath.

"Yeah," Roman agrees. "Banks didn't have evidence that Ed followed through on the idea, so he never came forward about it. Banks actually hired his own detective to make sure you weren't being followed."

I sink back onto the sofa, going back over our conversations and realizing Banks has been trying to keep Ed away from me this whole time. "So that's why Banks freaked out when he saw that Ed still texts me."

Roman chuckles, but it's laced with sadness. "Probably so. Banks has been in love with you for years, Kaitlyn."

At that, I bobble the phone, my thighs catching it before it falls between the sofa cushions. Olivia's voice comes out of the speaker when I finally get control of the phone. "Kaitlyn?"

"Yeah, I'm here," I croak. Banks is in love with me?

"Roman shouldn't have said anything, but now that he has, can you please just rethink things? If you drop Banks now, he's truly up shit creek without a paddle. And as much as you complain about him, I know you have feelings too."

Do I? I mean, I know I care for Banks. That's part of the problem. But *love* kind of feelings? That's overstating things just a bit, isn't it? How can I be in love with a client? Loving Banks would ruin everything. Then again, everything's kind of already ruined. Maybe not my whole career, but certainly his. Ed Presley won't get his comeuppance like he deserves, Banks will be forced out of the league over false rumors and no team being willing to pick up the hothead, and I...well, I'll be right here in Atlanta. Licking my wounds and trying to cobble together a life without Banks in it.

Olivia sighs. "Just sleep on it, okay? Don't make a decision until you've thought it all through. He really does love you and I bet, if you look past all the client/agent issues clouding your judgment, you love Banks too. That kind of thing is worth taking a chance. Believe me."

We hang up without me adding to the conversation. I can't. I have nothing to say to any of that. I need time to think about everything Roman announced like it's no big deal. It's a really big fucking deal if Banks loves me. It's a really big fucking deal that he was willing to blow up his career to defend me. Because that's what firing the great Ed Presley amounts to. Honestly, this changes everything.

The big question is what am *I* willing to do to defend Banks?

I toss and turn all night, getting a few hours of sleep some-where in the early morning hours, but I'm no closer to having an answer to that last question. I wake to my phone blowing up and a particular headline that makes me groan.

*Longtime NHL agent, Presley denies allegations.*

The headache turns to a migraine and I know today's going to be another shit show day. I have a decision to make. Am I going to stick by Banks's side and help him fight this? Or am I going to send in my resignation and walk away?

My doorbell buzzes and I freeze before realizing that the press can't get to me at my condo. They don't know where I live and my doorman downstairs is the human form of a pitbull. The shout through my door tells me I have bigger problems.

"Kaity-bug? Open up. It's your father!"

I throw back the covers and stumble through my condo, letting Dad in and hoping like hell I have some espresso beans in the cabinet that aren't expired. He busses a kiss across my cheek and starts ranting through my condo like he owns the place. I whistle to get his attention, turning into the kitchen, and his rant follows me in there. I do have beans and while they aren't the freshest, I'm desperate. I need caffeine. STAT.

"How'd you know I'm back in Atlanta?"

"Pfft. I can still track your phone, remember? Didn't you work for that zounderkite?" Dad settles his bulk on one of the barstools, like tracking your forty-year-old daughter isn't a step too far. I'll have to take a look at my settings once I get some caffeine on board.

I shake my head. It's too early for this. "I'm not sure what that is, but if you're referring to Ed, then yes. He's my former boss." The espresso machine chugs to life and grinds the beans. Within seconds I have hot black coffee in a mug. Only once I've taken a fortifying sip do I turn and lean my elbows on the granite island countertop.

Dad's face is red as a tomato. "He blackmailed an athlete? That would never happen in the NFL."

I roll my eyes, but stop when it makes the headache worse. "At least that you know about, right?"

Dad slaps his meaty hand on the countertop. "Kaitlyn. You worked for a guy who stooped to blackmail? That's despicable!" The barstool shoots backward as Dad hops to his feet. "Did that asshole ever hurt you?"

I come around the island and put my arm around his shoulders. "Only my feelings, Dad. And you and I both know feelings are bullshit." I parrot back the words he's told me all my life.

Dad considers that. "Well, that's mostly true."

I gape at him. "What do you mean? Remember when that girl in kindergarten stole my rainbow eraser and I came home crying? You said emotions are bullshit. Steal it back. That was your advice then and ever since."

Dad tilts his head back and forth, looking almost sheepish. "That was just because I didn't know what to do when my little girl cried."

"Dad!"

He throws his hands out. "What? I was a single dad doing my best, which was pretty lousy most of the time. *Crying* is bullshit, but feelings aren't. Without feelings I never would have fallen in love with your mother."

I put my coffee down on the counter and wave him out of the kitchen and over to the sofa. He plops down and grouses under his breath about the uncomfortable cushions.

"I thought getting sidetracked by love was the worst mistake you ever made?" How many times did he go off about everything in his life spiraling down after that? I know the story word for word.

Dad huffs, folding his hands over his belly. "Marrying your mother was the best decision I made. Getting distracted by the pregnancy and then her death, which led to the end of my career, was the worst mistake. A very important distinction."

I frown at the man who's been so anti-love he outlawed Valentine's Day in our house. "So if Mom had lived…"

Dad gets a wispy smile on his face. "If your mother had lived, I would have been happy my career ended. Love would be worth it. But that's not what happened and therefore I'm a bitter old man."

I sit there staring at the man I thought I knew. "Love is worth it," I repeat quietly, rolling that sentiment through my head. Isn't that what Olivia was trying to tell me? Isn't that what Banks believed when he fired Ed? Why was I the only adult in the room who didn't understand that simple phrase?

Dad pats my hand. "Now tell me all about Ed Presley. I want to hear the dirt straight from the horse's mouth."

I jump up from the sofa, headache a thing of the past. "Actually, Dad, I hate to break this up, but I have some very important phone calls to make." An idea is forming and so is the smile on my face. *Love is worth it*. Holy hell, I've fallen head over stilettos for a client. "And I have a zounderkite to destroy."

"That's my girl." Dad punches me in the arm and leaves me to my phone calls.

# Chapter Thirty

Banks

"You gonna eat that?"

At my question, Eli's eyes shift from his plate to my face, a look of mild disgust parking itself on his features. "Dude, there's more pizza in the kitchen. You don't need to snack on my crusts like a seagull."

"I don't have the energy to walk to the kitchen," I complain as I settle deeper into the couch cushions and pull my afghan tighter around me. Did somebody turn down the thermostat? Probably just inertia making me cold. After all, I haven't moved from this spot in almost forty-eight hours.

"Well, that's just plain pathetic." Eli sighs and drops his paper plate to the coffee table before striding on his long legs to the kitchen.

I narrow my eyes and pause the Magic/Hornets game. "Have you grown since the last time I saw you?"

My plate nearly falls to the rug when the soggy slice of meat-lovers lands on it.

"I've gained an inch since Christmas. Mom says I'm gonna be six feet by the time I start high school."

"Girls are gonna be all over you, man," I inform him. "But be careful. They're nothing but trouble." I frown at the remote in my hand. It's been over a week since Kaitlyn left, and despite my voicemails, I've gotten nothing but a few curt texts. I keep expecting official word that she's dropped me as a client, but it hasn't arrived yet. Probably got lost in the mail.

My phone dings from the end table on the other side of Eli, and he glances at it. "Beelzebub. Again." I've stooped to an all-time low having a twelve-year-old screen my calls, but I'm sick of picking up the phone hoping to see Kaitlyn's name on the screen and finding "Unknown Caller" or "Beelzebub" instead. Ed's contact name was officially changed earlier in the week to better represent his personality.

I've considered chasing after Kaitlyn, but she's such a stickler for boundaries, I decided it was wiser to stay put for the time being. Besides, the head office demanded I remain close at hand as they deal with the fallout from my press conference. The only good thing to come out of this debacle so far is knowing my teammates are behind me. Just about everyone has reached out to say they believe my version of events and can't wait till I'm back on the ice and we can put this behind us.

The only problem is I don't want to put Kaitlyn behind me. She's all I can see when I look at my future.

Sighing, I unpause the game and drop my eyes to my pizza. The cheese has congealed, and the pepperoni looks like it's been basking under a roller-dog lamp for a couple days. I abandon it on the coffee table and snuggle into my blanket like a five-year-old with a tummy ache.

"My friend Malik says you gotta know how to talk to them," Eli mumbles around a carrot stick. Yeah, Denise handed a whole bag of them over when she dropped him off earlier. It came with a tilted chin and a raised eyebrow, so I know Eli spilled the beans about our pizza and wings habit.

"How to talk to who?" I ask, my brain lagging.

"Girls." The *duh* is silent.

"Oh." Right. Girls. "Malik is right. It's like a foreign language."

The game goes to commercial, and Eli shoots a look my way. "What do you mean?"

Warming to the topic, I turn to face him, propping my arm on the back of the couch. "Okay, so say you ask a girl if she's okay and she responds, 'fine?' What do you do?"

Eli's brow furrows. "Is this a trick question?"

"Not on my part."

"Uh..." He thinks for a few seconds, rolling the carrot sticks around on his plate. "I guess I'd say 'good' or something like that."

"Wrong!" I jab a finger at him. "You just got dumped."

Carrots abandoned, he drops his plate on the end table and throws his arms out. "What?! But I didn't do anything."

"Aha! That's the problem. When a girl says she's *fine*, it means the *opposite* of fine. You either messed up—and need to apologize— or she wants to talk about something. Or she needs a hug."

"But why would she lie?" Oh, the poor naive grasshopper.

"She's not lying. She's speaking in girl code."

His face screws up. "Like a spy?"

"Kind of." I wave off his question and move on. "What about this one? A commercial comes on for some fake holiday made up by greeting card companies—like Sweethearts Day or Flower Day or some other BS—and she comments on how dumb it is. What do you do?"

"Agree with her?" He's got a lot of work to do.

"Wrong!" I jab another finger at him and his jaw drops in

disbelief. "Although agreeing with her is *usually* the right answer, this one's an exception."

Eli shakes his head and snaps another carrot between his teeth. "I don't get it."

"Nobody does. Don't worry about it. But the right move in this situation is to keep your mouth shut, mark that dumb holiday on your calendar, and get her a present."

"Why?"

"Because she's testing you, and there's no way she's going to let you in her p—I mean, it shows her how much you appreciate her."

"This is stupid. Doesn't sound worth it at all."

"Yeah." I turn back to the TV and readjust the afghan. The Magic turn the ball over twice and go down by six. I sigh. "Except if you find the right girl, it totally is."

The phone rings, and Eli glances at the end table again. "Unknown Caller."

"Send it to voicemail," I reply.

Two hours later, Eli is gone and I'm staring at twelve new voicemail notifications. Jesus, don't these people have hobbies? It's Sunday, for crying out loud. I listen to the first five seconds of each message before deleting or saving it for later. By the time I get to the last one, I'm ready to hurl my phone off my veranda. But the hesitant manner of the speaker on the line has me lifting my thumb from the trash icon.

*"Hi. Um, I'm trying to get in touch with Banks Bennet. I hope I have the right number. My name is Adrienne, and I live in Chicago. A friend, uh, sent me a link to the interview thing you did the other day, and I felt like I had to get in touch."* She takes an audible breath before continuing, *"You see, uh, I'm the girl in that photo."*

I drop the phone, and it crashes to the granite countertop of my kitchen island, the message going silent. "Shit!" I quickly snatch it up again and press play.

Her words pick up speed as she hurries to explain. *"I never got the guy's name, and I honestly had no idea who you were until today either, but I remember the whole thing. He came up to me on the street and said he'd give me five hundred bucks to play a joke on his friend. All I had to do was pose next to you while you were sleeping and make sure this little mirror with powdered sugar on it was right next to us. I mean, I guess I knew he was lying about it being a joke, but five hundred bucks is five hundred bucks, you know? Anyway, after I saw you on the news, I looked up this Ed Presley guy online, and that's definitely him. I'll never forget that awful hairpiece."*

Holy shit! Powdered sugar? Jesus, Ed.

*"So, um, it sounds like maybe you're in trouble because of that picture. I just wanted to call to see if there's anything I can do."* She leaves her number and hangs up.

My fingers shake as I hit the digits and wait for someone to pick up.

"Hello?"

"Adrienne?"

"Yeah?"

"This is Banks Bennet calling back. I can't tell you how happy I was to get your message."

She sighs. "It looks like I owe you an apology."

I shake my head even though I know she can't see me. "You're not the one who needs to be sorry, believe me. I'm not really sure where to go from here, but would you be willing to maybe talk to my team's lawyers? Maybe even the authorities?"

"Like the cops?" Her tone suggests I just asked her to eat a jar of moths.

"Okay, no cops then. What about the lawyer—or the team's PR manager?" Hell, they've got to be able to do *something* with this woman's information. If nothing else, it might convince them Ed's not the respectable agent they've thought him to be—even if it doesn't directly put him out of business.

"Um, I guess that would be okay."

I pump my fist in the air at her words. "Excellent. Thank you so much, Adrienne. Can I call you back once I've figured out a plan?"

We hang up a few moments later, and the first thing I want to do is call Kaitlyn. But before my thumb so much as twitches, my phone rings again, Roman's ugly mug splashing over the screen.

"Yo! What's up?"

"You're sounding a lot more chipper than the last time I talked to you," he responds.

Considering the last time we spoke, I was watching my team play without me and drowning my sorrows in beer and some ill-advised spray cheese directly from the can, that's not saying much. I bring him up to speed on my recent phone conversation.

"That slimy asshole! *Oh, we're going to bury him*," my friend promises, as only a true friend can. "You hear from Kaitlyn yet? I've got to imagine she'll be all over this."

"Nah, man. I think that ship has sailed." My stomach lurches as I admit it out loud.

"Shit."

"Yeah."

We're both silent for a few beats until he pipes up, "Oh! Shit, I almost forgot why I called. Guess who I ran into at a fundraiser last night in Raleigh?"

"The suspense is killing me."

"Shut up, dickhead. You'll want to hear this."

"Okay, fine, who did you run into last night while flaunting your millions of dollars in people's faces in Raleigh?"

"Ray Putnam."

"Putz? How the hell is he?" Ray Putnam was a longtime

player for the Silverkings and then the Blades. He retired a few years back. "Where's he at these days anyway?"

"Probably closing in on your front door if I had to guess."

"Huh?"

"He lives in Clearwater," Roman explains. "Pulled me aside last night saying he and the wife were on vacation this last week, but he saw the news about you when he got back to civilization. Said he had some dirt on Ed you'd want to know about, but he wouldn't discuss it with me without talking to you first. I gave him your number and address, and he said he was going to drop by tonight when he got home."

"What do you think it is?"

"No clue, but if you add whatever he's got to the story from this girl in Chicago, I'd say Ed is heading for an overdue retirement, possibly in a prison cell."

"It's not nice to tease the animals, LaFontaine."

"I'm assuming you're the animal in this scenario."

"Abso-fuckin-lutely." I can't help my grin. God, it feels good to smile again.

There's a knock on my door, making me spin in that direction. "Hey," I tell Roman. "Looks like Ray's here."

"Get back to me when you know what's up, yeah?"

"Sure thing." I hang up and stride to the door, dozens of scenarios surrounding Ed's misdeeds playing through my mind.

But when I swing the door open, it's not a retired hockey player on the other side. It's the love of my goddamn life. "Kaitlyn."

# Chapter Thirty-One

Kaitlyn

"Hey, hot shot."

He looks like shit and yet so, so good. If I were the type to express my feelings easily, I'd tell him how much I've missed him. It's only been a week and yet it feels like a lifetime.

Swallowing down the urge to throw myself into his arms, I brush past him into his condo, surveying the damage. There's a tattered afghan lying next to the Banks-shaped indentation on the couch. Cold pizza, take out containers, and a few empty bottles of water litter the coffee table and the floor. Video game controllers have been abandoned among the wreckage. "For fuck's sake, Banks. Did you even shower this week?"

I feel him come up behind me and the heat of him is enough to make me squeeze my eyes shut with longing. I can't cuddle into his broad chest like I want to though. I told myself I wouldn't. Told myself I'd get his life patched back together first. Then we'd talk.

"Kaitlyn," he says again, this time with less surprise and more of that longing I recognize so much.

I clear my throat, straighten my spine, and turn around to face him. "Well, at least you're not drunk." I wave my hand up and down in the air between us. "Go take a shower. Shave, find clean clothes a grown man would wear, and then meet me back out here."

Banks crosses his arms across his chest, a surly look on his handsome face. "Why?"

I match his stance, lifting my nose in the air. "Because I'm your goddamn agent and I run your life. Have you forgotten so quickly? Besides, we have plans and you can't show up like that." I wrinkle my nose for good measure.

One side of Banks's mouth tips up. "I've never been so happy to have a fucking governess."

I nod. "Damn right. Now go." If he starts smiling, the full force of his charm on display, there's no telling what I might do.

He spins on his bare feet and disappears down the hallway. My shoulders sag as I suck in a full breath. Shit. This is harder than I thought. After a few more measured breaths, I place my leather bag on the kitchen counter–thankfully free of half rotting takeout containers–and pull out the notes I'd made for Banks. Then I scrounge up some dishwashing gloves under the sink and collect the trash around the condo. The things I'll do for clients. I laugh out loud at myself. I would never do this for Bobby, Pete, or Alexi. More like the things I'll do for the man I've somehow, despite myself, fallen in love with.

When Banks emerges from his bedroom wearing a clean pair of jeans and a polo shirt, his wet combed hair giving him a boyish look, we can actually sit on the couch together without hazmat suits. He swivels his head about the place and then eyes me warily.

"I'm looking for the trap."

I lift an eyebrow. "A trap?"

Banks shrugs. "You made it clear you were dumping me last week and now here you are, in your favorite red soled stilettos, not even complaining about the lack of coffee available. I would also add you cleaned up my apartment, but that has to be beyond the realm of Killer Kaitlyn's duties so you must have smuggled in a tiny yet efficient maid in that bag of yours. In other words, what's the catch?"

I ignore his smart mouth and plow ahead. "I called a press conference for tomorrow morning. My lawyer will be there to field any questions we haven't already prepped you for. I have five pages of notes I need you to study and memorize tonight."

Banks holds up his hand, stopping me. "Wait, I have my own press conference to call."

I glare at him so hard he winces. "Have you learned nothing from last week's debacle?"

"In my defense, I thought you abandoned me and I needed to figure this out on my own from here on out."

"I didn't abandon you like some puppy on the side of the road, Banks," I snap, anger rising. "You didn't listen to me. You went off half-cocked and made your situation worse. You didn't trust me to do my job. That makes you exactly like my father and I refuse to tolerate yet another man in my life treating me like an afterthought."

Banks blinks multiple times before his face softens and he reaches out to grab my hand, thinks better of it, and sits on it instead. "I'm sorry, Kaitlyn. I trust you completely, I do. It's Ed Presley I don't trust, and I wanted to protect you from him." He shakes his head, a wry smile on his face. "An afterthought? Really? You're more like *every* thought, Kaitlyn."

That has the anger fizzling like my resolve that night he kissed me in the rain. "Banks," I murmur.

Instead of expanding on that further, he brightens. "I

actually just got off the phone with the woman in the picture. She says she'll come forward and talk to Sam and the PR department to get them off my ass. She can confirm the photo was staged and I had nothing to do with it."

His excitement makes the hundreds of phone calls worth it. "I know. How do you think she got your number?" Banks's mouth drops open, so I rush to explain. "I have another former player who will testify that Ed pulled a similar stunt on him. That's what the press conference is for."

Banks hops to his feet. "Roman also has a former player who wants to talk to me. He might be another one."

Excitement builds, knowing we have this fucker right where we want him. "Then this press conference is going to be another train wreck, this time for Ed."

Banks reaches down to grab my hands and pulls me to my feet. The movement has me stumbling into his chest. His blue eyes sparkle down at me with such hope and excitement I almost want to toss my promises aside. Almost.

"Kaitlyn," he breathes, his head dipping.

Heart pounding, I put my hand on his chest and give the slightest push. He freezes, just an inch from my lips. "Let's focus on this tonight and we'll talk after the press conference. Okay?"

His curt nod and visible retreat just about kills me.

Having given his brief overview of the situation, Banks steps aside, giving the microphone to Ray Putnam. Johan

Aaberg will be up next, a similar tale of blackmail and abuse by the one and only Ed Presley. With three players coming forward this morning, the Storm Chasers' PR team has promised me they will go after Ed with everything they've got, including pushing for criminal charges. I haven't heard if Banks's suspension has been lifted, but at this point I feel it's only a matter of time. When both Ray and Johan have told their stories, my lawyer and I take to the microphone to field questions. There's a lot of "no comment at this time" and "we'll let the authorities take it from here" but the tide has definitely shifted.

We go straight from the press conference to a handful of one-on-one interviews I set up for Banks with key sports reporters. The narrative has changed from a disgruntled hockey player off his rocker to Banks being a hero for evicting the cockroach of the hockey world. While Banks is in the middle of another one of these interviews that finally has him looking like the choir boy I always wanted for him, I get a phone call from Sam, the Storm Chasers' GM. I move further away from the interview and take it.

"Hello, Mr. Macalby. It's a beautiful day, isn't it?"

His deep chuckle is expected. "That it is, Ms. Phillips. I just saw the press conference and I have to say, you were right all along about Bennet."

I inhale audibly. "You always assume those words will make you happy, but it hits different actually hearing them, you know?"

Sam laughs again, but sobers quickly. "I actually called for a reason beyond inflating your ego, Ms. Phillips. It has come to my attention that there's been a breach of trust in my office."

I frown. "Oh?"

"One of our lawyers has been in cahoots with Ed Presley, giving him privileged information regarding our players and negotiations. Disappointing to be sure. He's been fired, of course, but I wanted to let you and all the other agents know that we'll be doing a deep dive in our office to make sure there's no future impropriety. There's no room in business for side deals and favoritism."

My brain is whirling, wondering at all the little details Ed always seemed to know about my clients. How much of my career has Ed been undermining and for how long? "I hope they all develop a serious case of insomnia due to their shoddy ethics."

Sam doesn't offer comment. "Now that most of this is behind us, I feel it best we schedule a meeting ASAP to finalize Bennet's contract."

"So, no trade then?"

"No trade, Ms. Phillips. We want Bennet to represent the Storm Chasers and all we stand for."

"I have time this afternoon," I offer, feeling on top of the world.

"I'll see you then, Ms. Phillips."

I turn around and march back to the interview, watching from behind the cameraman as Banks charms the interviewer. We've turned the ship around, getting Banks back in good standing while also taking down Ed Presley. We make a good team, Banks and I.

The only question left is if he and I are willing to do what it takes to make a good team outside of work. Or will acknowledging our feelings destroy everything we've each worked so hard for?

<h1 style="text-align:center">Chapter Thirty-Two</h1>

Banks

"I see he is no longer the big pine cone," Druggy says from behind me, making me tear my eyes from my phone screen to glance his way. It takes a second to mentally translate the expression before I smile.

"It seems not," I confirm, angling the screen so my teammate can see the online video of Ed Presley being led to a cop car in handcuffs. Time for champagne—after practice, that is. And preferably with my agent, who's a lot prettier than our goalie. I never thought I'd be so damn giddy to run drills, but I missed this place during my suspension. I haven't even needed Kaitlyn's banging on the wall to get me here on time since it was lifted. And now that Ed has not only been arrested but been suspended by the players' association, his career is well and truly over. Which means he can't touch Kaitlyn or mess with any other players' careers. A win for the good guys.

Druggy claps me on the shoulder. "Good to have this finished, my friend. We need you if we are to make playoffs again." My first game back was yesterday, and I ended up with two goals. Man, did that feel good.

"Good to be back." We fist bump, and I drop my phone to the bench to get my gear on.

"Yo, Druggy! I need to talk to you about your agent!" Money shouts our way, and Drugov trudges over to chat with him. My winger isn't the only guy shopping for a new agent now that Ed is out, so it should be an interesting few weeks in the league.

Kaitlyn's waiting outside the locker room when I head to the ice, and her smile tells me she's heard the news.

"It's a crying shame when bad things happen to such good people, isn't it?" she asks with a mischievous sparkle in her eyes.

I pause in front of her. "My favorite part was where the cop knocked his toupee off when she shoved him in the cruiser. I might take a screen grab and make it my wallpaper."

Kaitlyn snorts and closes the distance between us. It's all I can do not to haul her into me and kiss the hell out of her. But she's stood firm since the other day, so I can wait until the contract is signed if that's what she needs. As if fate just read my mind, Kaitlyn says, "Macalby wants to meet with both of us this afternoon, so shoot me a text after your post-practice workout, okay?"

My grin grows. From what Kaitlyn said about her meeting with Macalby the other day, it sounds like the Storm Chasers are going to offer me the two years and at least two mill each with a bonus. "I thought he was going to email the final contract."

She only shrugs. "Change of plans. See you later, hot shot." She turns to go but glances over her shoulder, completely busting me as I stare at her ass. "Oh, and make sure you watch that hammy. Time off probably did it some good, so we don't want to undo it."

"Yes, boss." I salute and head to the ice. If the contract comes this afternoon, it will finally be time to pin Kaitlyn down for that conversation she's been putting off. The woman can run, but she can't hide. For someone so straightforward and ballsy in every other aspect of her life, I find it almost amusing that she's still tiptoeing around the obvious. We're meant to be together, and we both know it.

Practice is as smooth as one of Dan-O's pickup lines at the club, and my body feels great. So, I'm actually whistling when I walk through Sam Macalby's door to find Kaitlyn already seated across from Sam. To my surprise, both Coach Bowman and Dave Wainright flank the GM. My whistle freezes on my lips at the sight.

Coach laughs. "Don't stop on our account. Far as I can tell, you've got a lot to whistle about today."

Unable to keep from being a smartass, I switch to whistling "Karma Police" by Radiohead this time. Coach and Dave chuckle, and even Sam's stern expression breaks. Kaitlyn rolls her eyes at me.

"Gang's all here, so let's get started, boys," she directs.

Sam wastes no time sliding a leather folio across the desk. "Three years. Three point five million per year. Seven hundred and fifty thousand signing bonus, paid upfront. The owners and management would like you to play out the rest of your career as a Storm Chaser, Mr. Bennet."

It takes a lot for my jaw to remain off the carpet. Three years? At my age? That's unheard of. And everything else is beyond what I hoped for. Looks like Beatrice is going on a shopping spree at Armani.

Kaitlyn somehow maintains a neutral expression as she responds, "That all sounds acceptable to my client."

"Benny, you done good," Dave says.

He's followed by Coach Bowman. "Conviction and moral fiber like yours are exactly what the younger guys need as an example. Add to that your work ethic, and I think you might just end up a co-captain."

"Wow. I, uh, thank you." I'm at a loss for words.

Luckily, Kaitlyn isn't. "Banks has always been your golden goose. He just needed a new alarm clock and a little dusting off."

"And a new agent, it seems," Macalby adds. "You had some very compelling arguments, Ms. Phillips." His gaze switches to me. "It took a lot to go up against Presley, and I for one thank you for putting your ass on the line to lance that boil." Uh, gross. "The owners, management, and I would all like to extend an apology for not catching onto his antics sooner. I see a lot of up-and-coming players—and agents—owing you a great debt."

"Happy to do it." It's all I can manage over the lump in my throat. Shit, I think Kaitlyn's mood swings might be contagious.

"Now, make us look good at the All-Star game, yeah?" Coach grins.

After handshakes all around, Kaitlyn sweeps up the contract and we leave the office. Neither of us says a word until we hit the parking lot. As soon as the door closes behind us, Kaitlyn literally jumps on me, letting out one of her ear-splitting howls that I often compare to that of a rhinoceros or other zoo creature. Her arms wrap tight around my neck while her legs lock around my middle.

"We did it!" She attempts to render me deaf, but I can only smile and hug her back.

"You're gonna be beating prospective clients off with a stick."

"And you're going to have endorsement offers filling your inbox!" she raves.

I squeeze her tight as I inhale her sweet floral scent and do my best not to get a boner. "We should celebrate." And talk.

She pulls back to gaze down at me with a brilliant smile, but it falters when she appears to only now notice the intimacy of our positions. Her stilettos hit the pavement as she untangles herself and self-consciously tucks a strand of loose hair behind her ear.

"Definitely," she agrees with less excitement than just moments ago. "But you've got that interview with Harry Rosen in an hour," she reminds me.

Damn. I forgot about that. "After, then. I'll grab some champagne on my way over and we can meet up at home."

"Sure." Her smile is a little more encouraging this time.

Three hours later, I knock on her door. Despite her declarations from a couple weeks back, Kaitlyn never actually gave up her lease, something I learned when half her shit was still at Pierre's condo upon her return.

When there's no answer, I knock again.

"It's unlocked!" Kaitlyn yells from inside.

I frown and turn the knob to let myself in. "You shouldn't leave it unlocked. I know we have a doorman, but Ralph is getting up there and is no match for a kindergartner, much less an armed robber."

At the sight of my agent and soon-to-be girlfriend, I halt. "What are you doing?"

She blows a lock of hair out of her eyes and bends to lift a large box, giving me a prime view of her gorgeous ass in a pair of tight black yoga pants. I can absolutely work with this. "Packing. Hand me that tape, would you?"

I grab the packing tape from the coffee table and approach. "What's the hurry? Pierre will be in London for at least another month." Not that she can't stay with me. In fact, I hope that's exactly what she'll do.

"I need to get back to Atlanta now that this contract is wrapped up and Ed is in the slammer. There's so much work to do." The tape dispenser lets out a loud screech as she seals the box and moves on to the next one.

"Oh." Okay, I guess that makes sense. Hell, I have no idea how she's kept up with all of her other clients while being my governess all this time. "Let me help, then." I rest the champagne bottle on an armchair and peel off my sweatshirt. "How did you manage to accumulate so much stuff over such a short period of time?" I ask, holding up a Tampa Bay snow globe from an end table.

But instead of answering my question, she responds, "You really don't need to. It's only a few boxes, and the courier isn't coming until the morning."

I frown at her when I realize she's avoiding looking at me. "Kaitlyn."

"Oh! The contract is on the dining table if you want to look it over. My lawyers are reviewing a copy as we speak, and I sent an electronic copy to your lawyer too. I don't foresee any issues, but you can never be too careful."

"Kaitlyn!" My voice is more forceful than I intended, but it manages to get her attention this time.

"What?" Her expression is guarded, and my heart sinks to the bottom of my gut.

"We need to talk."

She sighs and drops her hands to her sides. "What is there to say? I'm still your agent." At least she's not avoiding the topic anymore.

"You're fired." I step closer and don't miss the twitch of her lips.

"I thought you said clients would be banging my door down. And here I am getting fired?"

I shrug on another step. "I'm kinda high maintenance. You can get two clients to fill my spot."

Kaitlyn grins briefly before all amusement fades from her eyes. "It doesn't matter, Banks. I'd still be an agent and you'd still be a hockey player. There's nothing more to say." Her voice cracks on the last word, and I close the remaining distance so I can take her hand in mine.

"Yes, there is."

She bites her lip and shakes her head, and I can't stop this time, so I don't even try. I bend and take her lips with mine. The kiss feels like coming home, and I know she feels it too when she sighs into my mouth and lets her body melt against mine. The world falls into place when we're together like this, so I can't–no, I *won't*–let her deny us.

My tongue sweeps across her lower lip, begging for entry, and the first slide into her hot mouth has my cock thickening. Damn, I missed this. Kaitlyn grips my hair with impatient fingers, trying to pull me in closer even though there's not a millimeter of space between us. Our teeth clash in our urgency, and she practically gives me a split lip, but it's so hot I'd gladly go black and blue to have a lifetime of kisses with this woman.

When I finally tear my lips from hers, the words all tumble out. "I love you. I'm so fucking in love with you, I can't see straight. You're all I think about, all I care about."

"Banks," she hiccups my name on a quiet sob.

"I don't care what it takes for us to be together, I'm doing it. I'm not signing that contract or any other. You're worth more than hockey."

She gasps and grips my biceps with obvious desperation. "No. You have to! I won't let you throw away your entire life for me."

"Kaitlyn, don't you get it? *You're* my life. *You're* what's most important."

She's shaking her head like she's trying to get water out of her ears. "No! You can't mean it. You can't do it! Don't you see? We fight all the time. I annoy you and you annoy me. We'd last five minutes, and then you'd resent me the rest of your life for giving up what you love. It won't work, Banks. You've got to see that."

"I know what I want, and I'm willing to go all in for it." I draw in a deep breath, my heart pumping madly. "Are you?"

She exhales and takes a beat before responding in a quieter tone, "God, you're such a stubborn asshole. How did I forget that?" Her words have no sting because they're accompanied by a sad smile that has my stomach dropping.

"I mean it, Kaitlyn."

She reaches up to cup my cheek. "I know you do. But I... I can't."

Fuck. Did I misread everything? Does she not have feelings for me too?

No, I refuse to believe that. But the same determination and strength that have gotten her this far in life may end up being the nail in my coffin.

She swallows and continues, "You're leaving for Toronto tomorrow, and I need to get back home to catch up with work and give Bella room to breathe. Let's just get this contract wrapped up and put a pin in this conversation unt—"

"No." I cut her off. "No more stalling. No more excuses." If I don't make a stand, she'll string this out until we're both in Bay Villages with Beatrice. "I've told you everything you need to know. I love you, Kaitlyn Phillips, and I'm so confident in us that I'm willing to give up everything so we can be together. You either love me or you don't, so when you figure that out, you know where to find me."

It takes all I've got, but I manage to tear my eyes from her and walk out of the condo. I just hope I didn't throw away the best thing to ever happen to me.

# Chapter Thirty-Three

Kaitlyn

My storage unit in Atlanta smells like mothballs and old feet. I huff out a sad laugh and put down the box of Storm Chasers paraphernalia I collected these last two months. My limbs ache right down to my bones since Banks walked out of that condo in Tampa. Everything hurts and nothing feels right, which is weird. I'm on top of the world, professionally, with more clients than I know what to do with. The fallout of Ed Presley being arrested left me fielding call after call from clients wanting me to take them on. Within a single week, I've become the biggest hockey agent in the league. I should be celebrating, drinking champagne for breakfast and bathing in gold coins at night. Or at the very least, spending more time mentoring the two junior agents I hired just this week to help me with the overflow of work. Instead, I'm sulking, doing my best to ignore how much I miss Banks.

I dust off my hands and turn to leave when something catches my eye. I inhale sharply, recognizing that old red leather journal sitting on one of the stacked boxes. The teddy bear–Mr. Squishy–next to the journal was my favorite as a child. Dad made me rename him to Mr. Muscles after I screamed his name in front of a whole restaurant when I lost him under the booth. But the teddy bear isn't what's holding my interest. It's my mother's journal. I haven't read it in years, but something about the constant pang in my chest makes me grab for it now.

Sitting on a plastic box of Christmas decorations, I open the journal and read my mother's thoughts when she met my father. Her excitement about their wedding, her fears about her traditional Asian family accepting him, and her shock at finding out she was pregnant. *Your father cried when I told him,* she wrote. *At first I thought he was angry. Then he held my face, staring at me like he'd never seen me before. With his bottom lip trembling, he said, finally, the family I've always wanted. I knew then that everything we'd hoped and dreamed of was coming true. Because of you, my sweet baby.*

I snap the book closed, squeezing my eyes together. Those hopes and dreams were dashed when she died just a week after my birth. Dad has never been the same. I always thought he turned bitter and hard because of losing his career. *Because of you.* Mom didn't say his hopes and dreams came true because of being drafted. It was because of me. Because they were building a family.

I stand so fast the box of decorations almost tips over. Sliding my phone out of my back pocket, I open my notes app and go straight for the one pinned at the top. Kaitlyn's Goals. Yes, I keep a running list of goals in my phone like a good little Type A woman. I scan the first ten goals, realizing they've all come true the last few years. I look up at the dusty boxes in front of me and ponder how that can be right. I've hit all my major goals. I should be happy by now, right?

My brain flashes to Banks telling me he loves me and a

choked sob echoes off the back wall of the storage unit. I am decidedly *not* happy. Looking down once more, I see my eleventh goal, the one I put off in favor of one through ten. *Have a baby.*

I use my phone to hit the contact for Olivia. She answers after the third ring. "How happy did Livvies make you?" I ask by way of greeting. Olivia is extremely successful and owns her own company. If anyone can help me work through this, it's her.

"Um, well let's see. I could pay for my kids' college education and prove that I didn't need my ex. Is that what you mean?"

"I mean *happiness*. What makes you happy?" I pace the storage unit, heart galloping a mile a minute.

Olivia laughs lightly. "Well, my kids. Roman. Sharing a glass of wine on our deck after a hard day's work. Kaitlyn, what's this about?"

I freeze, realizing my heart is beating out of my chest because I'm fucking scared. Terrified is more like it. "I think I got it all wrong. Or at least I'm getting it all right now."

"Still lost, babe."

"I've been chasing external validation in the hockey world to make me happy. Now I have all the recognition I thought I'd want and I'm still not happy. Which means I did something wrong. What if my career alone can't make me happy? What if the things that do make me happy are the things I've been running from?"

"Which are...?"

"Love. Babies. Family. Connection." I shake my head, staring at nothing yet thinking of everything that lights me up inside. "Good coffee, a comfy couch, tattoos of tigers on my ass. Oh my god, I even wore a pair of Dunks to the store yesterday and I liked them." I whisper that last part, not quite sure I want to admit that stilettos aren't life, even while in the midst of an epiphany.

Olivia's laughter breaks me out of my fog. "Oh, honey. Sounds like you better get your ass up here to Toronto."

I spin in a full circle, not sure what to do first but knowing Olivia is right. I need to get to Banks. I need to tell him...something. That I'm choosing him over my career? That I'm willing to give it all up for him just like he's willing to do for me? That I love him more than coffee? Yes, to all of it.

"Holy shit, Olivia. I'm about to blow up my career," I breathe.

Like a good best friend, Olivia doesn't even hesitate. "Let me talk to Roman. I think he's got an extra ticket for the game. We'll sit together, okay?" Olivia's voice turns sharp. "And Kaitlyn? You better have a plan. A good plan to let Banks know you're all in."

I slam the door to the unit closed, fumbling with the lock. "Already on it, my friend. Text me about the tickets."

The arena is packed, people squeezing into every empty crevice, buying food and drink, merchandise flying off the shelves, and security doing their best to keep the peace among the chaos. I have a sign I labored on all last night before my early morning flight rolled up and tucked under my arm. I missed the skills competition last night and the semifinal games this morning, but have no intention of missing the championship game. With a hand to my stomach, I duck into the bathrooms and stand in line while my stomach revolts. Dear god, the vengeful bacteria are back. When it's my turn, I lose the lunch I grabbed on the way from the airport. Tears flood my eyes and I beg the universe to quell these nerves.

Now I know how Banks felt when he stood in front of the press and told the truth about Ed. I only love him more for standing up for what's right despite the fallout. I've always teased Banks about being a child, but the fact of the matter is I've been a bigger baby, always running from anything that might reflect poorly on my career. Running from Banks.

"I'm fucking done running," I mutter, washing my hands awkwardly with a poster under my arm.

"Yeah. Fuck running," says a woman at the sink to my left. She's got hockey puck earrings dangling and half the hair on her head shaved. The hair that's left is dyed a bright blue. "Girl, you're glowing."

I smile my appreciation at her support. Hockey fans are nuts but they're also the best people to have in your corner when you're about to torpedo your entire career in front of a televised audience.

My feet stop in their tracks halfway out the bathroom. Someone brushes past me in a hurry and I twist to the side and lean against the cool tile wall. Glowing? Throwing up? Holy shit. My hand automatically goes to my stomach and I mentally grasp for dates that escape me right now. Could I be...? When was my last period? Have I been searching for a sperm donor when I'm already knocked up? I look down at the poster curled under my arm and even bigger future plans slam into me. This *has* to work. Banks has to believe me when I tell him I love him. I was lying through my teeth when I said I didn't want him to be my baby's daddy.

I don't know how much time passes and how many women give me side eye for being dazed and confused in the bathroom, but I finally make my way into the concourse with extra pep in my step. I'll buy a pregnancy test before I leave Toronto and find out for sure.

It takes me a full lap, but I finally find my way to the section of seats indicated on my e-ticket. I see Roman's head and then Olivia next to him. The seats are ten rows up from the bench. The hockey players from both teams are warming up out on the ice and it only takes me a second to find Banks. He's focused, tight on the drills, and not bantering back and forth with his teammates. He's also not looking up in the stands.

"Kaitlyn!" Olivia squeals. She pushes Roman out of the way and slams into me for a hug. "Have you met Chloe Cooper, Coach Bowman's daughter?" She steps aside to let me shake hands with a short curvy woman around our age. I squeeze past Roman and have a seat between Olivia and Chloe.

"I filled Chloe in on the plan," Olivia whispers. I nod, too nervous to do much else. I can't seem to muster up my Killer Kaitlyn attitude. Not when it comes to something that actually matters to me. I'm back to being Kitten Kaitlyn, a meek little ball of fur hoping Banks will love her.

"Niko!" Roman shouts as the warm up ends and the Storm Chasers goalie skates by us.

He looks up and lifts his hand to Roman, then nearly wipes out on the ice as his gaze shifts down the row. He slams himself into the boards, his cheeks red already from exertion as his gaze freezes on Chloe.

"I did not know. I give you a tooth!" he shouts in that deep accent of his.

Chloe sinks down in her seat and looks elsewhere. Olivia and I exchange curious glances.

"Thanks for the tooth offer, but I'll pass," Roman hollers with a wink. "Niko and his Russian phrases." Niko glares at him and skates off the ice without another word.

"Why are these hockey boys so weird?" Olivia asks no one in particular.

Banks skates by, doing a double take when he sees me in the stands. He doesn't smile or even stop. He just stares, and like a fool, I stare back at him. He disappears off the ice and Olivia elbows me in the ribs.

"I hope your grand plan is better than that death glare," she teases.

I shake my head. "Shit. I need to pull it together."

"My dad says to always picture people naked when you get nervous, but I have a feeling that would backfire in this situation," Chloe adds, unhelpfully. "Maybe you can pretend it's just the two of you?"

An ear-splitting buzzer sounds, indicating the warm-ups are officially over. The crowd noise only increases as people start to find their seats. There's no way I'll be able to pretend we're alone. That's kind of the point. I need everyone to see me make a fool of myself so Banks will know I mean it. I'm done running, dammit.

Introductions happen and I hear some of it. Someone sings the U.S. National Anthem and then 'O Canada. The teams take to the ice and I bobble my knee up and down so badly, Roman reaches over to put his hand on me. I grimace and force myself to be calm. The two teams battle it out without a single point between them. It's not until late in the game that Rokowsky steals the puck and skates down the ice with Banks right beside him and not an opposing player in sight. The goalie tries to cover all sides, but can't when Rokowsky passes the puck lightning fast to Banks.

"Shoot it!!!" I bellow, along with half the fans in attendance. And Banks does, scoring a goal and making it look easy.

I lose my ever-loving shit, jumping to my feet and unfolding my sign, holding it high above my head. Banks skates past our side of the ice and looks up, doing another double take when he reads my sign. In sparkly letters that can probably be seen from outer space it reads *I heart Ben #29*. His face transforms into a blinding smile and then he's throwing a leg over the boards, letting other guys rotate in while he catches his breath. His gaze doesn't leave mine, even as all his teammates clap him on the back for the goal.

I mouth *I love you* and his grin only grows. Heads are swiveling back and forth between us and I don't even care. Let everyone speculate who Bennet is locking eyes with. Let them talk about me. Let them name me. I'm done hiding how I feel and it feels exactly like I'd hoped one-upping Ed Presley would feel.

The game continues and every time Banks has the puck I'm on my feet, screaming things that I'm sure he can't hear. The final buzzer shows that Banks's team has won, 3-2. Instead of celebrating with his team, Banks skates directly over to the bench, already pulling off his gloves. He crooks his finger, his smile turning wicked. I push past Olivia and Roman and bound down the steps to get to him. He disappears for a second, shoving open the emergency exit door and probably breaking some rule I won't be happy about later. When he's standing before me, I throw my arms around his neck and he pulls me back into the player's bench and slams the door closed.

"I love you!" I shout over the noise of the crowd, needing to get the words out more than I need to breathe.

Banks pulls back just enough to cup my face and kiss me, the heat pouring off his skin. The stands are going wild and I'm not sure if it's for the game or this kiss, but I don't care. All I care about is making sure Banks knows every single day how much he means to me. My head spins and time stops. Finally, it's just me and him in this huge arena.

"You're wearing the wrong shirt, woman." His blue eyes crinkle at the corners.

"Huh?"

Banks lets go of my face and pulls his jersey off. Then he shoves it over my head and I put my arms through the holes. It's huge even over my clothes, a tent on my slight frame. His smile is positively feral seeing me in his jersey. "That's more like it. You're mine, Kaitlyn Phillips, and now the whole world knows."

I stare up at him, so happy I could cry and probably will soon. "I don't care about the whole world. I just want you to know."

He tucks some hair behind my ear. "I know. I'm impossible not to love."

I roll my eyes but let him pull me into his chest again while the world carries on without us.

# Chapter Thirty-Four

Banks

For probably the first time ever, I'm more dressed up than my agent—or former agent, I should say. I tore off my gear and showered in record time after the win so I could get back to Kaitlyn where she waited with Roman and Olivia. Seeing her still wearing my jersey over her tee and jeans has the caveman inside me beating his chest.

"Nice work, man," Roman says as he sees me approach. Both women turn my way, but I've only got eyes for Kaitlyn. From the way her gaze sweeps my frame and her tongue pokes out to wet her lower lip, I'd say we're of like minds. Screw the afterparty.

"Damn, you sure do clean up good, hot shot," she says as I throw my arm around her shoulders. It feels good to be able to do that in front of everyone.

"Well, my agent told me that serious players dress seriously."

She grins up at me as Roman coughs out a laugh. "In all

the years since the team dropped the dress code, not once has my boy worn anything but gym clothes. You really are a miracle worker, Kaitlyn."

I dust the shoulder of my sports coat.

"Banks! Can we have a word?" someone asks from behind me, and I turn to see one of the network reporters standing a couple yards away with a mic and several cameramen.

Kaitlyn nudges me, and I step their way, not letting go of my girlfriend. I worry for half a second that she's going to pull away, but she comes right along, even snuggling into my side. I really hope I don't get a boner on national television.

"Drew Bentley from ASA," he introduces himself and sticks his mic in my face as soon as I'm near. "How do you feel after your big win?"

"Which one are you talking about?" I squeeze Kaitlyn's shoulder and pull her closer, laughing when she rolls her eyes at me.

The reporter looks almost relieved to have a new line of questioning to pursue. I mean, how boring must it be to ask the same three questions after every game? "You gave the fans something to talk about jumping into the stands like that. Looks like love is in the air. Care to make some introductions?"

I dip my chin to look at Kaitlyn with raised eyebrows, giving her one last chance to back out. She doesn't take it, instead leaning forward to speak into the mic. "My name is Kaitlyn Philips. I'm the sports agent to several of the guys on the ice tonight."

Bentley's brows spike as he side-eyes his own camera. "Must be handy having an agent as your partner." It's a douchebag thing to say, but it's not like we weren't expecting these kinds of comments. Best to ignore it and push through.

"Not just any agent–the best hockey agent in the game,

hands down. You can ask anybody." I smile down at Kaitlyn, and she shakes her head at me with a responding grin.

"Aww. You're sweet," she says, patting my chest.

"But you're not biased," the reporter responds with a chuckle to the camera.

"No bias necessary. Like I said, ask anybody." I gesture around us, and a few passing VIP fans cheer even though they have no clue what I just said.

"No bias, *period*." Kaitlyn eyes Bentley, using a tone that brooks no argument. "That's also why Banks is no longer my client." Kaitlyn's eyes lose their ice as she returns her gaze to me. "Winning isn't worth it if you're not playing fair, right?"

"Amen to that," I respond, bending down to drop a quick kiss on her lips. I hear Roman groan from a few feet behind us, and I steer us that way as the reporters find a new victim exiting the locker room.

I scowl at Roman. "Dude, you guys are all over each other all the time!"

Olivia snorts. "That's no lie."

"It's different when it's you, somehow." Roman looks almost confused.

"Well," Kaitlyn interjects. "Shall we go get a drink to toast the end of my career?"

All three of us frown at her, but I'm the first to speak. "Oh, I forgot to tell you, Dan-O, Rokowsky, and Fitzpatrick all want your card. I told them I'd drop a stack in the locker room before we take off."

Kaitlyn's expression falls even more, surprising me. "Oh no. It's worse than I thought. They all think if they sign with me, I'll sleep with them." She slaps a hand over her eyes.

Roman, Olivia, and I all look at each other for a few beats before we bust out laughing.

"This isn't funny!" Kaitlyn insists, the oversized jersey and pronounced scowl giving her the appearance of a six-year-old who's just been deprived of screentime.

"Oh, I disagree," Roman responds over his chuckle.

"Kaitlyn, you're a kick-ass agent. That's the only reason anyone needs for hiring you," Olivia tries, but I know Kaitlyn needs more than just her friend's opinion. This woman deals in facts and details.

"First," I begin, stepping aside so I can face her. "Rokowsky is married to his high-school sweetheart and the two of them are worse than these two." I throw a thumb at my best friend and his fiancé. "Second, Fitzy is gay. And third, you're missing the entire point. None of the guys care that you're with me, except for the possibility that I could put a good word in for them now that you're swamped with so many potential clients."

A thread of hope makes its way into her expression, and when both Olivia and Roman nod, her shoulders finally straighten again. "Oh," is all she says, sending the three of us into another round of laughter as I pull Kaitlyn close and bury my laugh in her hair.

Further proving that we're perfect for each other, Kaitlyn insists we go back to her swanky hotel to celebrate instead of joining the afterparty. But when we walk in, I'm surprised to see the penthouse unit is lit with small white candles on every surface, as if she's been expecting me.

"My, my. You were sure of yourself weren't you, Ms. Phillips?" I drawl, lifting an eyebrow.

Kaitlyn grins and nestles into my side. She feels strangely short without those stilettos I've come to love. "I wasn't sure of myself at all, but I always play to win. I was betting on you and me, hot shot."

I turn her so I can cup her face and stare into those gorgeous brown eyes. "Always a good bet." I give her a lopsided grin that I know makes her melt and pisses her off in equal measure. "This might be a little forward, but I think you'll like it." I waggle my brows. "How about you get naked–except for a pair of heels–while I get the champagne poured. Then we'll make a baby."

Kaitlyn's smile freezes as her eyes begin to shine. "About that. I might already be pregnant," she squeaks.

My heart stops for a moment, then starts beating again, the rhythm rearranged. Steadier. More confident that I'm on the path I'm meant to be on. "I could be a dad right now?"

Kaitlyn lifts a shoulder. "I mean, I don't know yet, but I'm late. That mighty sequoia of yours wasn't playing around."

I can't help the cocky grin. "We should definitely have sex again. Just to make sure. Right?" I shrug even though my entire body is drawn tight as a granite statue with the effort it's taking not to tear her clothes off. "Unless you want to watch a movie and snuggle instead..." I mean, I can make that work. Not my first choice, but as long as Kaitlyn is at my side, I can deal with it.

Kaitlyn backs up, her teary eyes giving way to a saucy grin that spells pleasure in my future. She leans down and chucks off her tennis shoes. Her shirt hits the floor next, and all my brain is thinking about is *boobs boobs boobs*. Not because I'm an immature asshole like some of the guys on my team, but because Kaitlyn's are just that spectacular. I take a step toward her but she puts her hand out, stopping me. The striptease continues, and I settle in to enjoy the show, loving how Kaitlyn's trademark confidence extends to everything she does. She's spectacular in every way, and somehow I'm the lucky bastard who gets to love her.

"You're going to make the best mom," I whisper out of nowhere. Not my best segue ever, but she doesn't seem to care.

Her hands pause on her jeans, the button and zipper already undone. "Don't make me cry, Ben."

I step closer, then drop to my knees to peel the jeans off her long, toned legs. "Cry, laugh, rage. Whatever you need to do, I'm here for it." My mouth gets jealous of my hands, and the second I have her feet clear of the jeans, I lean in and drag my lips up one thigh and then the next, inhaling the scent of her, memorizing the way her silky skin feels. Her breath catches and her fingers find my shoulders. I drop a kiss on her belly, just in case.

When I stand again, my legs are suddenly shaky, feeling a lot like when I overdo it on leg day. But I know it's emotion and not exertion causing these shakes. I came so close to losing Kaitlyn, and the fear is just now hitting me, now that the All-Star game is over. Or maybe her mood swings really *are* contagious because right now, all I want to do is pull her into my arms and never let her go until the tremors fade.

"Kaitlyn," I barely breathe. She sways into me, her arms sliding around my waist as she buries her face in my chest. My hands find her hips. "I love you."

She pulls her head back, long dark hair brushing against my wrists so she can look me in the eyes. "I love you too."

I dip my head and brush my nose across her cheek, my teeth catching the lobe of her ear. "I'll give you anything and everything you want. Babies, marriage, world domination, a fucking Tigers tattoo on your ass. Say it and it'll be done."

Her hands untuck the shirt from my slacks, sliding up my bare back while her nails drag across my skin. "Um, about that." She pulls back enough to shoot me a shy smile. "I may have already gotten the tiger." She pops her hip out and I crane my neck to check out her luscious ass cheek, newly tattooed Tigers mascot there, just like the ones we bought at the airport.

I feel like I'm in sensory overload. "I need to worship that ass for a couple minutes."

Kaitlyn giggles. "All I want right now is for you to make love to me."

I don't joke around, I don't even breathe, before I pick Kaitlyn up and carry her to the king sized bed where I lay her down. Then I peel my shirt over my head–because buttons would take too damn long–and push my slacks down my legs. The pants and shoes get tangled in my haste, but I finally manage to get them off and loom over her on the bed.

Kaitlyn smiles up at me, her hair fanning across the pillow. "I love you, hot shot, I really do, but you can't make love to me with just your socks on."

I look down my body, realizing my black dress socks still cover my feet. "What if my toes get cold?" I tease.

Kaitlyn hooks her thumbs in her lacy underwear and shimmies then down her hips, exposing the prettiest pussy I've ever had the pleasure of meeting. "With the things I plan to do with you, they won't have the chance, trust me."

My dick is so hard I'm in pain, but I take the socks off anyway. "Never knew you had a toe fetish, Killer Kaitlyn."

She reaches around to grab my ass and pulls me down onto her body. When my dick nestles perfectly between her thighs, I can no longer see straight. She's so hot and wet and perfect. "I have a Benjamin Banks Bennet fetish," she practically purrs.

It's with little finesse and a shit-eating grin that I slide into her heat. Her body welcomes me, and there's no more talking. No more teasing. No more distance between us as her hips lift and our hands roam. I barely get a nipple in my mouth before she's growling at me to keep thrusting. I don't, because I want this to last all night. Her frustrated growl is just a bonus.

Her muscles squeeze around me, and I nearly choke on my tongue. She glares up at me with fiery eyes, but the pink in her cheeks gives her away. I pull almost all the way out before slamming back in, hard. Her head falls back, exposing her throat, and she gasps. There it is. My greedy woman loves it hard and intense. My pace quickens and the bed creaks as she gives me little gasps and mewls that remind me of a kitten. Sweat beads on my back, and it takes everything I have not to spill into her right now. I grit my teeth and pull all the way out, my chest heaving. I roll onto my back and start reciting my career hockey stats.

"What the fuck, Ben?" Kaitlyn's breathing just as hard, but if looks could kill, I'd go out a very happy man.

"Climb aboard," I manage to say.

Kaitlyn's straddling me before I can catch my breath, her fist gripping me tight as she notches me at her entrance and then slides down. I'm back to chanting stats, though I have the wherewithal to keep my eyes shut and my thumb on her clit in a feeble attempt to make this good for her. If I look at her right now, I might lose my shit. Kaitlyn sets a fast pace, her thighs pressing into my ribs with each lift and fall. Goddammit, she feels so good. Better than any win in hockey has ever felt.

She stills and my eyes flick open. Big fucking mistake. Her head is tossed back and she has one hand on my abs and the other on her own breast. She begins to ride me again, and it's a magnificent sight watching my woman lost in her own pleasure. She's always been gorgeous, but seeing her use my body to chase her orgasm is my undoing. I surge upright and wrap my arms around her back, my hips lifting and thrusting so hard I'm sure my hamstring will be fucked up again tomorrow. My mouth latches onto one perfect nipple, and our damp skin glides against one another's in a perfect, dirty, uncoordinated rhythm until Kaitlyn screams my name, pulsing around me as she comes. And then, finally, I let myself explode, the orgasm so intense I swear I go blind for long minutes as we tremble together.

It's only much much later that I realize I forgot the champagne and the stilettos. Which is a good thing because if Kaitlyn's pregnant, she's banned from both for the next nine months. This baby daddy doesn't mess around.

# Epilogue
## FOUR MONTHS LATER

**Kaitlyn**

"Are your feet hurting?" Banks whispers in my ear as we watch Roman and Olivia out on the dance floor, their first dance as husband and wife.

The warm Bahamian breeze ruffles my side swept bangs, cut one day when the hormones got the best of me and I chopped my hair in a rage. Banks's arm tightens on my waist, his hand stilling on my belly. I put my hand on top of his and squeeze. Stilettos probably aren't the best idea given I'm four and a half months pregnant and finally showing. Not that I'll tell Banks that, given we've fought over my right to wear whatever I wanted on my own feet. We finally announced our pregnancy, mostly because Banks can't seem to keep his hands off my stomach, a dead giveaway to my condition. Since the moment we saw those two blue lines, he's been the very best dad-to-be, attentive and sweet.

"No, I just have to pee again."

I can feel Banks's laughter with his chest pressed against my back. "Come on then."

He escorts me into the resort where he stands watch outside the bathroom door. I swear, his protective instincts have gone into hyperdrive, but instead of annoying me, I find it adorable. He nearly lost his shit when a couple reporters printed innuendos about our relationship once we went public, but I managed to keep him under control, along with the help of his new agent. To my chagrin, Banks has rubbed off on me, making me see that what others think of me ultimately doesn't matter. I care about my reputation, of course, but my professional image is no longer my number one priority. Overall, there was nothing to worry about with going public. The rumors and remarks died down soon after the All-Star game. All the hockey players still respect me and my agency is at max capacity even with my two new female agents.

I dry my hands on the thick cotton towels and head back outside where Banks slips his arm around me. We stroll through the tikis back to the outdoor wedding reception. The song has just ended and Roman is kissing Olivia. Again. Those two are going to have chapped lips with all the kissing they've been doing today. Then again, it *is* their wedding day.

We rejoin the group, standing with Niko and Pete. Bobby, who somehow finagled an invite, is off at the bar, flirting with the captive bartender. None of them brought a date to the destination wedding, stating they didn't deserve to since the Storm Chasers lost in the finals yet again. I have high hopes they'll win the cup next year or they might all have to take a vow of celibacy for years to come.

"In my country, we have more drink at weddings," Niko states, looking disproportionately irritated. "Where is the vodka? Where is the kvass?"

"Easy, tiger," Banks drawls. "Why are you in such a bad mood? We're in paradise."

Niko turns his frown on Banks. "The crazy ex-wife tries to kill me with a thousand cuts."

My heart bleeds for Niko's situation. He intended to bring his daughter with him to the Bahamas, but his ex-wife refused to let her go at the last minute like they'd planned. He came alone, darting away to take frequent phone calls with his lawyer.

Banks holds up his hand. "Whoa there, buddy. Never call a woman crazy. She might just have hormonal mood swings like my lovely Kaitlyn." He looks far too pleased with himself.

I smack Banks's arm. "Hey, don't talk about me like I'm not here. But you're right. Never call a woman crazy."

"Actual crazy is that woman I met at Lodge X last week," Pete pipes in. "She went from feeling me up on the dance floor to slapping my face when I wouldn't give her the keys to my Maserati." He shakes his head, grinning like a fool. "She finally settled down when I told her she could take a spin on me and not the car."

I shake my head at Pete. "You better not have been photographed half naked with a puck bunny in your car."

"Nah," Pete cackles. "I barely got my dick out let alone my pants down. Sorry, Kaitlyn."

As if that quick apology at the end is sufficient for being so crass. I can feel my temper flaring. Sadly, getting pregnant has only made the mood swings more volatile.

"You know, it's truly amazing the audacity you men have calling women crazy when you're the fuckers who wore pork-chop sideburns for weeks on end thinking that would somehow determine the outcome of the Stanley Cup!" And they had. They'd taken up that tradition again and look where it's gotten them: cupless.

The guys all bark with laughter, none of them willing to look at my statement too closely because they know I'm right.

Roman comes over and Pete throws his arm around his shoulders, pulling him into our group.

"You look a little slow out there, Roman. Old ball and chain weighing you down already?" Bobby, having given up on the bartender, joins the group too.

Roman rolls his eyes and then turns his gaze on me. "You're needed on the dance floor, Kaitlyn. Olivia wants to do the bouquet."

I put both hands up. "Nope, I'm good. I'm already taken."

"Damn right," Banks growls.

Roman shakes his head. "Olivia insists all single women come to the dance floor." He leans closer. "There's only a couple women out there and Chloe is uncomfortable."

Niko snorts, but doesn't comment. I narrow my gaze at him for a moment. There's something going on there and neither of them is talking. Before this trip is over, I plan to get to the bottom of the tension between Niko and Chloe.

I kiss Banks on the cheek and head out onto the dance floor to help my new friend. Chloe moved to Tampa just before the All-Star game and has quickly become part of my inner circle. She finally told me her whole story a few weeks ago and suffice it to say, if she needs me, I'm there for her. The poor woman has endured more than any person should. Which is why I can't let Niko continue to give her a hard time. She gives me a relieved grin when I stand next to her.

"We're doing something different today," Olivia says to the six of us assembled on the dance floor. "I have the bouquet inside this acrylic box and six keys. Only one of them opens the box."

She swishes between us in her gorgeous wedding dress, handing each of us a small silver key. I take to the back of the line, not wanting to do this ridiculous stunt anyway. Each woman tries her key and it doesn't fit the lock. Olivia, standing on the other side of the box, starts to look worried. Chloe steps forward and tries to insert her key.

"You sure one of the keys works?" Olivia asks over her shoulder at the wedding planner.

Chloe's key doesn't fit either. She looks back at me. "Guess it's yours."

I suppress a groan and step forward to insert my key. For Olivia and Chloe I'll paste on a smile and pretend I care about receiving the bride's bouquet. The key slides in effortlessly and when I twist it, the lock springs free. Olivia gasps and then claps, looking so excited I don't even have to fake the smile. I reach inside the box and pull out the stunning bouquet. Olivia comes around the box and gives me a hug.

"Congrats, my friend. You deserve it all," she whispers in my ear. Seems a little over the top considering it's just a silly wedding tradition, but I go along with it, hugging her back.

Then a throat clears and I turn. The bouquet lowers to my side as my limbs grow weak. Banks, my handsome, kind, ridiculous baby daddy, is down on one knee, a lopsided grin on his face.

"Kaitlyn Phillips, I've loved you since the day we shared the Gouda grilled cheese at the airport. I love your strength, your beauty, your determination, and even your tears. There's nothing you can't do once you set your mind on it, and that kind of fire is addictive. If you'll let me, I want nothing more than to be by your side forever, fanning those flames and making you rest when you're about to burn out. Marry me, Kaitlyn with a K. Marry me and we'll ride those mood swings all the way into the sunset together."

His blue eyes are shining so bright I lose myself in them, blocking out both the aws and the groans of the crowd, I forget that anyone is around us. I forget that our baby is right here, listening to her father confess his love in front of our friends and family. All I can see is Banks, our future together, and all the happiness I almost missed out on.

"You gotta actually say yes or no soon because my knee is killing me," Banks says. The titter of laughter around us brings me back to this perfect moment.

I grin so hard my jaw hurts. "Yes. Absolutely, forever, yes."

Banks stands and I'm in his arms, our kiss one for the movie screen. The crowd cheers and I'm pretty sure Roman is the loudest. Tears slide down my cheeks and for the first time, I'm not embarrassed by them. I'm so damn happy I don't care who knows.

We refuse to let go of each other, even when Roman taps us on the shoulders. "You forgot the ring," he whispers loud enough for the people an island over to hear.

Banks pulls back and takes the box Roman hands him, clicking it open with one hand. A diamond flashes in the light of the tikis and I have to blink back tears to even see it when Banks slides it on my finger. Out of nowhere, my father strides up to us and smacks me on the shoulder.

"Congrats, Kaity-bug."

"Dad?" I gasp, looking between him and Banks. Dad was definitely not on the guest list. The two men thump each other's backs and then Dad pulls me into his arms for a surprisingly gentle hug.

"I love you, Kaitlyn." He pulls back and smiles at me proudly. If I'm not hallucinating there are tears shining behind those glasses. He sniffs and turns us to Banks, his arm still around my shoulders. "I always wanted a big family and thanks to you, I'll finally get one. Welcome to the family, son."

And then the DJ cranks the music and the servers pass out champagne. Banks takes my glass and drains it, like I was actually going to drink it, the silly man. Everyone comes by to congratulate us and Olivia finds my gaze across the crowd and shoots me a wink.

"Jesus, that was the corniest shit I've heard all year," Pete drawls, but he pulls both of us into a hug.

"I think it was beautiful and from the heart center," Niko says with a head nod of acknowledgment.

For once I don't give a shit what anyone thinks, because I'm finally truly happy. The reception quickly turns into a whole different kind of party and even Niko looks like he's starting to loosen up. I'm basking in the glow of pregnancy, newly engaged, and happier beyond anything I could have envisioned for my life. Banks doesn't let me out of his sight, which is fine by me. There's nowhere I'd rather be. No one I'd rather do life with. I know without a doubt none of those sperm donors made the cut because the very best man was skating right toward me the whole time. I just had to block out the noise of the crowd long enough to see him.

*Hot for more?? Grab the third book in the Hot Flash Hookups series: Night Sweats and Hockey Nets...coming September 2024!*

# Also by Marika Ray

Scan the QR code to go to Marika's Amazon page!

<u>Steamy RomComs - Blueball Band of Brothers:</u>

Grumpy the Bear - Blueball Band of Brothers #1

S'more Than a Feeling - Blueball Band of Brothers #2

Home is Where You Park It - Blueball Band of Brothers #3

Set My Heart Bonfire - Blueball Band of Brothers #4

Pining For You - Blueball Band of Brothers #5

***

<u>All Steamy RomComs Set in Hell:</u>

Grumpy As Hell - Hellman Brothers #1

Bro Code Hell - Hellman Brothers #2

Friend Zone Hell - Hellman Brothers #3

Cougar From Hell - Hellman Brothers #4

Falling First Hell - Hellman Brothers #5

***

Ridin' Solo - Sisters From Hell #1

One Night Bride - Sisters From Hell #2

Smarty Pants - Sisters From Hell #3

Ex Best Thing - Sisters From Hell #4

***

Love Bank - Jobs From Hell #1

Uber Bossy - Jobs From Hell #2

Unfriend Me - Jobs From Hell #3

Side Hustle - Jobs From Hell #4

***

Backroom Boy - Standalone

Steamy Small Town Christmas RomCom:

Grumpy Little Christmas

Steamy Hockey RomCom:

Hot Flashes and Hockey Slashes - Hot Flash Hookups #1

Mood Swings and Hockey Flings - Hot Flash Hookups #2

Steamy RomComs:

The Missing Ingredient - Reality of Love #1

Mom-Com - Reality of Love #2

Desperately Seeking Househusbands - Reality of Love #3

***

Happy New You - Standalone

Steamy RomComs with Delancey Stewart:

The Spare and the Single Mom

Head Over Cleats

Falling For Mr. Safety

*Carolina Connections Box Set 1*

*Carolina Connections Box Set 2*

* * *

*The Nerd Next Door* (*Carolina Kisses,* Book 1)

*New Jerk in Town* (*Carolina Kisses,* Book 2)

*The Last Good Liar* (*Carolina Kisses,* Book 3)

* * *

*Between a Rock and a Royal, Kings of Carolina, #1*

*Blue Bloods and Backroads, Kings of Carolina, #2*

*Stealing Kisses With a King, Kings of Carolina, #3*

*Kings of Carolina Box Set*

* * *

*Poppy & the Beast*

*Then Again*

*Full-On Clinger (FREE for a limited time)*

*About That*

*Nuts About You*

*Booby Trapped*

# Acknowledgments

Marika and Sylvie met years ago at a book signing, instantly hitting it off as they were both quite funny. Fast forward a few years and they were on the phone lamenting all the very real symptoms of peri menopause that were affecting their lives when they both had the grand idea that they wanted to write about it! The goal was to normalize conversation about the various side effects of the hormonal rollercoaster that is aging, while also reminding women of their inherent beauty no matter their age.

From Sylvie - A personal thanks to Allison, Carlie, and Annette for their support, and to my trusty neck fan for pulling me through my worst hot flashes.

From Marika - A huge thank you to the small handful of doctors out there who listen to our laundry list of menopausal symptoms and don't think we're crazy. Imagine a whole generation of 40+ women who have their hormones optimized and live the second half of their lives just as vibrantly as the first.

Thank you to fellow romance authors for their enthusiasm and support of this book. You make a girl feel less crazy.

Thank you to Contenta Schoenman, our hockey guru, for elevating our hockey vocab.

Last but not least...a huge thank you to Nancy Smay at Evident Ink for making this book shine with your editing and proofreading services!

# About Marika Ray

Marika Ray is a USA Today bestselling author, writing small town RomCom to make your heart explode and bring a smile to your face. All her books come with a money-back guarantee that you'll laugh at least once with every book.

Marika spends her time behind a computer crafting stories, walking along the beach, and making healthy food for her kids and husband whether they like it or not. Prior to writing novels, Marika held various jobs in the finance industry, with private start-up companies, and then in health & fitness. Cats may have nine lives, but Marika believes everyone should have nine careers to keep things spicy.

If you'd like to know more about Marika or the other novels she's currently writing, please find her in her private Reader Group.

If you want to take your stalking to the next level, here are other legal-ish places you can find Marika:

**Join her Newsletter** - http://bit.ly/MarikaRayNews

**Amazon** - https://www.amazon.com/author/marikaray

**Goodreads** - https://www.goodreads.com/author/show/16856659.Marika_Ray

**Bookbub** - https://www.bookbub.com/authors/marika-ray

**TikTok** - https://vm.tiktok.com/ZMJvnQ2Cv

**Instagram** - https://www.instagram/authormarikaray

**Website** - https://www.marikaray.com

# About Sylvie Stewart

USA Today bestselling author Sylvie Stewart loves dad jokes, dirty rom-coms, country music, and baby skunks—preferably all at the same time. Most of her steamy contemporary and romantic comedy novels take place across her favorite state of North Carolina, and her characters never run out of snarky banter or snacks. When her laptop closes, Sylvie is a sucker for hugs from her twin boys and a good laugh with her hot-nerd hubby. If you love smart Southern gals, hot blue-collar guys, and snort-laughing with characters who feel like your best friends, Sylvie's your gal. Stay up to date on all things Sylvie! https://sylviestewartauthor.com

**Join her Newsletter** - http://bit.ly/s-s-nl

**Facebook Reader Group** - https://www.facebook.com/groups/743238732533487

**Facebook Page** – https://facebook.com/SylvieStewartAuthor

**Instagram** – https://instagram.com/sylvie.stewart.romance

**BookBub** – https://bookbub.com/authors/sylvie-stewart

**Twitter** – https://twitter.com/sylvie_stewart_

**TikTok** – https://tiktok.com/@authorsylviestewart

**Pinterest** – https://pinterest.com/sylviestewartauthor

**Goodreads** – https://goodreads.com/author/show/15303783.Sylvie_Stewart

**YouTube** – https://youtube.com/@sylviestewartauthor